The Nature of Blood

THE
NATURE
OF
BLOOD

Caryl Phillips

ALFRED A. KNOPF
New York · *Toronto*
1997

THIS IS A BORZOI BOOK
PUBLISHED BY ALFRED A. KNOPF, INC.,
AND ALFRED A. KNOPF CANADA

Copyright © 1997 by Caryl Phillips
All rights reserved under International and Pan-American
Copyright Conventions. Published in the United States by
Alfred A. Knopf, Inc., New York, and distributed by
Random House, Inc., New York. Published simultaneously
in Canada by Alfred A. Knopf Canada, a division of
Random House of Canada Limited, Toronto, and
distributed by Random House of Canada Limited, Toronto.
http://www.randomhouse.com/

Originally published in Great Britain by Faber and Faber
Limited, London.

Library of Congress Cataloging-in-Publication Data
Phillips, Caryl.
The nature of blood / Caryl Phillips.
p.   cm.
ISBN 0-679-45470-5 (hc). — ISBN 0-679-77675-3 (pbk.)
I. Title.
PR9275.S263P47646   1997
823'.914—dc21   96-49641
CIP

Canadian Cataloguing in Publication Data
Phillips, Caryl.
The nature of blood
ISBN 0-676-97050-8
I. Title.
PR9275.S263P476 1997
823'.914   C96-932142-2

Manufactured in the United States of America
First American Edition

For Tony

ACKNOWLEDGEMENTS

In the course of writing this novel I referred to many works
which space does not allow me to acknowledge. I would, however, like to express my debt to two books: *Trent 1475* by
R. Po-Chia Hsia (Yale University Press), and *Portobuffole* by
Salomone G. Radzik (Editrice La Giuntina).

The Nature of Blood

BETWEEN us a small fire sputtered. When the wind rose, the flames occasionally danced. A pair of young men moved from fire to fire, carefully replenishing each nest of flames with sticks and twigs from a wicker basket which they bore with authority. They passed from one group to the next, eager to be seen to be efficiently carrying out their task. After they had finished with my fire, I thanked them and received their silent nods in reply. I watched as they strode away to the next group. The new kindling snapped, and the flames rose higher and illuminated the boy's face. He spoke quietly.

'Tell me, what will be the name of the country?'

'Our country,' I said. 'The country will belong to you too.'

The boy looked down at the sand, then scratched a short nervous line with his big toe.

'Tell me, what will be the name of our country?'

I paused for a moment, in the hope that he might relax. And then I whispered, as though confessing something to him.

'Israel. Our country will be called Israel.'

He looked up at me, the light from the fire reflected in his dark eyes.

Our country lay beyond this sand, beyond the black silk of the night sea, away to the south, away to the east. Distant, yet so tantalizingly close. Our troubled land. Palestine. Israel. The boy whispered the new word to himself, weighing it carefully on his tongue, rolling it from one side of his mouth to the other, until he was happy with its presence. He looked across at me.

'And in Israel the fruit is on the trees?'

'The fruit is on the trees. You may take the fruit straight from the branch.'

The formal part of the evening was over, and, together with this boy, I was sitting on a broad expanse of beach in southern Cyprus. Shoshana's concert had finished late, but the mood remained high and the atmosphere still resonated with the haunting melodies of her Yiddish songs. Mr Bellow, the camp director, had suggested that those of us who were staff might organize a picnic on the beach and enjoy the night air. We could talk and sing and, although he did not say this, he implied that those who already had some experience of the new country might educate those for whom the land beyond the water remained a mystery. We so-called staff members were all volunteers from Palestine, two dozen or so doctors, dentists, teachers and nurses, representatives of useful professions. Some linked arms as they walked through the barbed-wire gate and out of the camp, but being a little older than the others, and perhaps somewhat less idealistic, I chose to saunter by myself. Mr Bellow had arranged for a group of young men and women, trusted internees, to follow us down to the beach and light our fires. As it happened, I recognized one among them: Moshe, a tall, angular boy of Romanian origin. He had only recently arrived in the camp, and had been assigned work as a messenger boy at the makeshift hospital where I carried out my duties. Although we had passed only a few words, I invited him to forsake his fire-lighting duties and sit with me on the beach.

The boy was nervous, clearly worried about what his colleagues would think about his abandoning them in order that he might sit and talk with one of the doctors. I tried to reassure him, but the agitation in his eyes remained. Mr Bellow took a special interest in these young people – the orphaned and the unattached, as he called them – both bc ys and girls who were too old to be placed with families, yet too young to be treated

4

as adults. He was forever reminding his staff volunteers that, for these people in particular, the world must seem a very difficult place. *We must endeavour to treat them as though they were our own lost children.* He could have saved his words, for most had already been quietly recruited by armed emissaries from Palestine who regularly infiltrated the camp. The majority of the 'orphaned and unattached' were now *Hagannah* trainees, secretly preparing themselves for a life of military service in the underground army that they would join once they reached Palestine. However, the American Mr Bellow preferred to imagine his 'orphaned and unattached' as innocents in need of constant protection and education. With perhaps the exception of the newly arrived Moshe, nothing could be further from the truth.

Mr Bellow had been sent to Cyprus by a New York–based Jewish aid organization, the Joint Distribution Committee. He had arrived in the Mediterranean shortly after the British had initiated their policy of turning away refugee ships from Palestine, and off-loading the passengers on to their island of Cyprus. At first there were two camps, then three, then four, and now there were almost a dozen, containing over thirty thousand refugees of all ages and nationalities, whose sole aim in life was to escape war-ravaged Europe and reach the promised land. The benevolent Mr Bellow, a large, jocular man, presided over all the camps, attending to the health, education and general welfare of the displaced and the dispossessed. He faithfully promised each internee that they would eventually reach Palestine, but the British quota of seven hundred and fifty persons per month meant that thousands would have to spend weeks, if not years, under British lock and key on Cyprus. It was Mr Bellow who had arranged for trained professionals to journey from Palestine, both to attend to the sick and to assist in social welfare and language training. Quite simply, we professionals were to prepare these internees for their future lives.

Moshe had a head that appeared to be too large for his long, thin body. He sat cross-legged, a bundle of knees and elbows, and he quietly mentioned the name of the camp from which he had been liberated by the Russians. For want of anywhere else to go, he had returned to his village, but he soon discovered that another family were living in his parents' house. They were surprised to see him, but greeted him in a cordial manner and gave him soup to drink and a bed in which to sleep. And then, in the morning, a delegation of men arrived and pressed money upon Moshe. They told him that he should leave now, and if they ever saw him again they would kill him. Moshe related his story without once meeting my eyes. And then he smiled slightly and shrugged his shoulders.

'And so I left. What else could I do?'

Up on the hill, and crouched behind the barbed-wire fence, the camp stared down at us. A dishevelled collection of tin huts and tents were illuminated by bright floodlights. However, this shower of electricity, far from conferring any glamour, served only to confirm the pitiful nature of the whole shabby enterprise. The British had taken it upon themselves to imprison the defenceless. Around the perimeter of the camp, British tanks were stationed at regular intervals, and even down here on the beach there were tanks, their guns trained, the nervous soldiers alert to the task of guarding unarmed men, women and children. A foolish posting. Back up at the camp, I could clearly see silhouettes as people moved about nervously, visiting the latrines, taking the night air, pulling on a cigarette, dreaming. From where they stood, they could gaze down at the beach and see people sitting and talking and laughing, and then they could look out beyond the beach to the sea and imagine what lay over the horizon and out of sight. During the day, these people's lives simply marked time as idleness began to eat its way into their souls. However, their nights skirted an abyss, for they now recognized that in the inescapable intimacy of the camp, human dignity was beginning to decay. Inertia was ruining them, and the old values of discretion and decency seemed to count for little. Moshe waited until the pair of young men had moved off. The new kindling snapped, and the flames rose higher and illuminated the boy's face. He spoke quietly.

'Tell me, what will be the name of the country?'

Israel. Palestine. He knew of no such country. As yet, none of them did. Only in their minds. But at least he asked questions. And I answered. 'The fruit is on the trees. You may take it straight from the branch.' Moshe looked up at me as though I were holding something back; as though there were some awful secret about this imaginary country that I was refusing to share with him. But there was nothing. I was tired, for it had already been a long day. In fact, it had been a long two months. Tomorrow, at dawn, I would be returning to Palestine. But I was hiding nothing from Moshe.

'Do you have an army?'

I had heard this question before. From others who were newly arrived and, as yet, untouched by emissaries. So many of these young people were ready to fight. Determined to prove that, given a gun and a uniform, there were things that they too could do.

'Yes there is an army, and it is organized and well disciplined. It will be extremely important once we have a free country.'

Moshe looked up and adjusted his position in the sand. Now he was interested, his face radiant and alive. I worried about these young men and what they might do with a gun. Even some of the women, too. Luckily they seemed to understand that here, on Cyprus, the British were not the enemy. These reluctant soldiers were captors. They inflicted no punishment, and there was neither torture nor killing. The British were bored. Bored with their Mr Bevin, bored with Cyprus, bored with Jews. They couldn't care less about breaking the power of the 'Hebrew Resistance Movement'. The war was over and they wanted to go home. But Mr Bellow's 'orphaned and unattached' were acting as though their war had yet to begin.

Moshe stretched his legs and I could now see that his trousers stopped some way above his ankles. I looked and smiled, but tried to do so surreptitiously, hoping that Moshe would not notice. But I failed, because he quickly folded his legs back underneath himself and then looked into the fire. Suddenly there was an awkward silence between us and I found myself consumed with guilt. I chastised myself for my clumsiness, and searched desperately for some mollifying phrase. And then Moshe rescued me.

'Do you think I will find a wife?'

I laughed now.

'Moshe, you will be able to choose from hundreds of pretty women.'

'Do you have a wife?'

'No,' I said. 'At least, not any more. She is in America with my daughter.'

'Why don't they come and live in Palestine?'

'Well, that is a long story, Moshe. At present, my future lies over there.'

With a swift movement of my head I nodded in the general direction of the sea. Moshe looked out over the water as though he might see something.

'You see, that is my country now. The country over the water.'

I paused for a moment and tried to picture my country. And then I realized that Moshe was staring at me. My country?

'I, too, was in the army before I became a doctor. But, Moshe, the army is not everything. *Hagannah* is not everything. A wife and child, now that is something.'

I smiled at Moshe, for the moonlight was now illuminating his face in a manner that made him appear painfully young.

'Like you, Moshe, I too once left a country behind.'

I twisted myself around in the sand, and then gazed up the hill towards the floodlit camp. The boy turned and looked.

'Many of those people have come from my old country. Now, they have nothing. I remember many things about my old country. People. Places. Suddenly you couldn't do this, you had to do that. Then you couldn't do that, you had to do this. I left early, but even before I left there were people begging in the streets, respectable people. I remember the fear. But I do not have to tell you any of this. You have seen it, yes? You remember? It was the same in your country?'

Moshe continued to stare up at the illuminated vision that was the camp on the hill. He nodded, almost imperceptibly, for his mind was clearly lost in reverie.

'You will marry a beautiful girl and have wonderful children. And, sure, you will join the army if you wish.'

Moshe turned from the camp and looked at me. I tried to make him understand.

'The old world is dead. The survivors are here. Up there, gathered together on a hillside in Cyprus. The new world is just beginning, Moshe. And you are a part of it.'

I took the boy's hand and held it between my own. I felt we had become friends, the fire between us, the camp on the hill, the other volunteers scattered across the beach, the British in their uniforms, the young men and women distributing wood, the sea murmuring to us, our new country hidden beyond the dark horizon.

I could smell food and I now wanted to eat. Not this food. I wanted to eat the food that my wife would cook for me when I came home from the university at the end of the day. Waiting for me with our small daughter. In the old country. Before Palestine. Before America. In the old country, sitting with student friends in one of the small bars near the apartment. Drinking the full-bodied beer. Eating spiced sausage. Food. Drink.

Not on a beach in Cyprus. We had a country into whose life we slipped like a hand into a glove. I remember. Desks were rearranged. We now had to sit at the back, near the door. Soon after, there were young men in strange new uniforms. Saluting each other. Bright new flags. And now. Fruit on the trees. An army. Beautiful women. A new country to build. After two months in Cyprus, I was leaving at dawn. To go home. To go where? Away to the south. Away to the east. How much should I tell this boy? Truly I felt ashamed, for I had not described my country. I had described the country that might be his. The country that might belong to his children. The country that might belong to his children's children. My country? At dawn, going back to beautiful trees laden with fruit. But what about the joy of swirling snow on a cold winter's morning? And what about the thrill of being assaulted by an icy wind that charges its way towards you, down a narrow frost-ravaged street? And then, come springtime, the self-conscious flamboyance of impatient buds that burst into premature life. Watch me while I flower. No, watch me. In the parks, lakes and ducks and marching bands. And still the occasional chilly night, which requires a collar to be flicked skywards and the neck to be bandaged in a thick wool scarf. And then the sun-drenched courtyards of summer. And then later, in the autumn, a rose begins to unhinge its petals, and an apple lets go of its branch. In the old country. I left behind my brother and his dreams of our partnership. (*Why create another home? We can set up in practice together. The brothers Stern. We might become the richest doctors in the country.*) But Ernst, our lives are getting smaller. Shops and businesses are closing. You must go. (*To this primitive British colony of Palestine? I have dutifully bought the stamps to pay for the land that you buy from the Arabs. I have done my duty. Enough of this foolishness.*) But Ernst, America is not a golden land. They work like horses. It is difficult to make money. And Ernst, have you thought of your two girls? And if not the golden land, then where? Ernst, where are you taking them? And now in Cyprus. Where are they? Up on the hill with the rest of the refuse from old Europe? A futile and self-corrosive guilt. Wondering what else I might have done. Memory. That untidy room with unpredictable visiting hours. I am forever being thrust through the door and into that untidy room. Yes, my friend, the army will provide you with a port into which you might ultimately dock. Yes, the army. And the army will make sure that you continue to have a home. I was hungry. I wanted to eat now, but not in Cyprus. And not in the new country. How could I explain? Imagine any day of my old life. Walking on stone. Solid and secure. But now I walk on boards. Will they snap beneath my feet? A new world of boards. No stone. Nearly eleven years in Palestine. Two whole months in Cyprus. Boardworld. Imagine. Imagine. I still carry within me the old world that I once cast aside. (She is in America with my daughter.) And my two nieces. Dear Margot. Dear Eva. A world that I can never put down to rest. A world that, even now, I seem incapable of surrendering. Moshe, imagine. The snow. The full-bodied beer. The impatient buds. The stone beneath my feet. The icy wind of winter.

Moshe slips out his hand from between mine. Fruit growing freely on trees. Yes. Take it straight from the branch. Yes. He cannot understand. My years in the underground army. Enough killing. Now there will be a homeland. Yes. We can share. And so to finish my medical studies. And for some time now, simply a doctor. I never tried to find my wife and child. She wrote to me, saying that she respected my choice and she asked me to respect hers. She never wished to see me again. And now it is too late. I have let them go. Let them go. And in Cyprus, I have tried for two months to help those from the old world enter the new. The young with revenge in their hearts. Enough killing. Now there will be a homeland. We can share. But for these people on the hill, I imagined a smoother transition. A passage, not a rupture. In Cyprus, I have watched as Europe spits the chewed bones in our direction. (The flesh she has already swallowed.) I have encouraged my young Moshe to think only of the future. Here is some money. Go. And remember, we will kill you if we ever see you again. Tell me, what will be the name of the country? A good question. A fine question. It is difficult for me. My mind is tormented. You will marry a beautiful girl and have wonderful children. Israel. Moshe, think only of the future. My young friend, Moshe.

I WATCH as the trucks come roaring into the camp, dust and mud flying up behind their wheels. As the men jump down to the ground, they whistle and shout to each other. Then silence descends over them. They shield their eyes and look about themselves in disbelief. Silence. I count fifteen vehicles. The men are standing and staring at us. These men who are bursting with health. Some put their hands to their mouths and noses, while others pull handkerchiefs from their pockets and jam them into their faces. It is hard to know what they are thinking, but, whatever it is, they are struggling. This silent scene of us facing them. Skeletons facing men. Former prisoners facing liberators. We will no longer have to endure this captivity. We are free. These English men have arrived on this warm spring day and now we are free. Some among us begin to stumble and crawl towards the men. Weeping. Bodies twisted in bony gestures of supplication. I marvel at the fact that some of these men actually leapt from their vehicles. Leapt into the air. I sit with my back propped up against a hut, my spindly and scabrous legs stretched out before me, and I watch. Then I tilt my face so that I might soak up what little sun there is. I have no strength to be happy. My thin bones would shake and fall apart were they to be subjected to such an emotion.

It is some time before the man comes to me. I have been watching him. He is dressed in a heavy khaki uniform. He looks young. In fact, not much older than I am. He offers me some water and a piece of chocolate, both of which I take. And then he stands back and looks down at me as though unsure of what to do next. I want to tell him that it is fine. He can leave me now and attend to the others. I will be fine. There is nothing to worry about. I have survived this long. And then he speaks to me. Do you have any family? I swallow hard, and feel the brick of chocolate begin to slither its way down my throat. He continues to look at me and he waits for my answer. If I say, I don't know, will he think I am rude? I decide not to say this. Instead, I shake my head. His colleagues behind him are working furiously. The doctors wear gas masks, but we are used to the stench. People continue to die in their own excrement. Everybody is covered in lice. I am covered in lice. My body is withered. The light breeze fingers my stubbled head. The few teeth I have left are either broken or misdirected. I can feel them with my tongue. And still this man stands and looks down at me. Does he not understand that he can leave me? Because they have come today, and not some later day, I have survived. That is enough. I am grateful. But he does not move.

My Mama has left me alone. I do not tell this to the man who stands looking down at me. One morning, she did not wake up. She lay asleep and I spoke to her all day long in the hope that she might answer back. I had managed to convince myself that by the time the spring arrived, and the leaves were on the trees, Mama and I would be able to begin the task of forgetting. But, one night, her strength ran out. I spoke to her all day long, but I never received a reply. I wondered how, in the midst of all this misery, she managed to look so serene. And then, after my day of talking, the other women took me away from her and out of the hut. When I returned, there was another woman. My Mama was gone. The new woman understood why I could not find the words to talk to her.

I watch as he drifts away to join his colleagues. He stops and turns to look at me again. A nervous smile plays around the corners of his mouth. One of his fellow soldiers shouts at him, as though annoyed. He turns and breaks into a short run and joins him. And then I watch the friend point towards a place where men are carrying bodies. Now I understand. This is to be his job. To assist in the movement of dead bodies. Perhaps this will temper his idle curiosity.

Mama married beneath her. Of this she was sure. Her husband was a well-respected man, a young doctor, who eventually provided her with a beautiful four-storey house and two daughters. But Papa's was first-generation wealth. His parents were merely shopkeepers, and Papa had worked extremely hard to achieve his station in life. On the other hand, Mama's family were bankers, who, on both sides, were born to wealth and privilege as far back as one looked. Mama's sense of herself became the source of much of Papa's unhappiness, but Margot and I did not understand this until it was too late. Mama and Papa hid much from us. Perhaps we were too sheltered. It grew difficult for Papa to talk to Mama, and he spent increasing amounts of time in his surgery. And Mama grew to distrust her daughters, for her husband clearly preferred his children to his wife. She was isolated. She had married beneath her, and suddenly she found herself marooned between her distant husband and her difficult daughters. Mama never really knew how to talk to any of us.

. . .

14

On this first evening, they provide us with hot soup. Not hot water with a single potato thrown in to give it some body. This soup actually tastes of something, though of what I'm not sure. I sit by myself and marvel at the smell, the texture, and finally the taste of real food. Then I look up and gape at the disciplined manner in which my fellow inmates are lining up to receive their food. There is little pushing or shouting. All are hungry and anxious, but nobody usurps anyone else's position. Is this sheer fatigue, or have the good manners of the old world suddenly reimposed themselves? Darkness is beginning to fall, and the gloom casts a shadow across the camp. The sky, however, is streaked with red. Tomorrow will be a good day. I decide to drag myself to the end of the queue for more soup. Maybe tomorrow there won't be any. I don't know how to stop. At the moment, these men seem to possess an endless supply. In the distance, the soldiers continue to drag bodies towards the mass grave, the legs and arms forming convenient handles.

Papa hated taking us with him to the village near the border where his parents lived. Even as children, we could see that the poverty of his past embarrassed him. After all, what was his hard work for, if not to escape from such places and put this peasant life behind him? Some time in mid-afternoon, an impatient Papa would leave his parents' small cottage and stride across to the large oak tree. He would announce that we were returning to the city, but Margot and I would already know this. Long before he reached the oak tree, we would have pulled ourselves to our feet and dusted off our dresses. In the distance, his parents stood framed in the doorway, an anxious smile painted across their faces. Margot and I knew that Papa would have already prepared for our departure by bestowing a gift of money upon his parents; a gift which, I now realize, they would have gladly exchanged for more time with their son and their two grand-daughters.

Papa's parents were among the first to board the trains to the east. Word reached us after we had moved out of the four-storey house and into the small apartment. I was ashamed, for my first thought was of my grandparents' house, and how nobody would want a place in which there was no running water, and where the toilets were outside and did not flush. I tried to imagine Papa's parents nervously packing their bags with essentials, and then I looked across at Papa. The news of his parents' departure to the east seemed to have struck him a physical blow. Despite the fact that his whole life appeared to have been lived with a furious desire to heal the wound of his 'low' upbringing, I could see now that he clearly loved his parents. He knew only too well that his background would always be counted against him, especially by his wife. But now that a huge piece of it had fallen off and disappeared out of sight, Papa was lost and, for a moment, I feared he might cry. Mama was mixing flour and water, so that she might either boil it into a thin soup or fry it into pancakes. As yet, she had not decided which. Then she looked at her husband, and, realizing the full extent of his misery, she sat beside him at the tiny kitchen table and felt his brow with the back of her hand. Some years earlier, Mama's elderly parents had died in the comfort of their own beds, their world fortunately untouched by this present sorrow, convinced that their daughter had married in the manner that she had always lived her life: without patience. Their death had cast a temporary shadow across Mama's life, but it seemed that the news of his parents' deportation to the east had ushered Papa into a dark region from where it appeared unlikely that he would ever fully emerge. I stood up and left the table. Alone in my room, I hugged a childhood doll close to my chest, as though trying to smother the life out of her.

· · ·

I lay on my cot, surrounded by sounds of moaning and sickness. Through the window I can see that the red flecks in the sky have disappeared, and the night is now black. It must be the middle of the month, for the slender moon is cut into an unimposing shape. It is our first evening of freedom, but we continue to die. We are too weak to digest tinned meat or chocolate. The food that I pushed into my mouth now punches my stomach. The woman who took Mama's place has long since died, and tonight the new woman will die. She is burning with fever. I recognize the smell of death. I recognize the look of helplessness that marks a person's face as they prepare to pass over to the other side. And now the food rushes down the back of my legs towards my ankles. I roll on to my side and steer my thoughts towards Margot. She is all I have left. If I can find Margot, then perhaps together we might rebuild a life.

Four months in this place. Before this place, I worked. I struggled to keep death at bay. There were small ways of trying to stay alive. Cunning was a skill worth acquiring. As was endurance. Community formed the basis of our lives, but then came the long march, and yet another train, and then this place, which offered no community, no planning, no hope for survival. No work. Merely death. And waiting. I have spent most of the past four months on my cot trying to sleep. No work. And here, without community, without routine, only the strongest can survive. Every day I have stared death in the face. To become weak is to disappear. And eventually I felt myself becoming indifferent. Nothing bothered me any more. Those of us who have lasted until the arrival of these Englishmen, we have forgotten how to think of tomorrow. On this first night, I try to channel a course in my mind which might lead to the future. But it is not easy. I simply cling to the image of my sister.

· · ·

The sun rises, gloriously ignorant of the fact that a new day is not necessarily a good day. But perhaps today it will be warm. I now try to imagine ways in which I might prolong my life. In future, I must not gorge myself. I must drink only clean water. I must get in line to wash. I am acting as though I have already discovered a routine. As though I want to survive. I remind myself that this sunrise has already happened in some other place. And later, our sunset will be somebody else's sunrise. I look to the sky, where fully rigged clouds are already steering themselves towards some other destination.

He is approaching me from the side. I cannot see him, for I am sitting outside the hut and resting my back up against the wall. I can, however, hear him. My head is tilted slightly into the sun and my eyes are closed against the glare. I do not wish to see anything or anybody. I hear bulldozers. Too many bodies for bare hands. These Englishmen are learning to recognize the moment of death. When the lice crawl out of the hair and walk boldly about the forehead. That is death.

'Feeling any better today?'

I recognize the voice, but I do not open my eyes.

'Thank you,' I say.

There is a long silence, which I imagine will be resolved only if I turn to look at this man. But I decide to linger a while and choose not to turn. I do not hear him move off, so I assume that he is still here. And now, again, he speaks.

'More chocolate? I can get you some. Or something else?'

I open my eyes and turn to look at him. I cannot speak without exposing my ugly teeth.

'No chocolate.'

'Yes, I know,' he says. 'Some of the lads feel bad, but they gave it to you only because you asked. They didn't mean any harm.'

I wonder why he hasn't yet commented on my English. It's not too bad. Not everybody speaks English.

'Mind if I sit for a minute? I've got a break.'

He squats awkwardly next to me, then he lowers himself more purposefully to the earth.

'Where are you from?'

I lower my head, for now I'm anxious. I want this conversation to be over.

'Do you not want to talk? I can leave you by yourself, you know.'

'No,' I say. I have spoken too quickly, so I try to make up for my haste. 'My English is not very good.'

He laughs now.

'Your English is fine. I'm Gerry. From London.'

'Hello, Gerry.'

Already I have progressed too far.

'Hello,' he laughs. 'What's your name?'

This is enough. Gerry does not understand. I cannot possibly travel at the speed of this Gerry.

I stand under an open-air shower, naked in front of these men's eyes. But I do not feel like a woman, and I am sure that they do not regard me as one. The water is ice-cold, but no matter. It occurs to me that it will be years before I once more know what it means to feel clean. This first shower could last a week and still it would not suffice. I step clear of the water and a nurse empties powder all over my body. I am handed a fresh blanket which I drape around my shoulders. A doctor inspects my tufts of hair. A nurse cuts them off. Again, a factory line. Again, we are being processed. But this time for life. (Apparently, I weigh sixty pounds.) They give me women's clothing. I look around, but I cannot see Gerry. For some reason, I am sure that he can see me. I am sure that, somewhere in this vast camp,

Gerry is looking on with thoughts circling in his mind. He should show himself. Surely, I am no more hideous to look at than any of the others.

If Mama had been a more patient woman, it is possible that we might have gone to America. She could have talked quietly to Papa, instead of forever raising her voice and driving Papa into himself. Papa was the brightest of her father's medical students and, upon his graduation, he became a junior partner in her father's practice. It was then that Papa noticed Mama, for Papa was a frequent guest at their dinner table, and her father clearly enjoyed the knowledge and wit of this young man. But having secretly wooed the daughter, Papa was informed that not only would there be stern opposition to a marriage, but his services as a junior partner were no longer required. Papa was devastated, but Mama stood by him and they were married in a quiet ceremony to which neither set of parents were invited. Shortly before Mama's parents died, Mama and Papa were able to move from the small house they were renting into their own four-storey house, with their two daughters and the few pieces of furniture they had managed to buy.

Mama refused to employ a nanny, and raising her two children became her job. And then, as life deteriorated, she began to insist that they should leave for America, reminding Papa that if they left now they would impose no financial burden on the host country. But Papa was stubborn and Mama, instead of being patient, accused Papa of being typical of his class in his fierce attachment to his possessions. She raised her voice and accused him of cowardice, of not daring to begin again elsewhere, and of being happy to risk the future of his two daughters. This merely infuriated Papa, who could clearly see how impoverished and desperate the situation was becoming, but who refused to be ruled by a spoilt wife. And so he buried his head in his medicine and ignored his wife, and tried to pretend that nothing untoward was happening. But Mama talked incessantly about America, and about how important it was that she put our names on the list at the embassy, and when Papa refused to listen she would shout, and then sometimes scream, but Papa would simply close the door to his study. And then, of course, it was too late.

I watch Gerry. I stand hidden at the far end of the hut and peer at him through an open window. He is loitering about the place where I usually sit. To begin with, he paced about a little while smoking a hand-rolled cigarette. Now he sits and watches the world go by, occasionally relighting his cigarette and then coughing noisily. Today, the sun is too hot. I am taking shelter, although the smell inside this hut is loathsome. I am not sure what this Gerry seeks. His attention, while flattering, also causes me to worry. I decide that, in future, I will avoid this man as much as possible.

Tonight, we eat the same soup. It tastes familiar. After this soup I will wash.

Night falls and I return to my cot. I am cleaner, and my stomach has been satisfied. My bedding has been taken and burnt, so I must sleep on bare boards. There are fewer of us now. It is quiet. The seriously ill have been relocated to a tented hospital, and those of us who remain will not die with any undue clamour. The light from the moon casts a mournful pool on the floor. If only I could bathe my face in the pool, then surely I would emerge healed. I look around at my fellow women. All lie with their eyes open and their bodies broken. But slowly and silently, they are gathering strength. In the darkness, beyond the hut, I hear the sound of a soldier's raised voice. And then a nervous burst of laughter. But these noises aside, this night of freedom is tranquil. I continue to be bewitched by the moonlight on the floor.

I am awoken by a loud noise. It is bright outside. I realize that I am the only one left in the hut, and that I have actually slept peacefully. The noise outside is becoming louder and more raucous. I leave my cot and walk the few paces to the window. I look out. I see a long line of local townspeople. They are being forced to march past a huge mound of bodies. The English soldiers shout at them. And some of my fellow inmates shout at them too. But that is all. These miserable people continue to trudge by. I wonder how long this parade has been going on for? Hours? I notice that it will be a beautiful day.

I walk close to the barbed-wire fence and peer at the world beyond the camp. I touch the fence. I know where I am. I am suddenly appalled to realize that I am comfortable being confined. To remove the wire seems unthinkable. I know that I am free to trespass on the other side, to saunter out through the gate and bolt in any direction I choose. But looking at life through this fence suits me better. And then I realize that I cannot go back. I am sure that Margot will have found her way to America. Why go back? I am twenty-one now. I must begin to plan a future. Beyond the fence, a bird sets forth from a tree and soars into the air. But even while lost in flight, the bird remains beyond the fence. The bird never flies close to the fence.

I turn a corner and stop. Lying before me, encouraging me to step over it, is the battered corpse of a guard. His face is lumpy and misshapen, his limbs splayed. Near his body are a pair of freshly stained wooden staves. He wasn't a bad man. In fact, compared to some of the others, he was quite a good man. I step around the body and continue to walk. Why should the death of this one man affect me?

Margot loved the movies. Her room was plastered with pin-ups of the stars, but Mama did not like this, for she was concerned that both of her daughters should succeed at school. However, Papa said to leave her alone, for she wasn't harming anybody, and there was plenty of time to study. Margot was always trying to persuade me to come with her to the latest picture, and I envied Margot's preoccupation with the movies. Eventually it replaced her piano-playing, which she never really enjoyed. Compared to my sister, I was dull. I enjoyed school and studying, and Mama used to say, 'Margot is a dreamer, but Eva is like her father.' However, I could never understand whether Mama meant this warmly, or whether, deep down, this was a criticism of me. Eventually I realized that Mama's comment was born of both pride and disappointment.

I see Gerry walking towards me with his hands jammed deeply into his trouser pockets. He is pretending that he hasn't been looking for me, but a week has passed and I have been watching him. As he reaches me, he attempts a small but quickly abandoned whistle.

'Hello there. Feeling better?'

'Thank you.'

He's not a bad-looking man. In fact, he's quite handsome, although his thin moustache is a trifle old for him.

'Anything you need, you know you only have to ask.' He pulls an apple from his pocket. 'I saved this for you.'

Gerry holds out his hand and I take the apple from him.

'Thank you.'

'You haven't even told me your name. I told you mine. I'm Gerry.'

'My name is Eva.'

'That's nice.'

He fidgets slightly. I watch as he sways first left, then right, and then on to the outside edge of his boots.

'It must have been awful here. Have you been here long?'

'About four months.'

I have no desire to pursue this conversation with Gerry, but I feel as though the apple in my hand is some form of payment.

'On your own?'

I lie. 'Yes. On my own.'

'I see.'

Beyond the fence, the sun is beginning to set. A fiery, dramatic light on the horizon.

'We'll probably be here cleaning up for a while. But it's pretty much over for us now. Then back to civvy street.'

Why is this man talking to me as though we are friends?

'You can smile, you know.'

He laughs as he says this. He doesn't know that, should I attempt to smile, my face would break clean in two.

I sit outside the hut and stare at the sky. Tonight, I will not sleep. My head is full of worries. I worry about Papa. I worry about Mama. I worry about Margot. I worry about what else I might have done. Between torn patches of cloud, the sky is choked with stars. This night air is warm and clammy. I worry because there is nobody to help guide me in the right direction. I have never been alone. There has always been somebody. And now there seems to be just me and the night and the sky.

Gerry stands over me. All night, I have remained in the same place. He looks down with a concerned look on his face. I immediately sense that he wishes to say something, but he does not seem to know where to begin. I want to tell him that I like his silence. But before I have the chance to frame my statement, he moves slightly as though he is about to talk. The sun behind his head makes it difficult for me to look up and into his face.

Perhaps he has deliberately positioned himself so as to make me feel uncomfortable. I look past his legs to where his friends have slumped to the ground for a cigarette break. They appear to be relaxing, opening their shirts and rolling up their sleeves in order that they might attract some sun. I wonder what they think of their friend, Gerry? Is he regarded by them as some form of light entertainment? I wonder if they talk about him behind his back?

'Do you have any family? I mean brothers or sisters?'

Again, I squint up and in the direction of Gerry. What a strange question. I cannot understand why he would be asking such a question of me. Nevertheless, I start to answer.

'I have a sister, Margot. But I don't know where she is.'

I stop and wonder about my words. I measure their weight. I don't know where she is. And then I continue.

'Margot left us at the start of all this.' I pause. 'But I'm sure she's fine.'

Gerry shifts his weight from one foot to the other.

'Are you sure? I mean, you don't know where she is, right?'

I lower my eyes. I have compromised myself, for I had no intention of providing this man and his thin moustache with any insight into my life. Do not come any closer. My breath is foul with disease and tooth decay. I will say nothing further.

'I see.' He pauses. 'I'm sorry.'

I lie in the dark and listen to the noises of the night. There are less than a dozen of us in this hut, and most appear to be asleep. I hear a rapid volley of gunfire, then silence. Again, I hear a volley of gunfire. I slide from the cot and move to the window. A cloudless night. Behind the neighbouring hut I hear feet racing, and then I see a former guard break into view, his legs and arms pumping. And then again I hear bullets, and weapons are emptied. The guard tumbles gracelessly into the dirt, in much the same manner as I imagine an animal falls when it has

25

broken a leg. A group of men – former prisoners – run into view with guns in their hands. And then they see the body and stop. Among them are two English soldiers. And now I understand the nature of this approved slaughter. The group of men begin to walk slowly but purposefully across to the body. They look down at it, making sure that is it is truly dead. Clearly we are not beyond revenge. According to the Holy Scriptures, there should be more dignity than this. That much I remember.

At this point, the stream slows, then stops, then doubles back on itself. A large tree has fallen and all floating debris, all fish, even the water itself, have to find another way around this bulky obstacle. The tree has bent the stream. I walk further along the path, past this tree, and then scramble up the grassy bank. Once I reach the top, I look across the field towards the low profile of the town. All is quiet. I do not know what day of the week it is. Tuesday? Friday? Sunday? I long ago gave up any pretence of attempting to maintain vigilance over the weekly calendar. It may be that today is their day of rest. I simply do not know. I look back towards the stream, and on the other side of the water I see a group of children playing beneath the arch of a huge willow. They are boys, with one solitary girl among them. One of the boys is looking towards me, and I am suddenly aware of how I must appear to these healthy children. I am in possession of a strange body that bulges in unlikely areas, and remains painfully skinny in others. A comical, perhaps frightening figure. And then a pebble is thrown. I assume it will be the first of many. I stand and stare at the children, who laugh and point at me. I know they do not mock me. Eva. They do not know me. They mock what I look like, not who I am. And then another pebble. And another. I turn now and walk back along the top of the grassy bank, careful not to break into a run, careful not to betray any panic. I walk slowly, but with purpose and dignity. And I feel the pebbles fly past, the occasional one striking me a bruise-inflicting blow. But I do not hurry. I will not run.

My sister leads the way up the steep slope that lies just below the summit. I am struggling, but I do not ask her to slow down or stop. She will not leave me behind. I will not allow this. I lower my head and redouble my efforts, concentrating on each footstep, one foot in front of the other, slowly, first one foot and then the next, the incline working against me, the air thin, my legs screaming with pain, and then suddenly the hillside gives way and the ground is level. Margot is beaming at me, but I simply throw myself forwards and on to the grass. I roll over on to my back. I close my eyes, but we are so close to the sun that I feel myself being grilled. It is hot. Margot, water. I roll on to my side and can see that she has the bottle to her mouth, her head tilted back, and she is gulping deeply. Margot, water. She swivels her eyes in my direction, but still the bottle is to her mouth. Margot! I sit on her bed and watch as she picks up her suitcase. The snow continues to fall. (*Sister, will we two disappear like stones in a well?*) For a moment our eyes lock. And then Margot pushes me back on to the bed and starts to laugh. I still dream, one memory swirling into the other. Every night I endure an uncomfortable journey to a place of distorted and unnecessary recollection. And, come morning, I am grateful to be uncoupled from the night.

I find Gerry standing by the trucks with a group of his friends. They are all smoking cigarettes and they appear anxious. I approach Gerry, but I discover that as I move closer to him my nerve begins to fail me. I do not know what to say. Then Gerry sees me and turns from his friends.

'Eva.'

He throws his cigarette to the ground. He takes a step towards me and puts his hand on my arm. I understand. He is steering me away from his friends, for he does not intend to introduce me. He is smiling, and I am sure that he is genuinely pleased to see me. But he is hurrying.

'We can sit here.'

We sit on a pile of wooden boxes that look as though they probably contain supplies of some kind. I begin.

'I have to find Margot.'

For a moment there is silence. Then Gerry turns himself around so he is facing me square-on.

'Are you all right? You look like you've had a shock of some kind.'

'I'm fine,' I say. 'I just need to find my sister.'

Gerry stands and stretches his legs. He lights another cigarette, tosses down the match, then inhales and quickly blows out the smoke. He sits now, his cigarette carefully poised between finger and thumb.

'I thought you said you don't know where she is.'

'I don't.'

'I can look when I get back to England. They're bound to have some sort of agency for tracing people. And I can look here. The D.P. camps. They have some kind of system too.'

'Thank you.'

I look at him. I'm not sure what he will do, but I know that he wants to help. That's all I want. I just need some help.

There is a light tapping at the window to the hut. I am still lying down, my mind swirling about in a haze of dreams. Again, I hear a tapping, and now a voice. It is Gerry. At the window. A few days ago, the other women who shared this hut abandoned me. They became hostile and refused to talk to me. They accused me of stealing their food. They accused me of behaving without regard or concern for them. They accused me of being crazy. I am a twenty-one-year-old young woman. What harm could I possibly inflict upon these women? Why treat me in this way? I was no threat to them. I walk to the window and look at Gerry. He points to the door. He wants to come in. I smile and shake my head. He looks puzzled. He does not seem to understand that a lady cannot simply admit a man to her bedchamber in this manner. It would be unthinkable. He raises his voice.

'You must wait in the displaced-persons camp. I will get word to you about your sister.'

I nod my head.

'There are refugee committees both here and in England. I will find out about Margot.'

'Thank you.'

He smiles at me, but I know that he is unhappy. I know that he wishes I would open the door for him so that he might deliver his message in a more intimate manner. He wants to be my knight in shining armour. He wants to rescue me. And I suppose I am encouraging him a little in his quest. I see no harm in this.

I spend the afternoon sitting by myself. I have claimed a new berth, out in the open, in the full glare of the sun, close to the fence. I sit on a pile of discarded timber, squeezing myself into a crevice which holds me as though it were a comfortable chair. From this position, I can watch the sunlight moving like a cat along the palings of the fence. Since Mama left, I have grown accustomed to being solitary. But these days, even if I wished for company I would probably find myself alone. Tears begin to well in my eyes. These past years have hurt me in mind and body. I sit on this pile of wood. Close to the fence. On a warm spring afternoon.

Gerry stands and watches me while I drink my soup. I know that he will not approach until I have finished. I put down my still full bowl and walk towards Gerry. He begins.

'I wanted to talk to you.'

I do not express any surprise or concern. I know he wants to talk to me. This is why I have approached him. But I do not say this to him. I simply wait to hear what he has to say to me. He reaches into his pocket and pulls out a small bundle of notes.

'I want you to take this.'

I look at his money and begin to laugh. Money. I remember money. It is absurd to imagine that, for people out in the world, money has continued to be of value. I cannot control my laughter. Gerry does not understand why I am laughing. But he decides not to ask.

'There is a cinema in the town. You should go.'

I step back from him. How does he know about the movies?

'Please, take it. You have to get used to doing normal things again.'

For a brief second I hate Gerry. How dare he talk to me about normal? About what I have to do. I do not have to do anything that I do not want to do. He has no idea of what is normal and what is not normal. Just who, I wonder, does he imagine he is talking to? A child? I turn away from him, but I feel his hand on my arm.

'No. Eva. Take the money. Do what you want with it. Spend it on yourself, be selfish with it, I don't care.'

I look again at Gerry. Then at the money in his hand. He is trying to buy my affection. But if I am to find my sister, I need this man's help. I take the money. I speak as loudly as I can, but I know that it comes across as little more than a whisper.

'Thank you.'

Gerry smiles.

I have lain on my cot as long as possible. I can see through the window that the sun has almost reached the highest point in the sky. It is noon. The hut is empty. They continue to ignore me. I am too much trouble. I am naked. I decide that I will dress carefully. The clothes will, of course, be the same. But I will put them on as though they were the finest garments in the world. I will be new and I will look graceful. I let my head drop over the side of my cot. My fingers push into my shoe. I find the money neatly bundled up in its hiding place. It is not really a hiding place, more a place of safety. There is nobody here who will steal this money from me. There is nobody here. There is no reason to hide it. Sometimes I become confused.

A plume of smoke rises and twists through the cone of light. The sharpness and power of this cone of light seizes my attention. The picture is about America. A gangster picture with lots of shooting, and cars tearing after each other, and men shouting. In the gloom, I can see there are only a half-dozen or so other people in the cinema. But I watch the smoke. I watch the tall plume of smoke which rises slowly, twisting and turning through the cone of light.

The small park is surrounded by elm trees. I sit on a bench in the shade of these trees and stare at the fountain. There is no water. The park is deserted. Cloud-shadows slide past in a smooth parade. There is the kind of silence that convinces me that all around there are people. Watching and waiting to see what I will do. And then an elderly couple appear. They walk arm in arm towards me. They stare directly at me, then the woman looks from me and glances across at her husband. I know what he is thinking, but I do not care. He is free to think whatever he wishes. I have every right to sit in this park and enjoy the afternoon breeze. I am harming nobody, not even myself. As they pass by, she turns back towards me and smiles in my direction. But the man does not relax his severe expression.

I lie on my cot, but, as hard as I concentrate, I can hear no noise. This is the first night that I have heard neither shouting nor distant laughter. And it is a dark night. I lie suspended without sound, without sight, without distraction. Focusing on myself and my fears. Worried about everything. Simply everything. The tinned meat. A layer of lard on top, the meat underneath. Should I eat it? Can I eat it? And does the weight of the dead add itself to the earth? And if so, will the earth stop moving? Will it? Mama. Papa. There is not even a place where I might wear an uneven circle into the matted grass around your graves. And still I try to master these new gestures of life. How to use a toothbrush. How to fold toilet paper. How to say hello and goodbye. How to eat slowly. How to express joy. The rediscovery of smell. The smell of a tree. The smell of damp. The smell of rain. I worry about smell. A flower's perfume would knock me over. I worry about everything. The visit to the cinema has not managed to wash the anxieties from my mind. When I arrived back this evening, I looked for Gerry. I wanted to tell him that I did what he hoped I might do. I did not want to say, 'Thank you.' I just wanted to be able to let him know that I had done what he hoped I might do. But there was no sign of Gerry.

I look out of the window. The morning is overcast. The relative bleakness of the day causes my anxieties to resurface. I worry that there may be some return to the situation that existed before these men arrived. Camp life. The scream that deafens with its terror, the terror of deafening silence. The rigidity of motion, heavy stones weighing on everybody's hearts. Travelling daily beyond the frontiers of life with an obscene selfishness as one's sole companion. Forever hungry, no longer amazed at how quickly the body deteriorates, intrigued by the temporary peace with the skeletal, the unbearable pain of hunger, promising the shrinking body warm food, all night thinking of food. Killing only the lice, but not the eggs. Being bitten behind the ears and between the legs, in moist areas, little blood bumps that burst if you scratch. And always the violence of memory. Camp life. A return to the loneliness of this situation? There is no companionship in despair. But we are liberated and I choose to remain alone. (I want Margot. I want dear Bella.) I glance around at the empty cots, and I realize that I have created a prison. I have locked myself in this hut among the ghosts of strangers. Am I an offering? What is happening to me that I prefer to be in this hut? The humid atmosphere is foul, for the air has been trapped in this building for many days and many nights. But there are people who will talk to me. There are people who would be happy to talk to me.

I run to another of the men. He is climbing up and into the back of a truck, the engine of which is already running.

'Please. Where is Gerry?'

The man flicks his cigarette butt to the ground, and then continues to chew on his gum.

'Gone, love. Don't ask me where. Most of us are going.'

'Will you be back?'

By now, the engine is roaring and I can tell by the changing notes that the truck will soon pull away. I shout again, this time louder.

'Will you be back?'

'Dunno, love. But you'll be all right. You've made it.'

And then, almost as an afterthought, as the truck begins to pull away, he calls to me.

'If I see him, I'll tell him that you were asking after him.'

He waves, the canvas frame flapping around him, and then the truck begins to pick up speed. Behind me, the soldiers are trying to organize us into groups for processing. Everybody is on the move. Them. Us. People are leaving. And now I understand. Gerry gave me the money as a leaving gift. That was it. He wanted to give me a leaving present. I see a woman whom I remember from the long journey here. She looks at me, her dark eyes momentarily narrowed. I say nothing. I simply turn and walk in the opposite direction, back towards my hut.

I sit on my timber and angle my head towards the sun. My friend, the sun, has once more returned. And then I see them, in the distance. I rub the back of my hands into my eyes. A man with a camera. And other people, including a young woman. She is not much older than me. They are filming. She is fat. They are moving purposefully, like a slow train, towards me. I assume that they will want to know what life was like before the English soldiers arrived. I begin to undress slowly. We were happy. Every day was spring.

I stand by my window. I stare out at the world, then I turn and look around my empty hut. I rehearse in my mind the steps that have led me to this place. My empty hut. Then I disengage my mind from such disquieting thoughts and try to concentrate on the day at hand. But today there is nothing on which to concentrate. The film people are still here. I can see them through the window, wandering about in their sluggish manner. They did not film me. Cowards. I can see three soldiers (two men and a woman) who sit behind a clumsy wooden table. A single line of us queues in front of each of them. They are continuing to process us for D.P. camps. Slowly, they are emptying this camp. Gerry has already gone. I will stay in my hut today. I do not wish to be a part of their world.

I dreamt that nobody believed me. That I was in America and I was telling some people my story, the despondent words falling awkwardly from my mouth. Just *my* story. (. . . *dazed children wandering the streets, searching for their parents* . . .) They looked at me, their faces marked with respect, and they nodded with cultivated fascination. Nobody wished to offend me. And then a man looked at his watch. In America.

. . .

I like the way birds fly. At first you see the effort, how they flap
their wings frantically as they build up speed and direction. And
then they stop and glide confidently. And then comes my
favourite part, when they suddenly start to flap their wings
again and build up speed. That's what I do these days. I just sit
here on my timber and watch the birds beyond the fence. I
watch their communal flight. Every day, they beat a thin black
ribbon across the sky. There are too many to give them names,
or to get to know them personally. I just sit here on my timber
and watch them. Every day. My name is Eva Stern. I am
twenty-one years old. Just when I think I am going to fall, I flap
my wings.

Again I had the same dream. (. . . *dragging her child behind her
like a secret crime* . . .) This time I knew one of the people looking at me. Gerry. He was in America with all the other faces.
This time they were trying hard not to laugh, for they wanted
to hear more of my story. (. . . *the other woman was holding a tiny
baby that was wrinkled like a foot* . . .)

Today, Mama arrived back in the camp. At first I was angry, for I
thought the person lying in the cot next to me must have broken in during the night in order to steal something. And this
being the case, why lie down next to me? Why not go to one of
the other cots? Before I could say anything, the woman turned
her face towards me and I saw it was Mama. I wasn't frightened.
I was expecting her to return, for I never truly believed that she
had gone. And now she is back. I hold her hard and encourage
her to tell her story once more. Of how they took her from this
hut and left her for dead. Of how she took shelter in another
hut, among people who spoke a language that she simply could
not understand. But they fed her, and looked after her, and then
they forsook her, for they were part of the group that, upon the

arrival of the English soldiers, immediately fled. Mama tells me about how she struggled to look after herself on the far side of the camp. She touches my face as though still unable to believe her luck.

'But Mama,' I ask, 'why did you not come and look for me?'

Mama looks sad now.

'They told me that you were dead, and I believed them.'

'Dead?'

'Yes. They told me you were dead.'

I touch my Mama's face, her lips, her eyes, her nose. I stroke her wisps of hair. Mama is back with me. I can now begin to plan a future for both of us.

It is night. Neither Mama nor I have ventured out of this hut today. We are both hungry and thirsty, but we have spent the day together, talking. Mama is sure that Margot is fine and in America. Margot will not have stayed behind. We laugh at the idea of Margot in the movies. Dear Margot in Hollywood. Papa is dead. Mama and I know this. There is little further to say about this. We agree that we need not concern ourselves with how he might fit into our future plans. He simply does not. Outside, I imagine the night air is still heavy with the heat of the day. I tell Mama about my birds. I tell her about where I sit and watch them. I promise her that I will take her there. Maybe tomorrow. Maybe the day after. At present, I am concerned only with Mama and her words. She smiles at me and I know she understands.

The woman seems to be losing patience with me. I can tell by the way she looks down at the paper and taps her pencil against the desk. She is quite pretty, with short dark hair and hazel eyes. Even the drab, lifeless colour of her uniform cannot entirely detract from her glamour.

'Are you waiting for anybody from home?'

Stupid woman. Waiting where? Who knows where I am. I am not sure myself. I refuse to speak.

'Do you intend to go home?'

How can she use the word 'home'? It is cruel to do so in such circumstances. I cannot call that place 'home'. 'Home' is a place where one feels a welcome. For a moment, her eyes meet mine, but now she drops them again, and once more she resumes her tapping.

'I'll put you down for a D.P. camp. You can decide later what you want to do or where you want to go.'

She prepares to write, then she pauses. She looks up at me. When her teeth show they glisten beneath a thin coating of saliva.

'I have your home town and your family details. Is there anything else that I should know?'

I shake my head. I will not tell her about Mama. That is my business.

'All right, you may go.'

And now I understand that I am being dismissed and another person is to take my place. Fine. I understand the terms of this game. I am here, then I am gone. I matter only as long as I answer questions. I decide to stand my ground. She glances up at me, but this time with a puzzled look.

'You may leave.'

I will not torment her hazel eyes any further.

It is early evening, but the sun has not yet descended beneath the horizon. I am in another line. I am waiting for a second bowl of soup. I know nobody will question me. They have learnt when to see me, and when not to see me. How to ignore me effectively. I am a strange one. I know this is what they think. She is a strange one. But I cannot stop them thinking whatever it is they need to think. The man knows that this is my second bowl of soup, but these soldiers seem to take pleasure in our returning for more. He smiles and drops the spoon deeper into the pot. He makes sure that I get vegetables too. I smile back at him, then scurry off towards the hut with the bowl cupped between my hands. I do not look around to see if anybody is watching. My eyes are fixed firmly upon the ground in front of me. Mama is sitting on the edge of the cot. I hurry across and hand her the soup. She touches her daughter's hand as she takes it from me. Then she begins to drink the warm soup, and I edge back towards the door and lock it shut. Safe. Just mother and daughter. This is how I always want it to be.

Again, I hear the knocking on the door, but I remain where I am. I will not open the door. For two days and two nights, I have lain on this cot without venturing outside. Mama is worried that they will think something is wrong if they do not see me, but I do not want to leave her. I cannot afford to lose Mama again. Despite her pleadings, I have stayed with her for two days and two nights. The knocking begins again, and this time swells into a pounding. The man's voice is ordering me to open up. He assures me that he means no harm. Mama looks at me. The expression on her face is clearly designed to urge me to do as the man wishes. So I walk to the door and open it. Before me stand two men in uniform: an older man who is clearly responsible for the knocking, and a younger man who stands nervously behind him. It is the older man who speaks.

'Nobody means to intrude on your privacy, but we're worried. I'm a doctor.'

I stare back at him, urging him to continue.

'You have to understand that you must mix with people. You cannot allow yourself to just fade away. You've been through a lot.'

I hold the door so that it is impossible for him to see inside the hut. I do not want him to see Mama.

'I am fine.'

I say this quickly, for I now want him to leave.

'Are you ready to go to the D.P. camp? We need to evacuate this place. The air's not good, and it'll be better for you there.'

'I'm ready to leave. Not today. But I will leave.'

This seems to satisfy him. A smile creeps across his face. While I have the upper hand, I speak again.

'I will come and meet people.'

'Good. There are those of us who wish to help you.'

I nod curtly, then close the door against this doctor and his silent friend. I turn to look at Mama, who lies fearfully on her cot. She cannot continue to live like this.

I wait a few minutes before venturing out to get Mama another bowl of soup. Now I am back, but Mama will still not talk to me. I ask, 'Is it Margot?' No answer. I ask, 'Mama, what is it?' No answer. I ask, 'Mama, are you not well?' No answer. I ask, 'Mama, have I done something to offend or upset you?' No answer. I ask, 'Mama, is it Papa?' She turns to me and puts down her bowl of soup. It is Papa.

'Last night, Eva. I had a dream in which Papa told me that we were on our own now. Just you and me, my child.'

'And Margot?'

Mama begins to shake her head and sob.

'Just you and me.'

I hug Mama, but I am not sure if she is aware of me.

Neither Mama nor I have slept. We have stayed awake all night planning. And now, as the sun pours through the window, I watch as an exhausted Mama collapses into sleep. Tonight, she will leave. For the big city by the river. We will meet in the market square in two days' time. There is bound to be a market square. On this, we both agree. Mama will go first and hitch a ride with a military vehicle. English, American, it does not matter. I will follow. If we travel together, we will only attract attention. And then we will go on together to America. Despite Mama's dream, we both know that Margot is alive and living in America. (Dear Margot in Hollywood.) And it is to Margot and America that we will flee.

We see the young soldier by the gate. We crouch behind the small wall and wait until he turns and marches off to resume his patrolling of the perimeter. There are a few stars in the sky, but the night is uncommonly dark. Perfect for Mama to leave. The soldier passes from view, and Mama and I begin to half-walk, half-dash towards the gate. I ask myself, why this furtiveness if we are free? About one hundred yards down the road, Mama and I stop under an oak tree. This is as far as I will come, and Mama knows and understands this. I take her hand and squeeze. She looks beautiful under the night sky. Mama even manages a smile. I hand the small bundle to her, with its piece of bread and other meagre provisions. And then we embrace.

'Two days,' I say. 'I will see you in two days.'

I watch as Mama begins her adventure. And when I can no longer see her, I turn. I begin to wander back in the direction of the camp. But the young soldier has followed us. He steps from the gloom and presents himself. He says nothing, and simply looks at me. Then he takes a step forward and touches my left breast. He cups it, as though feeling its weight. And then he applies pressure. I hope that Mama does not find a reason to turn back and find me in this predicament.

I sit on my timber. Gerry stands over me. He looks older, as though he has passed through some terrible crisis. He tells me that there was another place to 'liberate'. He says the word slowly, carefully weighing it in his mouth as though distrustful of it. Whatever they have done or seen at this other place, it has marked them all. They seem somehow shabbier. But then it occurs to me that perhaps these are exactly the same men, but now seen through the lens of my own improved condition. Gerry tells me that I was the first person he came to look for. He was worried that I might have left. I think to myself, why should he worry? I tell him that I am going to find my sister, although I still don't know where she is. I tell him nothing about Mama. Gerry seems hurt that I am suggesting a course of action which excludes him.

'But I can help you find your sister. I'll be going back to England in the next few days, and I told you I can contact all the groups. People know about things like that over there. It's chaos here.'

I look at him. He's not a bad man.

'Thank you, Gerry.'

He seems relieved. But he does not move. He continues to stand over me.

It is evening. I am supposed to be packing a suitcase for a journey in the morning. But this is not my suitcase. To whom does this suitcase belong? It does not matter, for I have nothing to put in the suitcase. I will be holding my few possessions, much like Mama. A suitcase suggests a life. It seems appropriate that I should emerge into the world clutching a bundle. I kick the suitcase. I am not bitter. I just do not want to pretend. Not now. Not ever. Mama will be expecting me in the big city by the river. In the market square. But she will have to see me without a suitcase.

Gerry stands at the door to the hut. Behind him I can see people climbing aboard trucks. Engines are roaring and orders are being shouted. It seems that today is the day they have chosen finally to clear the whole camp. This morning marks the beginning of the end.

'I've brought you some food for the journey.'

Gerry hands me a paper bag which I take. I do not open it. I want to indicate to Gerry that I trust him.

'Thank you.'

'I have the address of your D.P. And here, this is for you.'

He holds out a piece of paper that is folded over twice, as though containing a secret.

'My address in London,' he says. He appears to be beaming with pride. 'You must write to me if you need anything. Otherwise I'll write to you.'

He pauses and looks around himself.

'You should come to London. I think you'd like it.'

I smile, and wonder just what it is that Gerry imagines makes this London so special.

'Here, take it.'

He thrusts the piece of paper towards me.

'Thank you, Gerry.'

'Don't thank me,' he says. 'Not till you've made use of it.'

It is almost evening. I am sitting on my timber. My birds still dare not cross the fence. And then I sense the presence of Gerry. I do not need to look up to know that it is Gerry.

'What happened?'

I do not turn to face him. I feel content. The sun has shed her final shell of heat for the day.

'There were too many people.'

'You'll have to go tomorrow.'

I look up at him. Poor boy, with his silly moustache. I know I will have to go tomorrow. Mama will be waiting for me.

'When you come to London, will you marry me?'

He pauses as though his own words have shocked him to his core. As the silence deepens, I can see that he desperately needs me to rescue him.

'Gerry,' I begin.

'Eva.' He pauses. 'When you're better, of course. Will you marry me?'

'I'm sorry. No.'

Gerry shrugs his shoulders in a theatrical manner. And then he begins to laugh.

'Nobody loves a loser. I suppose I'm just going to be left on the shelf.'

I do not know what he means, but I watch his attempt to enjoy his own laughter. There is something about this man that I like. But he can never understand somebody like me. None of them can.

It is morning and I am ready. After I leave, only the sick will be left behind. I carry my small bundle and climb up and into the truck. I seat myself at the back and look around. Of course, there is Gerry. And beyond Gerry, the camp. The soldiers still scurry about and try to impose themselves upon the place. Now that there is hardly anybody left, they are almost succeeding. Small fires are burning, and in some places the more energetic among the soldiers have begun to level the barracks. Others appear to be more fatigued, and they simply broom remnants into neat ridges. I want to tell them all, no. The camp must be renounced. Once we have gone, just walk away and leave it. See who comes to claim the remains. The engine thunders into life. As it does so, I cling to the side. Even before we have begun to move, Gerry starts waving. I smile in his direction. My liberator. Goodbye, Gerry. Goodbye.

We race through the countryside, turning heads as we do so. Myself and a dozen others, most of whom choose to ignore me, having no doubt been informed that I prefer my own peculiar company. I wish now that I had not sat at the back of the truck, for the fumes rise and curl their poisonous way into the vehicle

at precisely the point where I am sitting. It is particularly difficult whenever we idle at a junction, or when we slow down to
pass through a narrow lane. All around I can see the evidence of
war. The lanes are littered with long lines of defeated soldiers
and discarded vehicles. However, set against this there are strange
visions of normal life. Schoolchildren. Pet dogs. Newspapers.

After many hours we eventually slow down, then cross a
wooden bridge over a river, and now we are entering the outskirts of a city. Silence. And again, another of these strange visions. I see a woman pushing a pram in which I can see a baby.
We all stare. The child has healthy red cheeks. My fellow evac-
uees cling to their suitcases and stare. The woman to my right
offers me an English cigarette, which I take. She lights it. I am
not sure how to smoke, but it cannot be too difficult. But now I
feel it affecting me. My head feels light. An eerie feeling of in-
difference. I want to smile. I smile at her, my way of thanking
her. There are other strange sights. In front of us, a military vehicle. Not English. Perhaps American. A khaki-curtained vehicle, so we cannot see inside. Now my head begins to spin. Up
above, the poor clouds huddle together. And then they begin to
weep. Light rain. We have reached our destination.

I sit on the edge of a bed. On the bed are clean white sheets.
But the most disturbing sight of all is a pillow. I had forgotten
that such items existed. The other women from my camp are in
this makeshift dormitory with me, and they, too, sit on their
beds. They talk excitedly to each other, and one of them jumps
up and runs to a door. Another runs to a window and peers
out. Then they sit back down again. They are making nervous
plans. For Palestine. They speak with a sudden and miraculous
energy, and I listen to them in silent fascination. Apparently, we
have wandered long enough. We have worked and struggled
too long on the lands of other peoples. The journey that we are

making across the bones of Europe is a story that will be told in future years by many prophets. After hundreds of years of trying to be with others, of trying to be others, we are now pouring in the direction of home. I am not included in their plans, for they know not to waste their time. Neither Margot nor Mama are in Palestine. There is no need for me to go to Palestine. But, like them, I have feelings. I understand the passion that they must feel. I, too, have survived the storm. I, too, will soon be issued with identity papers. I, too, have dreamt of Palestine. And once we are together again, if either Mama or Margot wishes to go to Palestine, then to Palestine we shall go. And perhaps I will see these women again in the promised land.

I swing my legs up and on to the bed, and I stare through the window. It is evening now, and the light is fading. We have come to the right D.P. camp. We are on the outskirts of the right city. And tomorrow I will meet Mama in the square. But there is no reason for me to flaunt my good fortune. It is bad manners to do so. I try to let the other women know that I, too, like them, am happy. I do not want to dampen the atmosphere. I try to smile at them, but they consider me unreliable. I understand this. I am not angry. I listen to their planning, to their excitement, and I wish that I, too, had somebody with whom to share my joy. But all of us, in our own way, will now survive.

And now, at the end of the day, I have to admit that, again, there will be no Mama. For almost one week I have sat on this bench from sunrise to sunset. And then I walk back to the displaced-persons camp and take my meal with the rest of them. Men, women and children. I have my routine. I sit in the market square and I stare at the poster across the way. A splendid, colourful poster with a bright sun, a marine sky and bronzed shores. Come to Greece! I want to go on a voyage. What a temptation. What luxury. People pass by and glance at me.

Their lives are also miserable. Their eyes are filled with despair, their faces are glum, their heads are bowed to the ground. Their hearts are icy. I look at them and I whisper to myself. You deserve this unhappiness. You deserve it. In this city, people played in the park in the summer. In this city, people skated on the river in winter. At the end of the day, as the sun begins to set, I rise to my feet. It is a mile or so back to the camp. It will not take long. And when I return, there will be food.

It is simply another day. Why sit here any longer? There is no Mama. There never was a Mama, neither in this camp nor in the last. There is a place that I must find. A place to which Margot now belongs. A place to which I might travel. I am lucky. (Am I?) I am sorry, but I do not recognize this world any more. Why sit here any longer among these people who hurry across this market square, dragging their miserable lives behind them? They cannot know what I know. They can never know what I know. Full of their stupid importance. No, I will not waste my time enlightening them. No. Mama is gone from me and I am alone. For more than one week now, I have been afraid to face this. I have not wanted to see this. But now I see it, as clearly as I see my Greece at the corner of the square. These stupid, distressed people walking by me. Their bearing respectable but defeated, my imagination ruined. I have no Mama. And so back for more food. I must leave this bench before sunset and go back to the camp. I remain constantly haunted by food. Even though there is plenty to eat, I always carry a piece of bread hidden about me. I am ashamed.

I have spent a whole month avoiding impertinent questions. I eat with them, what more do they want from me? I am frightened to fall asleep at night in case I talk and reveal something about myself. Both day and night, I stare at the other women. Clearly I have unnerved them. But I am trying to be good. And whenever the women begin to sing in Yiddish, 'Pioneers prepare themselves for Palestine', I too join in, my voice weak, often mouthing the words, but I try. I still try. And then I received the letter from Gerry. And then I talked. I am going to be married. That was my announcement. In England. The camp authorities agreed to arrange my journey, but only after I showed them the letter. I told the women in my dormitory: He wants me to come to England and marry him, and so I will go. They were puzzled, but the camp authorities understood. We will give you money and arrange your passage. You're very lucky. Congratulations. My life here is dead. I lie down at night without a life. I rise up in the morning without a life. Mama, why did we not all hide together? Mama, why did Papa not turn around and look at me as he wheeled to the right?

Tomorrow, I leave for England and Gerry. I am to pass this final night in a new dormitory. With one other woman. This woman talks to me. She tells me that she went back and found nobody. That her family furniture had been burnt as firewood by the townspeople. That her family house was derelict. She tells me that she found a photograph in a frame. The glass was broken and the picture torn, but this is all she has left. (*I stayed one night and then ran for my life.*) She smiles at me. She says that she has heard. That they have given me some money and a ticket. She tells me that she simply wished to live long enough to witness the end of the war and then one hour more. But now she is happy. There is a new life. (*A new life for all of us, if we trust in God and believe again.* This is what she says.) She has a present for me. She slips it into my hand and then leaves the room. I know what I have to do. I wait for a few moments and then move across to the mirror. A stranger's face, with large puffy eyes. I do not want this anguished expression. How can this stranger be me? I look like them, ugly and ravaged. I begin to laugh at this mask. I smear the lipstick around my mouth. A jagged slash, red

47

like blood. Tomorrow, they will release me into an empty world with only Gerry for company. Gerry has never seen my true face. Oh Gerry, my heart is broken. Perhaps you can mend it a little, but it will never again be complete. Do you understand this? How can she give me this useless lipstick? How can she give me such a present? I am not like them. I am not.

In March of 1480, the people of the small town of Portobuffole, near Venice, were preparing their houses for the much anticipated arrival of relatives. The winter was at an end and the weather had already turned mild, but, more importantly, it appeared that the famine which had troubled the lives of these people for the past three years was now over. There were provisions for everybody, although the poorer members of the community could not afford to indulge themselves with luxuries. However, every household could boast either pork or eggs, or both, and the eager townsfolk now waited for the priest's blessing of house and food before completing their tables with delightful flowers and scented herbs.

The women, in particular, watched the streets in a state of anxiety, for the majority of them were looking for their men. The Most Serene Republic of Venice had recently made a reluctant peace with the infidel Turk and, once again, the Venetian army was being demobilized. Every day, the women expected to see their loved ones, and they contemplated the streets in anticipation of a joyful reunion. There was, however, a further reason why the streets were being scrutinized in such a concentrated manner. After raging for almost a full year, the plague had mercifully ceased, but the old suspicion of strangers remained. So, even as they looked for their men, the women also kept a sharp eye open for those they did not recognize. And then, on one evening, shortly before sunset, a young beggar boy entered the town, but sadly the women did not follow him closely. The boy's hair was blond and unkempt, his tattered linen skirt brushed his bare feet, and he carried a worn sack across one shoulder. One woman did speak to him, for he asked her the name of the town, and the woman remembered that the boy's difficult foreign accent reminded her of her husband's when he had first been recruited to the region by the Venetian army. There was one other woman who saw the boy, but unfortunately she did not speak to him.

The blacksmith claimed he had been busily shoeing a horse at the time that he saw the young vagabond. The boy approached him cautiously and asked him the way to the Jew Servadio's home. It was nearly dusk, and the blacksmith remembered that he simply pointed the wretch in the appropriate direction. The blacksmith then returned to the urgent business of shoeing the horse, in order that he might return it to its impatient owner before nightfall. It was important that the child had also been seen by a man, albeit the temperamental and somewhat unpredictable blacksmith, for in these times nobody would accept the word of a woman unless it had been substantiated by a man. This 'male' sighting of the boy became even more important when one considers that the innocent beggar child, who that day entered the small town of Portobuffole, was never seen again.

Portobuffole was a small town of less than a thousand people, some living inside and some outside the boundary walls. However, despite its small size, it was well known as an important administrative and commercial centre which had jurisdiction over fifteen or so neighbouring villages. Upon entering the town, one found a square, and in the town square, between the gates in the boundary wall and the town hall, was the hub of Portobuffole: the warehouse. The building boasted an ugly veranda, but beneath the veranda was a large counter, where one could negotiate for loans and securities. On the stone wall behind this counter was a list which plainly indicated the current taxes for those who wished to borrow. If one entered the town square and looked to the far left, one would see the synagogue and the large and comfortable homes of the principal Jewish money-lenders, Servadio and Moses. These homes were easily distinguishable by the cylindrical containers which held Hebrew scripture written on parchment. By law, these had to be placed to the right of a Jew's front door.

The leader of Portobuffole was Andrea Dolfin, a Venetian aristocrat, chosen by the *Signoria* of Venice. It was understood that he would remain in office for some sixteen months in return for a modest salary, out of which he had to support a deputy, a notary, three pages, three horses and a servant boy. Andrea Dolfin worked together with a local civic body which comprised members of the most important families, but, unlike other towns, these members were not required to be noblemen. The democratic ideals of Portobuffole determined that all men over a certain age could participate in the development of the town and, with some justification, the townspeople of Portobuffole were proud of the manner in which their town was governed.

The Jews had first begun journeying to Portobuffole in 1424, many of them migrating from Colonia in Germany. Back in 1349, the Christian people of that region had suddenly become incensed and irrational from fear of the plague, and the Jews began to suffer as this Christian hysteria manifested itself in violence. Eventually the Jews could take no more and they barricaded themselves into their large synagogue, set fire to it, and recited moribund prayers to each other as they waited for the end. The few Jews that survived this catastrophe remained in the region, but finally they were driven out. And then, a few years later, they were once more readmitted as though nothing had ever occurred. Such is the way of the Germans with their Jews. In 1424, the Jews of Colonia were finally expelled for good, and most decided to travel to the Republic of Venice, where it was rumoured that life was more secure.

Initially, the people of the republic accepted the Jews from Colonia with all the mistrust that is common among people who do not know one another. Sadly, as the years passed, this mistrust did not abate. It became apparent that the Jews wished to speak only among themselves. Further, they chose not to eat or drink with the Christians, and they refused to attend to their heavy German accents. They looked different, the average one being between thirty-five and fifty years of age, pale and heavy under the eyes, with a long untidy beard. And even at the height of summer, these men always wore their dark grey, heavy wool coats and their unseemly black hats. Although their women dressed with more propriety, occasionally wearing handkerchiefs on their heads like the Christian women wore in church, even these gentler creatures refused to join in the most innocent female talk about household matters or children. The Jews ate neither pork nor red meat sold from a butcher, prefer-ring instead to slaughter live animals and then drain the blood. They washed their clothes on Sundays and rested on Saturdays, and eight days after a son was born they had huge celebrations in honour of the boy's circumcision. Those who glimpsed the Jewish men praying claimed that they covered their whole bod-ies, including their heads, with a large shawl that made them appear both animal-like and foolish. These Jews arrived as for-eigners, and foreigners they remained.

In Germany they frequently murdered the Jews, because the Christian people claimed (and provided good evidence) that the Jews spread the plague by poisoning the wells with what-ever came to hand: spiders' webs, lizards, toads and, most com-monly, the severed heads of Christians. Not only had the Jews killed Jesus Christ, but during Holy Week it was common practice for them to re-enact this crime and kill a Christian child in order that they might draw out the fresh blood and knead some of it into the unleavened bread which they ate during their own Easter celebration, known as Passover. Their feast was designed to celebrate the moment in their history when they claimed that the Red Sea turned into blood and destroyed the Egyptian army, hence their need for fresh blood. However, this murderous act also demonstrated their hatred of Christianity. At the moment at which they stabbed the innocent Christian child, the Jews were known to recite the words: 'Even as we condemned the Christ to a shameful death, so let us also condemn this innocent Christian, so that, uniting the Lord and His servant in a like punishment, we may retort upon them the pain of that reproach which they impute to us.' In addition to using this blood in the preparation of bread, it was widely known that the Jews used fresh Christian blood for anointing rabbis, for circumcision, in stopping menstrual and other bleedings, in removing bodily odours, in making love potions and magical powder, and in painting the bodies of their dead.

Although the Venetian *Grand Council* sought to discourage the propagation of false ideas about the Jews (for these people were an important part of the republic's economy), the doge's inner *Council of Ten* nevertheless passed a law according to which the Jews were instructed to distinguish themselves by yellow stitching on their clothes. People detested the Jews for a variety of reasons, but the most often cited referred to their position in society as people who would loan money at an interest, more often than not requiring extravagant security from the borrower. To comprehend fully how shameful a trade this was, one had to understand that Christians were strictly forbidden to give out loans at interest to anyone. In fact, even Jews were forbidden by God Himself, taken from the word of the Scripture, to lend money to their 'brothers'. However, by interpreting this edict liberally, the Jews discovered that they could give loans to Christians, who were technically not their 'brothers', at whatever interest they deemed applicable. By obliging the Jews to lend money in exchange for permission to live in their territory, the Republic of Venice could pretend to be implementing a policy of some tolerance towards the Jews, while serving its own interests and ignoring the fact that it was further exposing the Jews to the multiple dangers of Christian hostility.

The grandparents of Portobuffole's principal Jewish moneylenders, Servadio and Moses, had begun to practise usury in Germany. Jews were unable to practise in either the arts or trades, no matter how skilled, for the various guilds had been deliberately established with religious affiliations to Christianity. Usury, however, because it was forbidden to Christians, remained a professional outlet for the Jews. The work was risky, and therefore profitable, but it was not physically demanding and it left time for both reading and studying. The Jews paid an excessive amount of tax on their profits, but plenty remained for them to live on. There was, however, little for them to invest in, so their money remained liquid, which further drove home the notion of the Jews maintaining a sybaritic lifestyle.

The Jewish moneylender offered to the public an indispensable service. In Portobuffole there was not a single working family who, every now and then, did not have to take out a loan in order to survive periods of poverty. However, a dependency upon the Jews was not confined to any one section of society. After the war with the Turks, the economy of the Most Serene Republic of Venice began to falter as the opportunity for expansion in the Orient appeared to have been blocked. This led young Venetian aristocrats to begin to explore the commercial and economic prospects inland, but only with the understanding that the Jews would be able to provide large-scale capital investment. However, despite their central role in Venetian society, Jews were ever-mindful that every debtor was a potential enemy, and that the goodwill of the usurer often fed the greediness of the borrower. It remained both easy and convenient for individuals habitually to accuse the Jews of wicked doing, and subsequently to confiscate their profits, but the doge and his *Council of Ten* realized that they could not afford to alienate these Jews completely.

The 'Contract of Moses' was the means by which the Jews were allowed 'freedom' to practise usury, but under strict controls. Whenever a town such as Portobuffole decided to grant a usurer's licence to a Jew, the contract between them, which was generally valid for five years and was renewable, had to be submitted to the Venetian *Grand Council* for ratification. The contract clearly listed the *rights* of the Jew proprietors and their collaborators:

- The Jews have usury rights (sometimes exclusively) in the town for the period valid in the contract.
- The Jews can live the way that they please and erect a synagogue.
- The Jews are not obliged to keep the banks open on Saturdays, or during other Jewish holidays.
- The Jews can refuse to lend to foreigners.
- The Jews can sell securities that have not been claimed for more than one year.
- The Jews are not held responsible for securities that are lost during fire, war, looting or robberies, or for securities that are gnawed by moths or rats (provided they keep cats in their houses).
- The Jews have the right to receive, from the butcher, living animals for the same price paid by Christians.

With as much care and precision, the 'Contract of Moses' listed the *duties* of the Jew proprietors and their collaborators:

- The Jews cannot keep banks open on Sundays, or on Christmas, Easter or Corpus Christi Day, or during any of the four feast days set aside for Mary.
- The Jews cannot refuse to lend money on securities with a value of less than ten ducati.
- If the Jews refuse to do this for more than ten consecutive workdays, then they have to pay a fine of ten ducati.
- The interest on their Jewish loans cannot exceed two and a half Venetian lire each month.
- In the case of loans given without securities, or, in other words, written loans, the monthly interest can rise to four lire.
- The Jews have to give loans up to one hundred ducati to the municipal government without interest.
- It is prohibited to take sacred furniture as a security; loans for weapons are given at the discretion of the Jew.
- A half of any fine is to be given to the town council.

For every object received as security, the usurer was obliged to write up a receipt in Italian, which indicated the place and date of the loan, the nature of the object offered as security, the weight of it, and whether it contained any gold or silver. In addition, each usurer generally kept a personal book in which he recorded confidential information. This private record book was usually written in Hebrew characters.

Whereas the state reluctantly admitted their need for the Jews, the church required no such diplomacy. The Franciscans, in particular, preached vehemently against the Jews, and urged that their avaricious monopoly of credit and usury be taken from them and given to a devout Christian group, who might operate without the base objective of profit. One among these Franciscan priests, a seventeen-year-old boy named Martin Tomitano of Feltre, gained much fame for his vigorous rhetoric.

He was a small novice of less than one and a half metres, who, when he preached, barely reached the parapet of the pulpit. However, like many small men, he was driven by a desire to achieve great feats in the world. As a young boy, Martin Tomitano had twice witnessed his father travel to Venice to protest in vain to the *Grand Council* against the Jews who wished to open a bank in Feltre. Martin Tomitano was in no doubt as to the primary source of evil in the world in which he lived.

Eventually, the boy took the name of Bernard, after a renowned Franciscan predecessor from Siena, and he began to travel from city to city, preaching in a clear, strong voice. He pronounced the language distinctly, slowing down and speeding up to good effect, accentuating the right words, making comparisons, relating pious anecdotes, techniques that he painstakingly designed, then practised, in order that he might keep the people's attention. He burnt with a love for God, and for God's people, whom he wished to help escape from the influence of the Jews, who were little more than merchants of tears and drinkers of human blood. During Lent, many cities recruited him to preach in town squares, because the churches could never hold all who wished to listen. As soon as he was done he would hurry away, for people would pull at his clothes to try to claim a relic for themselves. After his departure, people would light fires to burn what he had called the 'instruments of sin': playing cards, decorative ornaments, and even the emblems of enemy factions, were all cast into the flames. It was only after the feverishly righteous Bernard, formerly known as Martin Tomitano of Feltre, had left that the Jews would dare to show their faces once more, and they always did so cautiously and with the knowledge that the heated passions stirred up by this small man would take some time to die down.

The night of Saturday 25 March 1480 was the occasion of the first full moon of spring. In Portobuffole the atmosphere was merry, as many husbands had now returned from the Venetian army. The recently arrived men were happy in the arms of their loved ones, while those wives who still lived in anxious expectation of their husbands' return eventually tore their eyes from the streets and found solace in the company of their children. These highly spirited Christians were joyfully celebrating the Feast of the Annunciation and looking forward to the following day, Palm Sunday.

The Jews of Portobuffole had gathered in the house of Servadio to begin to celebrate the night of the fourteenth day of the month of Nissan in the year 5240 since the creation of their world. In common with all their holidays, this Jewish celebration began after sunset, with the men and children seated around a large table. In front of each person was a large illustrated Hebrew book of stories, which these Jews read from right to left. The men sat with their heads covered and with their elbows leaning against the table, and they read from their history about the night of the fleeing Jews.

At this time of the year, Jewish law called for these people to rid their homes of all fermented foods, and, beginning that night and for the next eight days, these Jews could not eat bread or anything leavened, for they were remembering when they had had to flee Egypt so quickly that their bread did not have time to rise. In place of bread, they ate unleavened crackers that had been carefully sheltered from any fermentation or external contamination. These crackers were placed at the centre of the table on a huge tray that also contained a hard-boiled egg, a thin leg of lamb, herbs, a small cup of vinegar, wine, and various other objects necessary to their Jewish rituals.

For many weeks, Servadio's youngest son had prepared with his tutor to ask in a high and confident voice, and in the Hebrew language, why this night was different from any other. And then suddenly the moment arrived for the boy to ask his first question, and then three further questions, and his mother, and the other women, left the kitchen with damp eyes and came to listen to this small boy who stood in front of the assembly of men. Servadio responded to his son's questions by reading from the Hebrew book of stories, occasionally interrupting his reading to make comments, and then stopping to listen to statements from those more learned than himself. Eventually everybody had a chance first to read from the books and then chant, 'This year, slaves; next year in the land of Israel, free', and the storytelling and chanting continued as the Jewish spirit moved each of them in turn.

For almost three thousand years the Jews had celebrated this holiday by reciting the same prayers, abstaining from the same foods, and reading the same stories as if reading them for the first time. This was the source of their safety, and the basis of their relative confidence and happiness. They repeatedly told each other about how the waters of the Red Sea were opened for the fleeing slaves and how, immediately after, they closed on the ranks of the Egyptians who followed them. Servadio watched his son carefully, and smiled as he recognized himself in the inquisitive young boy. And then Servadio was shaken from his proud contemplation as the hungry children shouted the last words of a prayer, which was the sign for the food and wine to be served. Jewish songs would continue to be sung, and Jewish stories would be joyfully recited, but most would now concentrate upon their feasting and the eager wolfing of Hebrew food.

The innocent beggar child with blond hair and a sack on his shoulder, who had appeared in Portobuffole at this time of Christian and Jewish festivities, was never seen again. Once Easter had passed, those who thought they had seen him began to talk about him. Those who had definitely not seen him also began to talk about him, and eventually the details of the stories became less conflicting. There was no doubt that the boy had entered the house of Servadio. Someone had noted an unusual number of Jews gathered in the house, and someone else had distinctly heard the sound of a boy sobbing and then suffocating cries, and yet someone else had seen a Jew walking the streets, dragging a sack behind him, at three in the morning. Nearly everyone remembered seeing smoke coming from the chimney of the house of Moses, but no one could remember the name of the boy. The image of the poor boy was clear, but the name was missing, and then one old woman retrieved his name from the corner of her mind. His name was Sebastian. The Jews had killed a beggar boy named Sebastian, and the precise details of this monstrous crime were on everyone's lips. The Jews had killed an innocent Christian boy named Sebastian New. They had dared to make a sacrifice in the Christian town of Porto-buffole.

I remember the afternoon when I first saw the woman. Mama and Papa were out in the streets looking for food, and, as usual, they had left me in my room, with my books, in the small apartment that we shared with the woman. The door to my room was firmly closed, the understanding being that it would remain so. In the past, Mama and Papa used to lock the door when they went out, but I hated this because I could never decide whether they were locking me in, or the woman out. Either way, I would spend most of the day crying. Some days I never bothered to open my books, and when they returned at the end of the day they would find me bleary-eyed and unable to tell them what I had learnt. They mustered hastily assembled excuses such as, 'It's for your own good,' or, 'We wouldn't do it unless it was absolutely necessary,' but still I cried and ignored my books, so eventually they agreed that they would leave the door unlocked. However, I was forbidden to venture out and into the small apartment. That was our understanding, that the door to my room would be closed – unlocked, but closed – and I would submit to voluntary captivity (for my own safety) until they returned at the end of each day.

I was standing by the high window in the tiny kitchen. It was my habit to abandon my books after an hour or two of studying, and looking out of the kitchen window had become my own special pastime. First, I would drag a small wooden crate across the floorboards to the window, and then I would mount it so that my chin could rest on the lower sill. From this precarious position, I looked down into the streets. It had been some time now since anyone in our community had witnessed splendid decorative hats upon women's heads, or gentlemen walking with canes. From my perch I observed only bent backs, bare heads and, littering the streets, lonely corpses. Occasionally I would see a scholar, an old man in a full-length coat, shamelessly dependent upon his walking stick, beard flowing, eyes damp, a pile of books tucked under one arm, his soup pot hanging idly from his waist. These men peered at the useless future without the aid of their round wire-rimmed spectacles, and they depressed me the most, for it was all too easy to calculate the extent of their fall, wearing as they did the outward garb of their former status. I hoped that Mama and Papa's daily search took them to a better place than this, but in my heart I knew otherwise. I assumed that every street was crowded with people with crazy, despairing eyes, and I imagined that they were all trying to sell something, or beg something. It could not only be this street. We knew that everything in our world had changed. In fact, everything in our world was collapsing all about us.

And then one hot summer day Rosa appeared, as if from nowhere. I don't know how long she had been standing behind me, but when she spoke I nearly fell from the crate.

'Can you see anything interesting out there?'

I turned quickly, then grabbed the tattered curtain. Rosa had about her shoulders a woollen shawl which she clasped tightly in front of her. I jumped to the ground and, as I did so, she took a step backwards. There was to be distance between the pair of us.

'Just people,' I said. 'Lots of people.'

I lived for nearly two years in that small apartment, abandoning my books, making daily visits to the high window in the tiny kitchen, and staring at the world which my parents had forbidden me to re-enter. They feared that, should I venture out, they would lose their remaining daughter, and so I was to remain hidden inside. I understood that we were fortunate, that most were living ten or more to an apartment, and that Papa's money, and what little influence Mama still had, had bought us this luxury of space. But still, I was unhappy and frustrated, and sixteen.

Rosa stayed in the room next to mine, but I had never heard a sound through the wall, or, until the afternoon she surprised me in the kitchen, caught a glimpse of this mysterious woman. However, during the day, when my parents were out, I often heard a man who came regularly to visit her. I would sit in my room and listen to him pounding up the communal stairs. Then I would hear the front door open, then slam, and then I would listen to the hurried patter of his feet as he scampered into Rosa's room. Soon I knew how to time my exit so that I would be in the kitchen by the time he curled himself around the front door. He would look down the short hallway and see me standing on the crate. An unshaven man, with dirty worn clothes, he seemed an unlikely visitor. Perhaps three times a week he would simply smile at me, and then he would disappear into Rosa's room.

· · ·

'A friend,' was Rosa's response to my question. 'Just a friend.'

'But why is your friend not living here with us?'

Rosa gave me a tired smile.

'He cannot be with us. He's fighting. In the underground.'

I looked down at her bony hands, then up again at her anxious face. She could only have been in her mid-twenties, yet she seemed so sad.

'I see.' I watched as Rosa tried to hide her hands in the folds of her cotton dress.

But, of course, I didn't really see. Rosa and I would spend long afternoons taking turns on the crate, and then Rosa would suddenly step down and disappear before Mama and Papa returned. No 'goodbye'. No 'see you tomorrow'. She would just turn and leave, as though in her mind an alarm-bell was sounding. I would climb back up on to the crate and once more survey the streets that were crowded with the desperate and the hungry. With each passing day, the women in the street grew to resemble men; by this time, it was often difficult to tell the difference. And then, later in the afternoon, I would once again step from the crate, drag it back to its familiar place, and return to my room and my books, and pull in the door behind me.

The day that Rosa surprised me on the crate, Mama and Papa arrived back early and were extremely angry to discover me sitting in the kitchen. Papa stormed off into their room, but Mama stayed with me. I explained in a low voice about Rosa, and how wonderful but frightened she was, and Mama listened patiently. However, I sensed that I should not be discussing Rosa. Before my discovery of her (or her discovery of me), Mama and Papa had seemed reluctant to answer any of my questions about the young woman in the apartment. Was she old or young? Did she own the small apartment that we had been forced to move into? Was she pretty or ugly? Did she know that we had had to leave nearly everything behind, including Mama's piano? Did she know that we were not poor, that I had a sister, that the things we brought with us were merely the things that we could carry? Did she know? Mama and Papa always evaded my questions with a polite smile. And then they would change the subject. And then, in the morning, they would once more go out into the streets to find whatever they could, and each evening they would return with the evidence of their labour. A single potato was a triumph. Or an egg. Or a misshapen loaf of illicitly baked bread. Papa was too honest to become involved in any of the smuggling rings, so there were never any treats. Never any fruit. Never any sugar.

After they discovered me in the kitchen, Mama and Papa must have talked. A week later, Papa came to me and announced that, because the heat was becoming more oppressive, he understood that I could not be expected to remain in a stifling room all day. Not only was the door to be unlocked, but I could occasionally leave. Finally, they were treating me as an adult. Papa continued and said he hoped that I knew that I would soon see Margot again. He also told me that they, too, missed her. Papa never said how, or where, or when I might see Margot again; he simply said he hoped that I knew that I would soon see her again. I almost believed him.

'Are they killing people today?'

I heard Rosa's voice and turned from the window. The early autumn light was catching Rosa's face and accentuating her pale features.

'Don't watch if they're killing people.'

I stepped down from the crate and smiled at my friend. I was the same height as Rosa. These days, she seldom seemed to venture anywhere without her shawl. During the summer, the shawl was occasionally forgotten, but now, summer over, she always wore the shawl across her rounded shoulders.

'I'm sorry,' she said. 'Please, watch if you must.'

'I don't like watching.'

'I know you don't. You're just curious. It's perfectly normal.'

I felt ashamed. There was nothing normal about watching a boy dancing barefoot, one hand outstretched, his brother's corpse curled at his feet, and people slouching around them both as though neither of them were visible. Normal? I had almost forgotten the meaning of the word. These days, Rosa and I talked more easily. She informed me that I was lucky, for my parents were relatively young. Even though the weather was turning bitter, they still had the energy to go out. They still had hope.

It was almost December, and snow had fallen heavily and settled. In the street it was thick and discoloured, and piled up like ploughed mud. Rosa had long confessed to me that she was married to her unshaven friend in dirty worn clothes, but that was all she told me. She opened and closed her confession in a single sentence. He is my husband. As I huddled in bed, and imagined the fearsome wind in some distant place stripping the remaining leaves from trees, I realized that these days I heard the pounding of his feet less frequently. I was disappointed, for I had become accustomed to his winking at me conspiratorially before he disappeared into Rosa's room. And then one afternoon, as the snow began to fall again, and while I stood on the crate wearing cap, scarf and gloves, I asked Rosa without turning to face her.

'Why does your husband not live with us?'

She did not answer. For a few moments, I was too nervous to turn around and face her. When I eventually did turn, she was smiling sadly.

'I told you, he's fighting on the outside.'

'He lives on the outside?'

She nodded.

'But he could get you out. You could live on the outside too. Both of you.'

'Yes,' said Rosa. 'That is possible, but then he would have difficulty visiting me.'

That evening, I dared to raise the name of my friend Rosa with my parents. Mama looked up at me and shook her head slowly and with resignation.

'She should forget him and live among her own kind. With them, she has a chance of a life.'

Papa looked across at his wife.

Spring arrived. It ceased snowing. In our streets birds did not sing, or trees bud, or flowers bloom. There were rumours that, within the year, we would be taken to the east. That the streets and houses would be emptied. And in the east? Work, of course. We would be required to labour like farm animals until we dropped. I had begun to question Rosa openly about her husband who seemed to be neglecting her. Three months had passed since his last visit. Had he gone away? Rosa simply smiled and shook her head.

'But why does he want to fight? Does he not see that it is hopeless?'

'It is not hopeless,' snapped Rosa. 'If we do not fight, then we have lost.'

(We? Always we. Rosa and her 'we'.)

'But we have already lost, Rosa. They are everywhere.'

I paused, for my friend was staring at me with a pained expression. I softened my tone.

'I'm sorry.'

'Eva, we have not lost. And I cannot go to him. I am a wife, so I must be where he can visit me.'

'But with us you are in danger, Rosa.'

'But with him I am in danger. It's all the same.'

'But you can save yourself. If they come in the night, there will be no time for explanations.'

For a moment there was silence. And then Rosa took my hand.

'Eva, I have made my choice. I have no regrets. Truly, no regrets.'

It was a long hot summer that second year, and the heat served only to increase the stench and the sadness. People continued to fall dead in the street from starvation, but an increasingly common practice was the taking of one's own life, and that of one's family. Jumping from a high window was a popular individual method, while rat poison administered to food was a common way of dispatching a household at one sitting. By utilizing these and other procedures, one remained master of life and death. A precious gift. Mama fell ill, so it was now Papa alone who left on the daily search for food. Rosa and I would sit together in the kitchen, the heat dripping from our bodies, talking and mopping our brows, while Mama lay alone in the cool darkness of her room. And then one day, Papa came home early, and he told Rosa and I that he had seen a girl of about my own age throw herself in front of a military vehicle. Papa's jacket was stained with blood. The horror of this girl's suicide had struck Papa a heavy blow. He waited a few minutes. Then he calmly told us that today he had also seen the son of a fellow doctor begging with open palms. Again, he waited a few moments, then he looked from Rosa to his daughter, then back again to Rosa.

'Some among us are behaving like animals. But we are human beings.'

And then he lowered his eyes. Papa's heavily fortified personality lay in ruins.

'It is written in the Holy Books,' he began, 'that a time will come when the living shall envy the dead.'

The summer heat gave way to grey skies, and then the freezing chill of a second winter. By now I had lost interest in my studies, although I occasionally still sought refuge in my books. An ailing Mama simply languished in bed and waited for her husband to return. One morning, she called me in to her bedside. With her stiffened fingers she touched my threadbare dress, and then, in a feverish voice, she began to try to explain the pain that she felt at not being able to buy clothes for daughters who were growing tall.

'I remember, you girls used to love to look at yourselves in the mirror. You used to try different hairdos, and secretly put on my make-up, and my jewellery, and my clothes. But of course, I knew. Neither of you could ever put anything back in the right place.'

Then Mama suddenly stopped, her face knotting before my eyes into a painful grimace. She turned from me. I left Mama and went into my cold room and locked the door. I sobbed all night. And then, in the morning, I began to keep a journal, but within a week I gave it up, for I could no longer summon the energy to maintain the daily pretence that I was writing to my sister.

I saw less of my friend Rosa. When I did see her, she seemed to be physically shrinking as the days became shorter. If her aspect could be used as a barometer of our general condition, then we were thoroughly exhausted. Out in the streets, the hostile noises and barked orders had begun to grow even louder. One morning, I looked through the high kitchen window as the bulky sewage wagon rumbled by. These days, it was pulled by men who were wrapped like mummies. The fresh snow and weak grey light made these thin figures appear ghostly, a state to which they would soon be reduced. There was no longer water in the standpipes, so people cleaned themselves in snow. And there were no tools to bury the dead in this frozen earth, so it was now acceptable for people to simply lie where they fell. By the time the spring arrived, we knew that our streets would soon be sealed. It was over. We were to be sent away on the trains, for we were needed elsewhere. The rumour was that, by the end of the spring, the whole district would be reduced to rubble. I wanted to discuss this with Rosa, but after the long hot summer I seldom saw her. My friend's increasingly reclusive behaviour, and her obvious physical decline on the few occasions that I did glimpse her, disturbed me greatly. I could not understand what was happening to her.

Towards the end of the summer, I had sat with Rosa in the kitchen and told her about Margot. About her being in hiding. About my sister, who was a year older than I, and who looked like them. (Apparently, according to Mama, I bore the stamp of Jerusalem.) I asked Rosa that if, by any chance, she should change her mind and decide to leave, would she please find my sister and be sure to tell her that Eva loves her and is thinking about her. Rosa clasped her bony hands around mine and whispered, 'Of course.' And the longer I talked to Rosa, the more I found myself speaking to her as though her leaving were inevitable, her discovery of Margot only a matter of time, her reclamation of her old life a certainty. Yet Rosa said nothing further. She simply listened as I retold tales of Margot's escapades, and of how I was sure that my sister was harbouring a boyfriend named Peter, and I talked on until I noticed the sad smile on Rosa's face. And then I fell silent in embarrassment. And then again, Rosa squeezed my hands between her own.

'Don't worry,' she whispered. 'It will be all right.'

· · ·

This turned out to be the last conversation that I ever had with Rosa. At nights I heard her walking around her room, and during the day, although I stationed myself in the kitchen so that I might see her should she venture out, Rosa seemed determined to be by herself. And then, one late spring day, we received the fateful news that at six-thirty the next morning we were to report to the train station with clothes for a journey. All valuables were to be surrendered, and all who failed to report would be punished. I watched as a defeated Mama and Papa prepared themselves in silence. I could see the terrible truth in Papa's dead eyes. His flame of hope had gone out long before the arrival of this latest gust of wind. And Mama, having reluctantly removed her wedding ring and her mother's antique necklace, simply sat with her head bowed.

But my thoughts were not with my parents. I wondered about Rosa. Had she truly been abandoned? I turned my mind back to that first afternoon nearly two years ago, when Rosa caught me standing on the wooden crate, a shaft of light illuminating her face, a young woman waiting for her husband. And I remembered how, after she had gone back to her room, I had again looked out of the window. However, unable to concentrate, I had climbed down and sat at the table and simply stared at her closed door. When Mama and Papa arrived back, they were extremely angry to find me sitting in the kitchen. Papa stormed off into their room, but Mama stayed with me. I explained in a low voice about Rosa, and how wonderful but frightened she was. And Mama listened. Then, having heard me out, Mama looked in the direction of Rosa's room and spoke quietly, but firmly. 'She married outside of her people.' Mama spoke as though she wished me to understand that this was the greatest crime that a person could commit. Then she smiled at me, rose to her feet, and left me by myself. It was our secret. I had no idea that Mama possessed such attitudes. That night, I lay in bed and listened to the immensity of the silence coming from Rosa's room. Nearly two years later, the same silence.

I discovered the body. We were packed and ready to go. By now, my parents possessed little of value that had not been hidden, or confiscated, or sold. Just their wedding rings and the necklace. Papa decided to hide these treasures, although I don't believe that he truly expected to reclaim them. However, at the darkest hour of the night, a floorboard had been lifted and carefully replaced. But it was futile. Even I knew this. And was it worth the risk? They had promised that for every item discovered, one hundred would be killed. But these days. One hundred. One thousand. Who was counting? As we stood with a suitcase each, I asked Papa if I might say goodbye to Rosa. Quickly, he said. Quickly. I knocked and then carefully opened the door. I sensed immediately that it was rat poison. Rosa was fully dressed and lying on the bed. Beside her lay her suitcase. She was ready to leave. Then, at the last minute, she couldn't leave. Abandoned. She stared at me from her deep, long-suffering eyes. Then I felt Papa's hand on my shoulder.
'Come, Eva. We have to go.'

In the sky, there shone a solitary morning star. The three of us joined the flood of people pouring down the street towards the train station. A human river of shattered lives, and at eighteen I now understood how cruel life could be. The men who lined our way with their machine guns and angry dogs were unnecessary. All of us knew that at this stage we had little choice. I gazed up at the church clock. It read five o'clock. It was the same clock that I could see from the kitchen window. For almost two years, it had read five o'clock. Here, among these houses which had become our prisons and our tombs, there was no midnight, there were no bells, there was no time. I

70

looked around at the miserable and crumbling buildings, knowing in my heart that those who were hiding would soon be found. And killed. Buildings would be looted, contraband discovered, and whole streets burnt. In time, there would be no evidence that any of us had ever lived here. We never existed. According to Papa, we had followed the advice of our prophets. 'Come, my people, enter thou into thy chambers, and shut thy doors about thee: hide thyself for a little moment, until the indignation be overpast.' But it appeared that there would be no end to the indignation. Mama and Papa marched on with grim resolution, and I scurried to keep up with them. My suitcase was heavier than theirs, for it was filled with books, but I was determined that I should carry it myself. I knew that they did not want to talk to me about Rosa. For them, Rosa was already a thing of the past. My eyes were full of tears. Their eyes were firmly trained on the future.

During the winter when we sorted through our family belongings, in order to prepare for the move from our four-storey house to the small apartment on the other side of the city, Margot and I came across the old photograph album. The black one with the gilt trim and the specially reinforced edges. Mama kept it on the top shelf in the drawing room, where she imagined that it was out of our reach. Well, it used to be. Mama had forgotten that Margot and I had grown up.

Mama took it from us and then swept her hand along the shelf to make sure that nothing else was up there. Then, instead of stuffing it into a suitcase or a bag, or leaving it on the huge pile of materials whose fate was yet to be decided, she set it down on the drawing-room table and dusted its cover with a cloth. Beneath the skin-like layer of dust, a new object appeared. Mama opened it, and Margot and I gathered at her side, eager to see who or what it might reveal.

There were pictures of people we had never seen before. Old formal portraits, with photographers' names embossed at the bottom of the print. Portraits of old ladies perched on the edge of white wicker chairs, profiles of bearded men, people about whom, when Margot and I asked after them, Mama simply shook her head. They must belong to your Papa. The fact that she could remember neither these people nor their names clearly disturbed her. She looked particularly closely at a yellow-edged photograph of an old man in a suit. He had a doughy face, and an ugly sack of flesh which swelled beneath his chin, yet he insisted on leaning against a cane in a dandyish manner. No, she couldn't place him, either.

In the photographs of Margot as a child, I noticed that she always flirted with the camera. Head thrown back, eyes deliberately bright – she played the coquette.

'Look at you, you show-off,' I said. 'Always looking up at the camera.'

In my photographs, I had a tendency to look down. My head was always lowered, but my eyes looked up, as though I were framing a timid request. Such a contrast in manner.

And then we saw the photographs of Uncle Stephan. He was tall and strong, and he stared confidently into the camera with his soft eyes. Seeing him again sent my mind spinning back six years to when he visited the house. I was about to speak, when I felt the outside of Margot's shoe scuff my ankle, and I knew that I should not comment upon these photographs. Five of them spread across two pages. Uncle Stephan. Always on his own. Always staring directly into the lens of the camera. Always standing.

Uncle Stephan was Papa's only brother. He had journeyed to the British colony of Palestine, for he wanted to defend the new

Jewish settlements against attacks from the Arabs, and to prepare the land for large-scale settlement by Jews of all ages and backgrounds. However, his journey was made all the more arduous by the fact that in order to visit this so-called promised land he had to leave behind a young wife and child, and break off from his medical studies. If I think now of Uncle Stephan, I can see a man who, if truth be told, did not know how to handle us children. There was a part of him that was secret and inaccessible, and we could always sense this. Children are able to pick up on such weaknesses and they can be ruthless. As time went by, Uncle Stephan learnt to protect himself against his nieces, although he never held himself distant from either one of us. He had about him a warm detachment, which must have been his way of enduring the pain of his life, but I suppose the truth is that we girls did not really know him. But then again, we did not make much of an effort.

I remember the day when I returned home from school and saw the fancy leather valise in the hallway. Hanging from a peg was a strange khaki-coloured coat. We had a visitor. In the drawing room sat a tall sun-tanned man, delicately holding a cup of coffee between his broad hands. Papa sat opposite him, the two men engaged in an animated conversation. When I walked in, Papa looked up and Uncle Stephan turned to face me.

'Ah, and here she is. Little Eva. Eva, do you remember my brother, Stephan?'

Of course, I didn't. I smiled nervously.

'Uncle Stephan has returned to us from Palestine.'

After dinner that evening, Mama dressed Margot and me in clean white dresses and we were ceremoniously marched into the drawing room. Twice before, Papa had insisted on parading his daughters in this manner, and on both occasions we had cried and begged him not to humiliate us in this way. This time, Mama said, it was different. It was just Uncle, and we could play as little or as much as we wished. As we walked into the cigar-smoke-filled room, Papa cried out with delight.

'Margot! Eva!'

He slapped a knee and jumped to his feet. Then he turned from us to his brother.

'Margot is quite a little pianist. Eva, however, is a newcomer to the violin. You must forgive her mistakes.'

The shock of this betrayal chilled my blood. I looked across at my sister, who, to my dismay, was beaming.

That summer, my parents seized the opportunity of Uncle Stephan's visit to go to the east for a short vacation. Uncle Stephan was left in charge of Margot and me, plus three of our friends. It was understood that we would study in the mornings, and then be free to play for the rest of the day. However, we contrived to turn the mornings into a nightmare for poor Uncle Stephan, who was constantly labouring up the stairs and encouraging us to stop shouting and return to our books. Once he had left, Margot and I would begin again to make up stories about him for our three friends. One day, he might be a pirate who sailed the seas of the world looking for treasure; the next day, an African explorer. We transformed poor Uncle Stephan into anything we thought appropriate, and when we became bored with our games, we simply shouted at each other in order to make him climb the stairs so that we might giggle at him. But he never raised his voice, or left us without a small, if some-what tired smile.

'I know you're good children.'

And then the door would close in, and we would listen to the thumping of his feet as he made his weary way back down the stairs.

During those long hot summer evenings, Margot and I would sit with Uncle Stephan and question him about fashions, and movies, and movie-stars. But he knew nothing. He had seen nothing. He had never seen a Valentino picture, or even a Chaplin picture. Margot knew more than I did, therefore her sense of disappointment was greater than mine. I simply followed where she led, sighing after her, throwing my hands into the air a moment after hers, and letting them come to rest a few seconds after hers had settled. Uncle Stephan would reveal little about where he had travelled, or what he had done, except to confess that he had been in Palestine and that it was hot – hotter than even our hottest days. His reticence only served to add to his mystery, and yet Margot and I grew very fond of our strange uncle. And then, in the morning, our friends would arrive with their books and papers, and the five of us would again conspire to produce a kingdom of chaos at the top of the four-storey house.

After Mama and Papa returned from their vacation, things were never the same again. In the evenings, Papa and Uncle Stephan would sit together, their conversation growing louder and more heated as the evening wore on. It was so hot that Mama allowed us to keep the doors to our bedrooms open, which made it a simple matter to follow the tide of argument that flowed up the stairs. Papa was adamant. Uncle Stephan had given up on his medical studies, discarded a wife and daughter, and gone off to fight for what? Why create another home among these Arab people? His wife was right to refuse to uproot her life and expose her child to these barbarians. Papa and he could set up in medical practice together. The brothers Stern. They might become the richest doctors in the country. Why had Stephan suddenly become a fool who evaded his responsibilities? Let some other idiots risk their lives for this self-styled new country. Uncle did not like being a called a fool, and this epithet generally produced a vocal storm which raged and bellowed as long as the pair of them had the energy. Had Ernst forgotten that they were Jews? That they remained the only people on the face of the earth

75

without their own home. Did he know this? Papa would eventually drag his tired body up the stairs towards his bed, but he always remembered to stop by and give his girls a kiss goodnight. I usually pretended to be asleep, but sometimes the unusual smell of alcohol disturbed me and my eyes met those of my Papa.

After a week of acrimony and raised voices, Uncle Stephan crossed a bridge and passed into the world of himself. He spent long hot afternoons sitting on a wooden bench in the garden, simply staring at the trees as though introducing himself to nature. He would sit perfectly still in the searing heat, nothing on his head, barely blinking, until the daylight had faded and the trees had begun to blacken. Somehow Margot acquired a map of Palestine and, one afternoon, we went together to Uncle Stephan and asked him to show us exactly where he had been. He looked at the map, then drew his finger aimlessly across it, pausing at various places, and then he continued to drag his finger this way and that, as though he were touching some precious object. Then he squinted up at us, the sun obviously causing his eyes some difficulty.

'Thank you.'

Margot and I glanced at each other. Thank you for what? we thought. Then a frustrated Margot asked him.

'But Uncle, what were you doing there?'

Uncle Stephan fed his own enigmatic personality by simply smiling and shaking his head. He had no desire to share with us the secrets of the world to which he was committed. Margot was exasperated.

'But Uncle Stephan, why won't you tell us?'

What neither of us fully appreciated was that poor Uncle Stephan was not talking to anyone. For him, there had already been enough talking. Papa had told him that unless he returned to his wife and child, Papa would help them to leave and settle in America. Uncle Stephan's wife had written her husband many letters, all of which confirmed that she remained adamant that she would not live in the desert with Arabs bearing down on her from all sides. At least, in America, she and her child could begin anew. And so Uncle Stephan decided not to return to his wife and child. He loved them dearly, but he feared that his resolve might break were he to see them again and try to settle this issue face to face. Papa laughed at his brother, and then spat in disgust. Sitting on the wooden bench in the garden, and these days simply staring at the yellowing grass between his feet, Uncle Stephan tried to minister to his broken heart. He had made his decision. He would be returning to Palestine.

Uncle Stephan was carrying the same khaki-coloured coat, and standing beside the same fancy leather valise, that I had noticed when he first arrived. Mama and Papa stood with him in the drawing room. Uncle Stephan seemed rested, serene even, and he smiled at the two girls who stood together in the doorway. Perhaps the sight of his nieces caused him some further regret, as he imagined his own child growing up without ever knowing her father. It turned out that his wife had written to him and informed him that she understood from his silence that he preferred Arabs to his own child. To her mind, the serious responsibilities of family were incompatible with the responsibilities of this self-proclaimed new life of his. This being the case, she had no desire ever to see him again. She was respecting his choice, and she asked him to respect hers.

Papa flagged us into the drawing room, where we were encouraged to say goodbye. Uncle Stephan gently stroked the top of my head, and then he let his hand slip down on to my shoulder. And then he did the same to Margot. We stood on either side of him, but he said nothing. It was Papa who spoke.

'I shall walk with my brother to the end of the street.'

I cannot remember any formal leave-taking, any shaking of hands, or kissing or embracing. I do, however, remember Margot and me peering out of the drawing-room window as Papa and his brother emerged from the house. For a moment they paused, and Papa glanced up at the window. And then they turned and began to walk away from the four-storey house. Tall Uncle Stephan, with his long strides, and a frustrated Papa scurrying along beside him. Papa liked to have his own way. Even as I watched the pair of them walking, I sensed how much pain his brother's departure was causing Papa. But Uncle Stephan walked with a firm step. A decision had been made.

Once Uncle Stephan returned to Palestine, he disappeared without trace. The police would occasionally visit and ask after him, and Mama would always make these men coffee and offer them cakes. I remember Papa's patient tone. Everything was polite and civilized while they were here. No, he had still not heard from his brother. Yes, he would most certainly let them know if he did hear. But after these men had gone, Papa would fly into a rage at the thought that his brother could place him in a situation that required the police to visit the house. And then there were the men who turned up either early in the morning or late at night, and who invariably needed a bed for a night or two, a meal, a bath and some money, before they went on their way. Neither Mama nor Papa ever turned these idealistic young men away, knowing full well that they were either on their way to, or on their way back from Palestine and Uncle Stephan. However, when asked, none of them ever delivered any news of Uncle. They were being schooled in the same methods of evasion which Uncle Stephan had mastered, yet they remained pupils. Uncle Stephan would never have shrugged his shoulders as these men did. He was both more skilled and kinder.

And then, some two years after Uncle Stephan's departure, a gaunt-looking man arrived one morning while we were still having breakfast. He was inadequately dressed for the cold, in a thin jacket and with a long scarf wrapped three or four times around his neck. His eyes were watering and his cheeks seemed to have been hollowed by the wind. He stood at the door to the kitchen, grateful that some warmth was seeping into his bones. Papa asked Hannah first to give him a cup of coffee and a piece of bread, and then to show him to the spare room where he might sleep.

That evening, Papa asked the man to dine with us. Clearly this was a special man, for Papa had never extended such an invitation to any of the others. The man sipped gingerly at a glass of red wine as he ate, but soon the bottle was empty. However, the man kept his tongue and spoke only when spoken to. Once the plates had been cleared, Papa and this newly rested man retired to the drawing room. I asked Margot what she made of him, but all she would say was that he was not as old as he looked. To her mind, he was a young man who had thrown away his youth. Mama and I stared at Margot, who began to colour. She then stood and asked if she might be excused from the table.

Papa had used all his contacts and resources to let it be known that he would happily reward anybody who might help him solve the mystery of what had happened to his brother. It transpired that this man, who now sat in the drawing room, clumsily sucking on one of Papa's finest cigars and introducing himself to a second bottle of red wine, was prepared to help Papa solve this mystery. Margot and I eavesdropped by the door to the drawing room as the man explained to Papa that Uncle Stephan was one of the leaders of the Palestine underground army, and that among these young idealists he was something of a legend. As the story of brave Uncle Stephan's exploits began to be told, I found myself thinking that perhaps Uncle had been right to try to make a new home in Palestine. Things in our country had raced rapidly downhill since the morning when Papa had walked with his brother to the end of the street.

According to this man's report, Uncle Stephan had not been seen or heard of for six months, but the man was sure that nothing adverse could have happened to Papa's brother. Apparently, the nature of Uncle Stephan's work meant that occasionally he would have to undertake secret missions, but he had always emerged at the conclusion of his duties as though nothing untoward had occurred. Papa seemed painfully unconvinced, but the man pressed on and began to speak now of the world he was rediscovering, with its restrictions and new laws, and he expressed both surprise and anger that we should be treated in this fashion. Fortifying himself with the dregs of the second bottle of wine, he encouraged Papa to abandon the land of his birth while he still had time. Papa glared at this scruffy young man, who clumsily pawed at the expensive cigar and who swilled down his fine wine as though it were water. And then, as though a cloud was suddenly lifted from his evening, it occurred to Papa that the vulgar rogue was simply waiting for money. Papa reached for his wallet, and Margot and I looked at each other. And still the young man puffed away.

Later that same evening, Papa told his wife and daughters that his brother Stephan might be dead in a hot country, among people who did not know him, or love him, or care for him. Papa paused, the look on his face so poignant that only now do I realize how desperately unhappy Papa must have been. Papa needed his family. He needed his wife. He needed his daughters. He needed his brother. At this stage, he even needed his parents. Mama looked on helplessly, and then she smiled in the direction of her girls.

I think of Uncle Stephan sitting on the bench in the garden and making his decision while the night blackened the trees. Uncle Stephan trudging up the stairs to pacify the children who teased him relentlessly, but only because they were so proud of him. Uncle Stephan steeling himself for a life of commitment, trying to justify to himself the enormity of the crime of leaving his wife and daughter. Perhaps he saw something that we did not see. Perhaps he knew that he had to throw himself into the building of another world, even if this meant setting himself adrift from those who loved him. Including us. Two annoying young girls. I like to think that, wherever he is, Uncle Stephan might sometimes remember Margot and Eva. Two annoying young girls.

It was raining heavily now. Through the window of the café I could see passers-by bent almost double, leaning into the wind and trying to shield their eyes from the rain. Occasionally the wind would roar and catch an innocent, holding him or her for a second or so, a single leg hanging half-suspended, and then the wind would stop its foolishness and let the victim fall back to the ground. I felt particularly grown-up as I observed the world bustling by on that dark November afternoon, for I was out with Papa. I looked across at him, but Papa had no interest in anything beyond his own thoughts. He idly stirred the spoon in his coffee, seemingly intrigued by its circular journey.

A drenched couple stepped inside from the rain. They peeled off their coats and hung them on the brass hooks by the door. Then they looked around and began to push their way across the café towards us. Once they reached our table, the man took off his glasses and asked if anyone was sitting opposite us. Papa looked up and shook his head. The man bowed quickly and asked, 'May we?' meaning, would it be all right if they shared our table?

'Of course.'

For a moment, Papa became the old Papa, courteous and charming.

'Please,' he said, and gestured with his hand to the empty seats. The couple smiled, but their smiles marked the onset and conclusion of their engagement with us. The man replaced his glasses, while the woman dabbed at her face with an embroidered lace handkerchief. And then they sat and quickly angled themselves so that they faced each other.

'But the larger hotel. On the lake. It's so pretty.'

The woman shook her head firmly. I could see that she was considerably younger than the man, perhaps by some thirty years, but they talked intimately and as equals.

'A larger hotel is better.'

Again, the woman shook her head.

'Too much money. A waste.'

She was dressed simply in a brown sweater and matching scarf. Her hair was pulled back tightly and fastened with a clip, and she wore just a little make-up under the eyes. He, on the other hand, was attired more formally in a dark suit and tie, but it was the additional elements – the tie-pin, the cuff-links and the trouser-braces – which betrayed both his age and his manner. He was used to doing things in his own precise way, and her refusal to obey him was causing him some distress.

'Are you all right?'

I looked at Papa and nodded. I could see that he was embarrassed that the lovers were making no allowance for my presence, but I was thrilled with this development. I began to imagine this woman as the most glamorous person in the world: a French cabaret star who had travelled from Paris and deposited herself in our country, in a café in our city, at our table.

'Papa, may I have some coffee?'

'Are you sure?'

Again, I nodded.

The café was becoming increasingly crowded and noisy. The rain showed no sign of letting up and, although people continued to arrive and wait in the doorway by the cashier's till, nobody appeared to be leaving. The two waitresses were being run off their feet and, as they dashed around taking repeat orders, they pointedly removed cups and glasses from in front of those who had clearly finished, and with their most commercial smiles they pacified those who waited impatiently. Papa held up his hand.

Eventually, the waitress returned with a cup of coffee for myself and another large glass of wine for Papa. The couple barely noticed as the waitress set two coffees in front of them.

'But the spring is my favourite time of the year. We cannot risk waiting until the summer.'

The woman looked disappointed.

'You know this is difficult for me.'

Papa snatched up the glass and gulped a hasty mouthful of wine. I glanced across at him in surprise, but he was staring at the couple opposite. He seemed nervous at the prospect of what they might say next, and then I heard the clasp of a hand-bag being unfastened. I looked over as the woman produced a blue cigarette case with gold trimming. She pulled clear two cigarettes, handed one to her companion, put one into her own mouth, and then lit them both. The smoke billowed across the table and I stifled a cough. Again, Papa whispered, 'Are you all right?' I smiled and nodded. Poor Papa. He picked up his glass of wine.

Papa and I had stopped at the café on our way home from the funeral of one of his colleagues. Over the weekend, Dr Singer had suddenly died from heart failure, and his death had shaken Papa badly. Two years younger than Papa, there had been no sign of illness, no shortage of breath, no putting on of weight, nothing. After hearing the news, and sharing it with his family, Papa sat slumped at the kitchen table. We left him to his thoughts and followed Mama into the drawing room. Three days later, neither Mama nor Margot were interested in venturing out on a cold November day to attend the funeral of someone they barely knew. Papa looked so lonely that I simply could not bear the thought of him leaving the house alone, so I pulled on my coat and boots, and slipped my arm into his.

There were only three others at the funeral. An old woman dressed in black, who I presumed to be the doctor's mother. A younger woman in a worn coat and ill-matching hat, who I imagined to be his faithful receptionist or housekeeper. And an older man, about Papa's age, who I immediately presumed to be another doctor. It soon became clear that Papa knew this man, for, once the brief service was over, they shook hands warmly and Papa introduced his daughter to a Dr Lewin. This done, Papa turned to the two women and introduced me to Dr Singer's mother and his housekeeper, and then we stood together, a small awkward knot of people, until it began to rain and hasty excuses were proffered. For some reason, Papa and I were the last to depart. We stood together on the stone steps and watched the three mourners fan out in their separate directions.

As we began the walk home, the rain became more insistent. I looked across at Papa and knew that his mind was churning. We would soon have to give up our beautiful house, and most of our possessions, and move to a special part of town. Papa had already been forbidden to practise medicine, and, although people still sought him out, he was able to prescribe only patience. These days, he spent his time at home either staring into mid-air or trying to occupy himself by reading a book. What little money remained was slowly draining away. All of this he tried to hide from his children, but there are some things that cannot be hidden. And then it occurred to me that perhaps Papa's friend did not die of heart failure. Perhaps Papa's friend had no one to live for. Like Papa, he was no longer permitted to practise as a doctor and, his elderly mother apart, had no family. What else was there?

There was humiliation. There was the daily anxiety of being easy prey for groups of men who ran through the streets yelling slogans. There was the torment of their cruel laughter. There was the fear of being betrayed by a gesture, a slip of the tongue, or an accent. There was the waiting and the worrying. There was the knowledge that you might be pointed out by classmates or friends or colleagues. There was the constant bullying. (Remove your hat!) I knew why Papa stared into mid-air. I, too, stared into mid-air. I, too, had tried to bury myself in books. There was blackmail. An earring. A watch. There were muffled tears at night. Margot and I both understood this. There were those who had already gone into hiding. The classroom was shrinking. And everybody dreamt of escape to America. But in the meantime, there was humiliation. Forbidden to ride on a trolley-car. Forbidden to sit in a park. Permitted to breathe. Permitted to cry.

The rain continued to fall, and there was now a sizeable cluster of people huddled in the doorway waiting for a table. Occasionally the door would open and one or two would leave, having decided that they should try elsewhere. I turned from both the drama by the door and the antics of the couple sitting opposite, he now pressing her smooth, well-manicured hands between his own, and I began once more to observe life in the windy street. As the afternoon gave way to early evening, there were fewer people struggling against the wind. I imagined that most had either reached their destination or had decided not to venture out at all. The streetlights were now lit, and the mysterious half-world between day and night fascinated me.

'What do you want, Eva?'

Papa's voice was tired. I turned from the window and reached for the menu.

'No. What do you want. In this life?'

I panicked inside, realizing that Papa was asking me an adult question. In fact, an impossible question. I searched his face for some clue as to how I might answer him, but I discovered nothing.

'I want to be happy, Papa. To marry. To have two children.'

And then I stopped, disturbed by the realization that I was answering as a child might answer. But what did Papa mean? Really, what kind of a question was this?

'You want to be happy?'

Papa smiled as he asked the question. I nodded.

'That is enough, Eva. That is a fine answer.'

The woman opposite glanced across at me. I was sure that she had overheard some part of our conversation, but she smiled quickly, then averted her eyes. Meanwhile, her friend released her hands, broke off a piece of bread, buttered it, and then placed it on her plate. The woman looked quizzically at him and I wondered if my glamorous woman was truly happy with her old man.

The door opened wide and cold air rushed in. It was now dark outside and the rain was cascading down. A tall, elegantly dressed woman, in a thick black coat with an elaborate brown fur collar, made her entrance. Quickly, somebody moved to close the door behind her and keep the heat inside. The woman hardly broke stride. She was led past those who still congregated

86

in the doorway to a space where a single chair and small table suddenly appeared. Papa looked up at her.

'That's the singer, Leyna,' whispered Papa.

Other heads turned.

'She's going to America next week. It's all arranged.'

The woman opposite reached into her handbag and again pulled out her cigarette case. She gave a cigarette to her friend, lit it, then took one for herself. One of the two waitresses bolted the door to the café, turned the sign in the window, and drew across a curtain. But the large windows to the street remained undraped. Papa turned from Leyna, raised his hand, and beckoned the waitress who had previously served us. She was tired. It was nearly time to go home. Papa ordered another large glass of wine and a coffee and then, with his eyes fixed firmly on Leyna at her single table, he idly wafted smoke from his eyes with a slow branch-like movement of his arm. The old man immediately stubbed out his cigarette, but the young woman did not appear to notice. I looked at Papa and realized that his family and his dead friend were far from his mind. Papa continued to stare at Leyna.

I sat on the side of the bed and watched as Margot packed her suitcase. I wondered if I should tell her about Mama's strange behaviour, but I decided against doing so. It seemed better that Margot should leave without this additional burden. As she folded her clothes, Margot spoke loudly and with the recently acquired confidence that her new friends seemed to have instilled in her. 'You see, Eva, in spite of everything that we have lost, they still hate us, and they will always hate us.' I did not want my sister to see me cry. I looked at the window where the snow was banking into the corners and beginning to obscure the view. 'Papa must not wear spectacles in the street because they love to hit such people straight in the face. And men will probably start to ask you to prostitute yourself for them. They pretend it is a joke, but there is more to it than this.' Margot closed the lid of the suitcase and sat next to me on the bed. For a moment, she followed my gaze and looked up and out of the window. 'You see, in some ways it is easier for us women.' Margot shrugged her shoulders. 'There is no trouser check, for one thing.' I wondered if Margot might talk now about her boyfriend. I knew that she must have one. But Margot stood up. 'You too must go into hiding. But we mustn't be apart for too long.' I tried to smile, but I couldn't. 'Peter says it is painful to have to walk on earth that is saturated with the blood of our people. He says we should have seen what was coming.' I looked at Margot. 'Peter?' For a moment our eyes locked. And then Margot pushed me back on to the bed and started to laugh.

Yesterday they beat me. Having wiped my tear-stained face, Mama insisted that, in future, she would walk with me to school and then meet me again at the end of the day. And so this morning we had set out together, with Mama tightly clutching my hand. I looked around as we passed through a grubby court-yard, a short-cut that Mama was introducing me to. The truth was, I was ashamed that I had let Mama know the true nature of my distress. I had run home, my face streaked with tears, but once she had cleaned me up, Mama simply sat me down and changed the subject. Three boys had pushed me and kicked me and called me names, but it appeared that all Mama wanted to talk about were her daughters. About how different we were from each other, and how I was the more studious and deter-mined, and Margot the more fanciful. And then, when Margot returned from her club, the three of us sat together and Mama told us about the problems of young girls, and how they differed from the problems of young boys. And then, looking closely at Margot, she began to share with us her understanding of the many difficulties of love, and offer advice as to how best to cope with boys. She even spoke about Papa's courting of her, but this was a story that she had related to us on many occasions, although Mama seemed to have forgotten this fact. As the candles burnt low, and Mama began to revel in the warm glow of her private memories, it began to upset me that she never once referred back to the fact that I had just been beaten. Finally, after Mama's anecdotes and advice had run their course, and as Margot and I began to make our way to bed, she looked at me and confirmed that, from tomorrow, she would be accompanying me on both the journey to school and the journey back home at the end of the day, but she mentioned this as though it were an afterthought.

We passed out of the filthy courtyard and turned right on to the main street. On this broad thoroughfare the destitute former musicians gathered, and all day the place was awash with mournful song. In a week or two, I knew that most would have been forced to sell their instruments, and they would be reduced to merely standing on street corners. But there were always new musicians to take their places, with old violins wedged hopefully under their chins. Mama quickened her pace and then, from a small alley, a column of men swung into view. They walked in perfect step under the assiduous scrutiny of a pair of youths in uniform. The prisoners' faces were emaciated, the details of their crimes almost certainly invented. Mama tugged at my hand to tear my attention away from these men. But what else was there to look at? The skies were grey, the buildings dull, and the other people who walked these streets did so with their hands pushed deeply into their pockets and their eyes peeled, searching for crumbs and morsels that they knew did not exist. All about me, shoulders were habitually hunched and hats were worn with sad resignation, for there was nothing rakish or jaunty about people's lives. What else was I to look at besides this column of prisoners?

As we neared the school, we passed the place where the boys had cornered me on the previous day. Assaults in the street were becoming increasingly frequent, and even decently dressed people were being waylaid by uniformed brutes and ordered to scoop up dog filth with their bare hands, or lick clean the windows of a nearby shop, or simply hand over their money and valuables. Only the previous week I had witnessed the sight of a lady in a fur coat being forced to remove her lower underwear and scrub the icy streets with the garment. She was then made to put the dirty wet rag back on and proceed on her way. Mama knew about such incidents, but they were not to be talked about. And then something had happened to me. It appeared that even this was not to be talked about. Just before we reached the school, a uniformed man passed by. Mama stopped, and there was silence. In fact, everybody stopped until this man had passed from sight, and then, as though being awoken from a hypnotic trance, we all resumed our lives.

At school I always sat near the window, for, when the teacher was not spying on me, I liked to look outside. From my classroom window I could see the street, and I could therefore follow the lives of the people down below. Mama had warned me about dreaming at school, but these days she did not seem as interested in how well my studies were going. We both knew that I would soon have to leave this school. Last night, when talking to Margot and me, she again told us of how she had given up her studies at the university to marry this serious young doctor. He was a young man of medium height, bespectacled and shy, a man who dreamt of a future he could not afford. She told us of his diligence, his determination to learn to dress himself in the fashion of this big city, and his desire to secure for himself and his family a life of leisured comfort and happiness. And in spite of her parents' feelings, Mama had insisted on marrying this man, and, having done so, she watched her own future walk away from her. Mama paused at this point, and she looked closely at her daughters. And then she reminded us that although she loved this shy, bespectacled man, she had prepared her own girls for something else. Hadn't she always encouraged us to dream beyond marriage and children? The world would be ours in a way in which it could never be so for her generation. Mama reminded us of this.

It began to snow. I looked out of the classroom window and watched the ground receive a thin sprinkling of what appeared to be sugar. However, I knew that, should I taste it, the snow would be bitter. I watched people huddling under arches and stairwells, with a profound fear of the forthcoming winter etched clearly across their faces. In the summer, I would look out at this same street and see men with abandoned jackets and loosened ties lounging about idly. The windows to the apartments would be thrown wide open and the curtains tied back, creating wide holes that were desperate to suck in fresh air. I imagined these same windows at dusk, after I had left school and gone home, beginning to close, one by one, a thousand eyelids slowly shutting. But today, as the snow continued to fall, they were all tightly sealed.

This morning, before I left for school, I heard Papa shout at Mama. I was lying half-asleep in bed, but I clearly heard him asking her for something that he claimed she had taken. And then I heard Mama begin to cry, and then Papa evidently discovered whatever it was that he had been looking for. There followed a quiet period in which I assumed that Papa was begging Mama for her forgiveness, which I knew she would eventually give. I rolled over. Relations between them were not good. A week earlier, they had left their two daughters and gone together to the woods. On their return, they had told their daughters that today they had buried some precious family objects beneath a large oak tree, and that Margot would have to go into hiding. Margot looked dumbfounded. Both she and I had assumed that she would be coming with us to the small apartment, and, in a peculiar way, we were both looking forward to this new enterprise. But a grim-faced Papa went on and reminded us that, these days, people were hiding in every imaginable place. People were building tunnels under hallways, widening cellars, creating hiding places inside furniture, in woodsheds, in fact anywhere. Until these ugly times passed by, it was better to be safe. In less than a week, we would have to leave the four-storey house for the apartment on the other side of town. It made sense that we should take precautions now, for after the move it might be too difficult. Luckily, Mama and Papa had found a family who would take Margot. They were still looking for a family who would take me. And then, before either daughter had a chance to protest, a tired-looking Mama and Papa left the room together.

The Mama who met me at the end of the school day seemed suddenly older. A week had passed by and nothing further had been mentioned about Margot's imminent departure. As we began to walk home, a fatigued Mama started to speak, but she spoke in a manner which suggested that she was wandering in her mind. I knew immediately that today was the day we would lose Margot. 'Remember, Eva, you are a guest in this country. And you must never speak with your hands.' Mama stopped and began to demonstrate. A man whose pride remained intact, despite his unshaven face and his unwashed skin, looked on. Only in his expensive clothes, now filthy, could I see the quality of his past. He stared, and for a brief moment his eyes met mine.

Mama did not notice as she finished her demonstration. And then, without warning, she began to walk away from me. I turned from the man and chased after Mama, who by now was speaking aloud to herself. 'Eva, where in the world is the United States? Where is Russia, even? One day you are neighbours, the next day they spit on you. We are stupid for being proud to be what we are not, do you understand? Stupid.' I took Mama's hand, but she did not seem to notice. 'In this world, you do not shoot people without a reason. There has to be a reason. How is it possible to be so angry with people who have done you no wrong?' The afternoon light was prematurely fading, and the snow continued to fall.

Margot pulled on her coat and picked up her suitcase. The man took the envelope from Papa, tucked it into his pocket, and said that he would wait downstairs. 'No,' said Papa. 'There will be no farewell scenes. This is only a temporary measure.' Papa quickly kissed Margot, and then Mama hugged her eldest daughter. Over Mama's shoulder, Margot winked at me. And then she was gone. That night, I lay in bed and listened to a volley of dull thwacks as, somewhere, a restless housewife beat the dust from a hanging rug. But above this sound, and dominating the night, was the sobbing of Mama, who had now lost one daughter. Through the window I could see that it had stopped snowing, although the sill remained thickly crusted.

On Good Friday 1480, the Christian faithful of Portobuffole began to congregate in large numbers at the Church of St Marie of Settimo. The altar had been carefully dusted many times over, and the crucifix was covered with a black veil. Three purple cushions had been placed on the altar steps, and the failing light at the end of the day evoked the darkness which covered the earth during the death of Jesus. As ever, the service was both austere and moving, and towards the conclusion the priest joined his hands together for prayer and exhortations. The first oration was said for 'Omnipotent God', and then six more followed.

- For the Pope.
- For the clergy, the virgins, the widows and the people of God.
- For the Most Serene Doge of Venice.
- For the catechumens.
- For the sick, the imprisoned, the travellers and the navigators.
- For the heretics and schismatics.

And then there was a brief pause, and the voice of the priest changed in tone, in order that he might fully capture the attention of the faithful.

'We also pray for the malicious Jews so that You, God, can take away the venom of their spirits so that they may come to recognize Jesus Christ.'

Before these words had time to settle, there was a call for one last oration for the salvation of these Jews.

'Eternal, omnipotent God, who does not refuse mercy to the Jews, grant us prayers that we might pray for the blindness of these Jews so that, recognizing the light of your truth in Christ, they may soon be taken from their darkness.'

At the conclusion of their Good Friday service, the Christian faithful of Portobuffole, their souls contented, spilt out on to the dark streets of the town and began to wander home, but not before casting a stern look at the houses of those who carried evil in their hearts.

Easter passed, but left trouble in its wake. The doge's representative, Andrea Dolfin, felt obliged to mention, in his periodical re-

94

port to the *Council of Ten*, that a certain discontent had broken out in the town, but he did so in a manner designed not to raise alarm. The doge was consumed with problems in the Orient, with the Pope, and with the extension of the Most Serene Republic's business affairs inland; civil disorder in his domain was the last thing that the doge desired. However, much to Andrea Dolfin's disappointment, the ferment would not seem to pass, and the situation was further exacerbated by the fact that the frightened Jews were now refusing to open their banks. People came from surrounding regions both to pawn and to redeem their personal belongings, but, upon discovering this Jewish recalcitrance, they voiced their opinion that the Jews should respect their commitments and not be permitted to live outside the law. Andrea Dolfin ordered the civic council to meet, but, before they could do so, the Jews, fearing that they were about to suffer physical assault, returned to their work. However, the reopening of the banks failed to quell the wave of anti-Hebrew sentiment.

The unresolved question of the abduction and murder of the blond beggar child, Sebastian New, was clearly a matter so serious that the public was not going to let this issue pass until justice had been served. However, as a Venetian aristocrat, Andrea Dolfin could not allow a civic council comprised principally of plebeians to by-pass Venetian authority and take reckless measures against the Jews, which they were threatening to do. This would serve to enrage not only the doge, but also the *Grand Council* of Venice. Andrea Dolfin had little choice but to act swiftly and according to the law, therefore he decided to order the chief of police and his army into the houses of the Jews.

Servadio, usurer, was taken.

Sara, his wife, was put under arrest along with the children, *Fays*, their tutor, and *Donato*, the servant boy.

Moses, usurer, was taken.

Rebecca, his wife, was arrested.

Giacobbe from Colonia, Germany, was taken.

Four 'wanted' men could not be found and they were declared fugitives.

To guarantee the legality of the trial against the Jews, Andrea Dolfin insisted that a lawyer be engaged on their behalf, whose duty would be to explain fully anything that they could not follow. The Most Serene Republic of Venice not only boasted of its severe justice, but was also proud of its flawless procedure. No one could be arrested unless there was already evidence against them, and no one could be condemned to death unless his crimes could be verified by proof or confession. The Republic had faith in the Latin inscription that was to be found over the entrance to the courtroom in the Doge's Palace in Venice.

Before everything, always investigate scrupulously to find the truth with justice and clarity. Do not condemn anyone without a sincere and just trial. Do not judge anyone based on suspicion, but research well and in the end find a merciful sentence. And do not do to others what you would not want done to yourself.

At the onset of the Portobuffole investigation, the accused Jews were obliged to take an oath that they would freely volunteer the truth. If, at any point during the course of the investigation, the judge suspected either perjury or reticence in the accused, he could order the individual to be tormented. Both the judge and a lawyer were obliged to attend the torture session, which most commonly involved the employment of a mechanism known as the *strappada*, which featured a cord, a pulley, and the optional use of weights of twenty-five, fifty, or one hundred pounds. The accused would raise his hands behind his back and they would be tied together with the cord, which was then strung up to the pulley firmly attached to the ceiling. He would then be hoisted up and left hanging for an hour, the abnormal stretching and stress producing a pain that became more atrocious with each pull. If the accused did not confess, he would be given a few additional tugs of the cord, and weights would then be attached to his feet. In smaller country towns, something else, such as a live ram, might be used in place of the weights. In certain cases, the accused could be additionally tortured with a flame or a piece of charcoal that was placed on the bottom of his feet.

As they dragged the chief Jew, Servadio, from the Portobuffole prison well, where for two days and two nights he had been secreted, the flash of sunlight blinded him. Servadio tripped many times as they pushed him into a room where he slowly began to discern shapes and voices. The Jew was introduced to the lawyer who was deemed appropriate for people of his religion, then a piece of paper was produced and he was instructed to recite an oath.

'I, servant of God, who am a Jew; I swear on the almighty father Sabaot, and on the God who appeared to Moses in the bramble-bush, and on God Adonai the Father, and on God Eloi – I swear that, should I be guilty or a perjurer, then may I be lost among enemies, and die in an enemy land; may the land swallow me, as it did with Daton and Abiram; may plague seize me, as it did with Naaman the Syrian; may my home be deserted; may my ancestors' and my own sins fall on me; may all the curses written in Moses' and the prophets' laws rest on me; and may God curse me, as an example for everybody.'

Servadio read the written words mechanically, but with little difficulty. He had lived an anguished life, but one he regarded as honest, so he did not fear judgement by God. But here on earth, in the eyes of Christians, he knew it was easy for a Jew to sin. One could sin even without knowing it. As he looked around himself, Servadio wondered if these people realized that, so far, no one had even accused him of a crime.

On 14 April 1480, the bell rang nine times in St Mark's Square to indicate that the doors to the Doge's Palace were closing. The last few senators were arriving, flushed and out of breath, and they were hurrying to avoid a fine. The adjacent rooms were already empty and everybody was in his place. The Most Serene Doge, the members of the *Council of Ten*, the Superintendents of St Mark's, the Officials of the Senate, the Officials of the Commune, and all the numerous other government officers were gathered. Business proceeded as usual, with the recitation of letters, telegrams and petitions, and, as was common, towards noon other issues were discussed, the order of the agenda being determined by the importance of the matter to the republic. Andrea Dolfin began his report with the news that the people of Portobuffole firmly believed that during Holy Week their Jews had sacrificed an innocent Christian boy as part of their rituals. Under normal circumstances, no one would have given much weight to a report from Portobuffole which referred to certain accusations by the people against their Jews. But this report went further and included details of the recent trial of the foreigners principally involved before the Court of Portobuffole, and the subsequent passing of death sentences against three Jews.

The report was received in silence. Its contents worried the *Grand Council*, for this trial had already attracted much public attention. It now appeared that the popularity of the judgement had begun to cause civil unrest across the whole region, as people were becoming increasingly hostile to the Jews. The *Grand Council* had, over the years, repeatedly declared that the Jews could live in the Most Serene Republic, and that, if necessary, they would severely punish anyone who either bothered them or caused damage to their persons or their property. Clearly, the

Grand Council would have to restate their position. Accordingly, three days later, on 17 April, the *Grand Council* drew up and dispatched a bill whose contents specifically addressed the problems at Portobuffole. It read:

With displeasure we have heard that, in our homeland, the Jews are objects of insult, beatings and other damage because of accusations made against the Jews of Portobuffole. Since we want the Jews to be able to be at home in our domain without being insulted, we are furnishing the following in writing: We desire and order that each district launch a proclamation that no man, woman, minor or servant, either with words or actions, may either molest, assail or provoke any known Jew. If this occurs, a punishment will be set up for those that are of an adult age. Those younger, however, will be punished with a whip, and the damages that they have inflicted will be made known to their fathers, tutors and teachers. No one should be pardoned. We intend to tolerate some bullying and maltreatment towards the Jews who reside among us, but we want them to be able to stay and live under our domain without being submitted to excessive damage and insults. You must all abide by what has been said if you wish to continue to merit Our praise.

On this very same day, 17 April 1480, a long statement from Andrea Dolfin was delivered to the *Council of Ten*. Enclosed was a copy of the notes from the trial against the Jews, plus a full report of the behaviour of the three Jews – Servadio, Moses and Giacobbe – who now languished under sentence of death. It told of how they were first scornful, then resentful, then fearful when made aware of the nature and the number of testimonies against them. The report made mention of their torture, and of how they were stripped, bound and hoisted up, and of their many confessions, some taken back, some repeated, and then all eventually confirmed in front of the Court of Portobuffole. And finally, the details of the sentencing. Of how the judges had condemned them all to make honourable amends and then die in varying ways: one to be burnt alive, another trampled by four horses, and a third to be shot with arrows. Having, by means of torture, loosened the Jews' tongues to a full confession of their wickedness, the appalling details of their crime continued to cause great indignation among the people of Portobuffole, so much so that Andrea Dolfin was now begging for the intervention of the *Council of Ten* in order to preserve public order. Andrea Dolfin concluded his urgent report with a written summary of the crime, according to the Jews' own testimonies.

Everything began on a day in September during the previous year, when the Jews were celebrating a holiday known as the Feast of the Tabernacles. It was Servadio who, after a few glasses of wine, found the courage to turn to Giacobbe of Colonia and say, 'You know that, before Easter, we will need a little Christian blood for our bread. My friend, produce a young child, for you know how to do it, and in return I will give you ten ducati in cash.' Giacobbe of Colonia happily agreed, but another Giacobbe, this one from Verona, overheard the conversation and also offered to find a child. A few months passed and, as Holy Week approached, Giacobbe of Colonia decided to begin his search in the largest nearby city, Treviso. He looked closely at every young boy he met; some seemed well nourished, but were not alone. Others were alone, but appeared too thin and hungry, and were clearly in need of milk and honey to fatten them up. Eventually, in the market, Giacobbe of Colonia found a healthily complexioned boy of about six or seven years named Sebastian New. He quickly enticed this boy into his company with promises of bread and wine, and took him to the house of a fellow Jew, where he chanced upon Giacobbe of Verona. The two Jews, having arrived in Treviso for the same purpose, decided to progress together. First, they bought a new basin from the barber into which the fresh blood would eventually be drained, and then they trained the boy to walk some half-dozen paces behind them so as not to arouse suspicion.

Under cover of night, they left Treviso and began the journey back to Portobuffole. The boy tired quickly and eventually Giacobbe of Colonia had to carry him. However, whenever they reached the outskirts of a town, the boy was set down and ordered to make his own way through the place and to meet the two Jews on the other side. He was rewarded each time with bread and apples, and offered a long drink from their hipflasks. Once they reached Portobuffole, the boy was instructed to follow behind at a reasonable distance. The two Giacobbes made their way into the house of Servadio, where his wife was busy cooking matzah for the forthcoming feast day. They informed Servadio of their successful mission, and then Giacobbe of Colonia stole outside and ushered in the boy. Both Giacobbes received their ten ducati, along with praise for the fine choice they had made. The young innocent was inspected and then ushered into the kitchen where, in order that he might be quickly fattened, he was fed an egg and a piece of matzah, and then given some wine. Thereafter, he was taken to a small room where he slept soundly.

In the meantime, the Jews arranged that the word should be secretly passed among them that they would soon have to present themselves at the house of Servadio. On the night in question, Donato, the servant, was sent to guard the entrance to the house, and when all the Jews had arrived, the young boy – now plumper after a generous diet – was brought from the room where he had been held captive and was stripped down in the kitchen. He was frightened, for the Jews had about them an evil quality which, in their excitement, they found difficult to disguise. Then, without warning, Giacobbe of Colonia fixed a handkerchief to the boy's face so that he could not see, and then he clapped his hand over the child's mouth. Mercifully he was not quick enough, for two or three screams were heard on the outside, although none of the Christians, at this time, knew the true nature of their origins. The new basin was produced by Moses and he placed it under the boy. Thereafter, Giacobbe of Colonia quickly struck the little mammal a blow near his heart and watched as the fresh blood collected in the basin. As the sacrifice bled, the onlookers hissed blasphemies aimed at the Saviour and his mother, calling her a whore and the Saviour 'the dead one born out of wedlock'. Some went further and stuck out their tongues and exposed their private parts in an attempt to scorn and further disrespect the innocent young Christian victim.

Once the basin was full, and Sebastian New's veins drained of blood, its contents were evenly distributed among the many jugs proffered and then greedily drunk. Some was saved, for it would be dried into powder and sprinkled on Seder wine and matzah. There followed some consultation as to how best to dispose of the useless body. One among the Jews suggested the river, but another Jew argued that, should the body float to the surface and be discovered, the nature of the wound would give them away. It was Moses who produced a sack and suggested that the body and clothes be bundled inside, and he could be trusted to burn the contents in his huge oven. And so it came to pass. But the Jews were not careful, and the evidence against them was overwhelming. There were witnesses who saw the two Giacobbes on the road from Treviso in company with the boy. There were the women in Portobuffole who also saw the boy, and, of course, there was the blacksmith who spoke to him. There were others who clearly heard the screams of the innocent at the moment of death, and an inspection of the contents of Moses' oven produced evidence that something organic had recently been burnt. However, having been subjected to torment, the most compelling evidence of all fell from the lips of the three principals in the form of their confessions. Although fantastic and monstrous in detail, they were consistent. All of this Andrea Dolfin duly reported in the hope that his words might stir the *Council of Ten* into action.

On receiving the magistrate's report, the *Council of Ten* found themselves in an impossible position. The severity and unusual nature of the punishment would not enhance the judicial reputation of the Most Serene Republic, and might well destroy her carefully cultivated relations with the Jews. But what could they do? Deny the work of the local judges and repeal the sentences? To do so would be to imply that half the population of Portobuffole had given false testimony. On 19 April, the *Council of Ten* placed the problem before a particularly animated meeting of the *Grand Council*. After much debate, it was finally decided that the executions should be suspended, and an emissary dispatched to Portobuffole to unearth further evidence.

The Venetian emissary gathered his new evidence in the company of Andrea Dolfin, and he discovered that some of it proved contradictory. However, a great deal of it confirmed the original allegations and the emissary felt compelled to rearrest Servadio's servant boy, Donato. Shortly after this heinous crime, the boy had forsaken Judaism and become a Christian, assuming the name of the murdered child, Sebastian. Under new examination by the Venetian emissary, this *new* Sebastian spontaneously confessed, without recourse to torture, and accused his master Servadio of the alleged crimes. He claimed that, before conversion, he had been privy to all the secrets of the enemy Jew, and he confirmed that it was written in the ancient writings that, without the shedding of human blood, Jews could neither obtain their freedom nor ever return to the promised land. Therefore, it was laid down that every year they must sacrifice a Christian to the Most High God in contempt of Christ, for it was owing to Christ's death that they had been shut out from their own country and were in exile in a foreign place.

Sara, the wife of Servadio, and Rebecca, the wife of Moses, were also rearrested, and because they refused to confess they were submitted to torture, but they denied every allegation. They further claimed that because Jews regarded women as weak, they did not allow them to assist in certain rituals, therefore the emissary showed mercy and decided not to continue proceedings against the two women. During the course of their investigations it became clear to both Andrea Dolfin and the Venetian emissary that the people of Portobuffole were not only continuing to abuse and insult the Jews, but there was a danger that they might begin to attack Jewish houses in order to repossess their securities and recover the files that recorded where the remainder of their belongings were hidden. Time was doing little to soothe the inflamed passions of the populace, and the emissary hurried back to Venice in order that he might report his discoveries.

On the night of Saturday 6 May, a messenger from the *Council of Ten* delivered the following brief to Andrea Dolfin, and to others in similar positions of authority in neighbouring territories.

Because of the recent case in Portobuffole regarding the Jews who are said to have killed a Christian child, it is hurtful to them and their relatives if people continue to create rumours about them. We have decided to write this to you because we know you will read it and can obey secretly, and with discretion, and without public demonstration, but yet with diligence, as we order it. You shall live and respect their goods. They shall not be treated poorly, not in this world, or in any other place, and everything, namely their securities and goods, shall remain where they are without the slightest alteration or addition. We advise caution. Violence, theft or transportation of underwritten goods for any reason is not permissible. We give you this order in great confidence and great trust.

That same night, while everyone was asleep, an armed body of men arrived in Portobuffole and took into custody the three condemned prisoners and three other Jews who had been arrested in the course of the supplementary investigations by the emissary and Andrea Dolfin: Fays, tutor of Servadio's sons; Solomon, the domestic servant of Moses; and Donato, the new Christian who now wished to be addressed as Sebastian. During the night, the six Jews were transported to Venice, and, on the morning of Sunday 7 May, they were all locked up in the Doge's Palace in rooms situated under the Rooms of Torment. It was here that they languished while the *Council of Ten* decided their fate.

Some six weeks later, on 22 June, the members of the *Grand Council* received the following order from the *Council of Ten*.

Considering that this case with the Jews is full of evil and goes against the honour of Jesus Christ, it is necessary to draw some conclusions with the maximum amount of application. It has therefore been decided that anyone who sits on this Council has to come tomorrow at the sound of the ninth chord. At that time, the doors will be closed and he who has not arrived will have to pay a fine of ten ducati that will be inflicted immediately. He who does not pay will be sent to sign the Book of Debtors. This goes for all who have a seat in the Grand Council.

After four days of heated debate, the honourable members of the *Grand Council* finally decided that the Jews of Portobuffole should submit to a second trial, this time in Venice, beginning on Tuesday 27 June 1480.

She sleeps peacefully, her dark hair a gown about her neck and shoulders. This young woman can never have imagined that fate would have deposited her into such a predicament. No longer a secure station in life, underscored by the most powerful of traditions. No longer to be gazed upon as desirable, yet unattainable. All will now imagine her easy prey for their lascivious thoughts. Truly, what am I to make of her? She lies here among twists of white linen sheeting. In her chastity, loyalty and honour, she is the most un-Venetian of women, yet is there some sport to this lady's actions? I am familiar with the renowned deceit of the Venetian courtesan, yet I have taken a Venetian for a wife. Has some plot been hatched about me? I am a foreigner. I do not know. My ceiling is high, the tall window shuttered against the moonlight. Out in the world, night has fallen and reduced the city to a succession of wintry reflections and whispered echoes. Beneath my window, I hear the soft plash of an oar as a boatman goes about his chilly business. I hear his laughter, then anonymous footfalls on stone, then water slapping against cold brick. In the distance, a shrill voice cries from a hidden balcony and the icy water gurgles as though in reply. I turn from the shuttered window and, once more, gaze upon my new wife.

I arrived in the spring and was immediately enchanted by this city-state. I approached by water and found myself propelled by the swift tides across the lonely empty spaces of the forbidding lagoon. I stepped out on deck and observed the grey choppy seas, the high arch of the sky, and then looked across the distant low horizons to the monasteries, forts and fishing villages of the surrounding islands. Above me, the sails and flags snapped in the damp Venetian wind, and then, to our side, I spied a boatman hurrying back to the city ahead of the oncoming storm, with swallows flying low and skimming the water to either side of his unsteady vessel. As we neared the city, the air became warm and moist, and its smell somewhat like the breath of an animal. Then the water began to lap less vigorously, and bells began to sound, and I suddenly found myself to be surrounded by the raised voices of gondoliers; and then, as though following strange music, I discovered myself being sucked into the heart of Venice. What ingenuity! Nothing in my native country had prepared me for the splendour of the canals, but it was not only these waterways which seized my attention. The magnificence of the buildings that lined the canals overwhelmed my senses, and upon the grandest of these buildings, proud images of the Venetian lion were carved in wood, chiselled in stone, or wrought in iron. I could barely tear my eyes from the genius of these palaces, for they suggested to me the true extent of my journey into this fabled city. I had moved from the edge of the world to the centre. From the dark margins to a place where even the weakest rays of the evening sun were caught and thrown back in a blaze of glory. I, a man born of royal blood, a mighty warrior, yet a man who, at one time, could view himself only as a poor slave, had been summoned to serve this state; to lead the Venetian army; to stand at the very centre of the empire.

Upon my arrival in fair Venice, a retired merchant – a man somewhat advanced in years, but with considerable experience of trading in different parts of the world – was appointed by the doge and his senators to watch over me. This good fellow was pleased to offer me lodgings within his own modest house, and, by conversing with me, he was soon able to understand the serious nature of the predicament in which I initially found myself. I possessed only a rudimentary grasp of the language that was being spoken all about me, and I lacked fluency in dealing with issues which related to common Venetian practices and matters of custom. Furthermore, I was naturally suspicious of the motives behind the simplest actions on the part of those who professed that they wished to help me, for I knew the world to be full of those who sought to increase their status by strutting beneath the outstretched wings of their superiors. My kindly retired merchant, although keenly aware of the magnitude of the obstacles that littered the path along which I would have to travel in order to gain a more substantial understanding of Venetian society, seemed unable to help me. In fact, he grew somewhat frustrated by the persistence of my questioning and his own inability to supply me with satisfactory answers. Accordingly, after little more than a month, it was decided that I should develop in my own direction and he in his, and in this manner we might one day reap the benefits of the seeds of friendship that we had begun to sow.

With the help of my merchant, I soon obtained new lodgings on the Grand Canal, in a house that had formerly been opulent. Sadly, over the years, the house appeared to have fallen into a state of neglect, but it possessed all the necessary conveniences, and the owner promised faithfully to make good certain deficiencies. From its windows I peered down at the teeming life on the Grand Canal, which caused me great joy, for I had previously been rewarded with little more than a view of a muddy tributary. I quickly learnt to explore the streets of my quarter, passing from alley to alley, crossing bridges that were arched like camels' backs, noticing crumbling houses boarded up by rotting planks, being surprised by abandoned churches, stretching my legs in empty squares, and looking up to windows where ragged clothes hung out to dry. I enjoyed watching the unloading of blunt-nosed ships, their decks piled high with loads of firewood and tangles of cordage, the air redolent with pungent wood-odours; and I learnt to recognize the gondolier's cry, a half-salute, half-warning, which always seemed to be answered from somewhere within the labyrinth that is Venice. I soon came to understand that, behind the gaudy façade, much of Venice was quite different from the pretty city of the watercolours. But this caused me little concern, for whether it be the clumsy little garden perched half-way up a crumbling wall, or the chipped marble steps of a lonely church which descended directly into the canal, or the filthy, narrow street in which wretched-looking children played noisily, each picture of the city occasioned me pleasure, and I learnt to hold these various images close to my dark bosom.

I soon settled into the house, and frequently observed my landlord as he repaired what he had clearly not attended to for years. I surmised that the house must have once belonged to a wealthy Venetian family, for there were traces of splendour about its balconies and the mouldings of its windows. However, among its more problematic imperfections were the shutters, which were beginning to part from their rusty hinges so that, at night, when the wind blew, the combination of the unfortunate woodwork and the squally weather created the most unpleasant ghostly noises. My landlord claimed that, only some few years past, the walls of his 'mansion' had been hung with arras and gilded leather, and sumptuously decorated with armour and portraits of the finest quality. Apparently these items, plus the red velvet armchairs, the mahogany tables and the iron lanterns that adorned each room, had been stolen by a rogue who had secured the place on favourable terms and then fled into the night, once his debts had mounted beyond his control. These furnishings had, of necessity, been replaced with inferior pieces. At first I listened with sympathy to my landlord's many tales of woe, but sadly I soon came to understand this man to be a dishonourable vagabond. I became aware that a great number of the deficiencies that he sought to remedy, and for which he presented me with a hefty demand note, were, in fact, part of his general responsibility and should have been attended to without the 'present' of money from my pocket. This I learnt from my merchant, who, on visiting me, seemed anxious to know why my daily peace was disrupted by this man's tiresome labouring. Together we challenged my landlord, who pleaded ignorance of our charges, but who none the less refunded a sum amounting to a healthy figure. At this juncture, my merchant suggested that I should engage a fellow of his acquaintance who might act as an attendant and help me to avoid such unpleasantness in the future.

It happened that my attendant was a man whose family were traditionally gondoliers. He confided to me that his class, the gondolier class, were frugal in their habits, spending little on food and drink, preferring a routine of sustenance that seldom varied. Apparently, some gondoliers neglect to cover the wood on the arms of their chairs, and often tolerate beds that are little more than narrow cots with iron bedsteads, while others mix water with the wine in their hogsheads, which renders it either dead or sour. By living life in this manner, gondoliers are able to indulge their weak side, relating to their love of fine clothes and costume. According to my attendant, when exterior show is deemed necessary, a gondolier never hesitates over cost. If the fashion dictates extravagance, then a gondolier will display extravagance. Sadly, it transpired that my man, being the third son, was unlikely to benefit from the family 'business', so, to his great disappointment, he was forced to enter the service of the army where, for twenty years, he had occupied himself without rising in anyone's estimation, either on or off the battlefield. On our first evening together, he spoke endlessly and with passion about the lives of gondoliers, and he confessed his regret that he had not been able to pursue this family profession.

. . .

The gondola, he informed me, was unique to Venice, its great and impressive length obeying the impulse of a single rower, or sometimes two. It had only recently been decreed that these boats should be painted black, and black only, for some among the richer families of the city had begun to offend dignity by painting their vessels in a variety of gaudy colours in the hope of drawing attention to themselves. I was, of course, familiar with these vessels which dominated the waters of this city of the sea, but I listened eagerly as my attendant expounded upon their unique features. He gave me to understand that it requires only a delicate turn of the wrist for these artists – gondoliers – to guide their boats wherever they will, and he suggested that, with the sea and sky in one's sole possession, and the opportunity to indulge in contemplation that was afforded by both solitude and space, surely this was the perfect way to travel. Apparently gondoliers become very devoted to their boats, studying their characters and temperaments, and a large part of their skill depends upon this intimacy of knowledge. Many hours of each day are spent sponging, scrubbing and drying the boat so that every scratch, nail or blemish is known and recorded. A gondolier who attends lovingly to his boat can expect it to last him for five years or so, after which time he can sell the hull for a decent sum, and this former gondola will probably do duty for some years as a ferry on a back canal, all the while losing its graceful curves as the woodwork fails. The gondolier, however, will ensure that he keeps about him the canopy, the cushions, the carpeting and seats, and other fixtures, for these are often individual in design and part of the family inheritance. I listened with great interest, and felt that we were establishing the beginning of some form of understanding, but regrettably this conversation marked both the onset and the conclusion of our amity, for the next day an incident occurred that seemed to change this man's opinion of my character.

.   .   .

It had been the custom of a Venetian woman of middle years and frantic passion to visit me occasionally while I stayed at my merchant's house. Indeed, it was my merchant who suggested that it would be quite unnatural for an unattached man of my station not to have some legitimate avenue in which his pleasures might be indulged. For the aristocratic Venetian marriage was a carefully controlled economic and political ritual, and it was therefore important to keep the bloodlines pure. This being the case, prostitution was not only tolerated but positively encouraged, for it enabled the aristocratic man to indulge his desires without endangering the sanctity of his class. The woman whom my merchant deemed suitable to play host to my natural instincts was pleasant enough, and conversation formed part of her trade with me. However, on her first appearance during my new attendant's service, she found herself being rudely dismissed from the doorstep, despite her pleas that she had most definitely arrived at the correct house. I overheard this disturbance and was shocked by the vulgar intemperance of my attendant's tongue, therefore I intervened on the side of my woman friend and quickly ushered her into my chamber. I immediately endeavoured to engage her in some conversation in the hope that the unpleasantness of what had just occurred might be quickly forgotten. Fortunately, after some tedious pouting and a predictable display of hurt emotions, she soon calmed down and, upon my urging, began to explain to me the rules of courtship that are peculiar to Venetians of all classes.

I learnt that, in this city of Venice, courtship is both lengthy and expensive. Young men attempt to find their future loved ones by sailing the canals, or walking the streets, all the while looking up to windows and balconies. Having identified an object of attraction, the young man has to discover whether she is available to be approached by him, and this he is able to do in a variety of ways. He might continually pass by her house and observe whether he is being watched, he might offer flowers, or he might even sing to her. She will, if she is interested, soon let him know this fact by her continual appearance, or perhaps by bestowing a smile upon him. At this signal, the suitor dresses in his best clothes and, together with his closest friend, he will call on the father of the girl and formally request permission to court her. If the father is satisfied with the boy and his profession, he will set a time limit – usually two months – in which the pair might meet and decide whether they are suited. At the end of this time, if love does not prosper they will part and nothing further is mentioned of the matter. However, if love blooms, the parents of the girl nominate a day, and the young man and his whole family are invited to a supper at which the two families will be formally introduced. After the food, the lover requests the hand of the girl and he presents her with a gift. The father will usually give his consent, then make a speech on the blessings and important duties of the married state.

I listened, somewhat dumbfounded by the complex details that my woman friend seemed to be delighting in sharing with me, but to my astonishment there was yet more to this performance. A day or so after this supper at which the families meet, it seems that the father of the girl has to organize yet another supper which the young man must attend, this time bearing a wedding ring, and other rings, all of which pass into the girl's keeping. Apparently, should she abandon her suitor at any point after this, she is obliged to hand back the rings. Should, however, the man find reason to change his mind, then the girl keeps everything. At this point my woman friend showed me her richly bedecked fingers, from which I was able to surmise that, on more than one previous occasion, a young man had found reason to change his mind. Between this day of the rings and the wedding itself, many further presents are exchanged between would-be bride and bridegroom. The girl is expected to furnish silk handkerchiefs or neckties that are traditionally embroidered with her lover's initials, or his name, and the man is encouraged to give simple gifts such as fruit, raw mustard seed, cake, and, at Christmas, roast chestnuts. However, on no account must he give a comb, for this is deemed to be a witch's instrument, and books or pictures of saints are thought to bring misfortune. And then, my woman friend announced with a smile, there is only the wedding.

At the conclusion of her story, my friend began to prepare herself for the main purpose of her visit, but I stopped her, then reassured her that she would nevertheless be paid in full. She seemed confused and somewhat hurt, so I let it be known that I would have to explain my situation with her to my attendant, and, having done so, I imagined that all would be as before. This seemed to reassure her and she began to repair her clothing. However, upon her departure I immediately sensed a new tone to my dealings with my attendant. I gave this matter some thought and decided that, in order to protect my new and undoubtedly more important relationship, I could happily forgo the pleasures of the flesh, particularly as I held no real affection for the woman. However, it soon became clear that in my attendant's eyes I had seriously transgressed, and it would be difficult, if not impossible, for me to amend the damage of this woman's unannounced visit. I had no doubt that, had I been a foreigner of his own complexion, he would have had little difficulty in accepting my desire to engage a courtesan. I suspected the problem was that he objected to one such as I coupling with one of his own, even though she who entertained me was merely acting out the rank and station of her life.

My daily routine developed and involved much exploration on water and foot, and then private study, as I grew to master this new language. My tutor, a scholarly Venetian of advanced years, undertook the task of working with me for purely financial motives. He lived in a particularly desolate part of the city, in an area whose sluggish canals were choked with refuse and whose many wharves were busy with boats that were repaired daily in thick clouds of black smoke. His crumbling house, like those all around, seemed to have been idly passed from one generation to the next without regard to maintenance. The grey plaster barely clung to the outside walls, its shutters were made of ancient rotten wood, and balcony railings had come adrift and now hung over the canal. In fact, not just this house, but the whole district gave the impression of having been eaten away by time and inclement weather. To reach this man's house, I had to carefully cross many tottering bridges, the flimsy structures of which were carefully balanced on piles of loose stone. From these edifices, one could clearly see the green line that the stagnant water of the canal had painted along the side of all the buildings. However, once I entered this man's book-lined study and began to follow his instructions carefully, I left behind the mournful atmosphere of his quarter and attended to the pleasures of the new world which this language opened up for me. He paid me compliments and claimed that I was a fine pupil, and I believe he was correct for, after some few weeks, I came to the conclusion that there was little more that this man could teach me.

Each week, my solitary migrations through the streets and along the canals of Venice would suddenly achieve a focus as I would journey to the Doge's Palace and present myself to the senators. My weekly visits to the palace generally involved my stalking the waiting rooms and ante-chambers until the grand men were ready to receive me. Once I had been ushered into their presence, they would again remind me that, as a revered leader of military men, I was to serve only in a time of crisis, and that I would not be troubled with the petty affairs of the state. In the meantime, I was to reconcile myself to the fact that I was a man of leisure, occupying the same status as a cannon or a breastplate of armour during a time of peace. There was, however, much rumour abroad which referred to impending conflict with the ever-vengeful Turk, and although none of the senators ever spoke directly to me of this matter, I knew that, should this situation deteriorate, I would be immediately pressed into service.

Spring gave way to summer, and summer, in turn, to a strangely melancholic autumn, and many times I wondered if I had not chosen gold and self-advancement above the more important consideration of my own happiness. The great majority of my days passed off without incident, and a large portion of my time was taken up observing the customs of these Venetians who, perhaps owing to the unique isolation of their state, seemed to obey their own special code. My former language teacher had explained to me how Venice was controlled by a small heredi- tary aristocracy, and how, because of the republic's power and achievements, most foreigners respected her but none would ever choose to love her. Flamboyant and lavish displays of her wealth stirred hostility and envy in the hearts of visiting digni- taries, but the Most Serene Republic was skilled at protecting herself from problems both within and without. My own posi- tion in Venice could be explained by the fact that the republic preferred to employ the services of great foreign commanders in order that they might prevent the development of Venetian- born military dictatorships. In fact, it was common practice to humiliate and break outstanding Venetian soldiers so they did not rise above their station. When the lion of Venice roared, all – outside the small circle of the doge and his immediate ad- visers – knew that they must bow and acknowledge her power.

. . .

After a long summer of isolation, I found it difficult to reconcile myself to this new emotion of loneliness, and, for the first time in my life, I found myself battling bouts of despondency that could persist for weeks. One late autumn afternoon, I was forced to confront my fears and insecurities in a most dramatic fashion. I engaged a gondola and rode, with a light and pleasant breeze born of the vessel's progress stirring my face, down towards the cluster of islands that populated the lagoon. It was my intention to find some location in the mouth of the lagoon from which I might observe the passing sails of the ships of the world, and, in this manner, while away the afternoon hours in a pleasant reverie. At first all was bright sunshine, and my colourfully clad gondolier posed gracefully against the blue sky and rowed with easy strokes. However, we had passed only a small part of our journey into the heart of the lagoon before the wind turned against us and we laboured to a jetty, where our boat was so violently rocked that it made it difficult to land. The rains began to fall, at first only a delicate lace curtain, and then the noisy whirring of seagulls overhead signalled the imminent opening of the heavens. The sky blackened and shrugged off the day, and suddenly there was an ominous silence. Moments later, the silence was broken by a distant roar, then a shrill whine of wind stung my ears, and soon after the inevitable lashing and blinding rain began to cascade, and presently the lagoon was a tempest of sound and movement. My gondolier, a frail-looking fellow with the prematurely puckered throat of an old man, took some comfort in the shadows of the monastery upon whose steps we had alighted. I drew into my lungs the faintly rotten smell of swamp that rose from the lagoon and watched as, before my eyes, nature quickly erased vain beauty.

Suddenly the world was muffled in mist, and from many different towers, both distant and near, came the various notes of the bells: alarmed, angry and finally arrogant city bells. I realized that this city was betraying me, and I was betraying myself. Only so much strength slept in the arms of a warrior, and I had wasted near two-thirds of a year in the rapture of foolish enchantment. I pulled my General's cloak tight about my shoulders and watched as grey fog began to march in from the sea. And then my attention was seized by the loud slapping of water against my moored gondola, and I noticed that small waves were now breaking over the sides and filling the vessel with water. I looked around in search of my gondolier, but my eyes were greeted by the wet masonry of the monastery's outer walls, and the sight of a miserable dog slinking away from me and around the corner. I had made no friends among these people, and my standing in society rested solely upon my reputation in the field. My reputation. It was to be hoped that this one small word might lay to rest any hostility that my natural appearance might provoke. My reputation. Some among these people, both high and low, were teaching me to think of myself as a man less worthy than the person I knew myself to be. My own people, although degraded and without the sophistication and manners of these Venetians, at least regarded me with respect and dignity, and among them I had many friends, and some few enemies, all of whom were easily identifiable. Among the Venetians, all was confusion as I attempted to distinguish those who beheld my person with scorn and contempt, from those who simply looked upon me with the curiosity that one would associate with a child. The storm raged for many hours until, watered to the bone and distraught in mind, I finally decided to join my oarsman and seek shelter among the smoking candles and soft light of the monastery. Thereafter, all memory was lost to fatigue until I awoke some hours later as the faint light of morning touched a distant wall and the Venetian bells began a silver chant. Through the high windows I was able to see a bright and clear sky, by which I judged the peril to have passed and a new day to be spread before me.

And then, only some few weeks past, one among the doge's most trusted senators eventually rescued me from this dull routine of isolation. He was a senior man who was rumoured to be held in high esteem by his peers, and I imagined that he must have often observed me on the many occasions when I visited the Doge's Palace in search of an audience. I suspect that, on this particular occasion, the trusted senator must have taken pity on me because, before I was able to engage a boat for my return journey, his messenger sought me out and delivered his master's request that I might, that same afternoon, visit his residence. This would be my debut inside a grand Venetian home and I immediately determined to present my person with a dignity and charm which might befit the occasion. Sadly, I judged myself to have failed, for, although I endeavoured to behave in a manner which might endear me to my generous host, the look of boredom which marked his face, from the moment I crossed his threshold to the moment I left, caused me to feel certain that this invitation was one that would never again be repeated. When, a few days later, his messenger called upon me with another invitation, this time to dine and meet his good lady wife and children, my first thought was to wonder whether some prank was being played at my expense.

I had taken care of how to dress and hold myself on my first visit, but clearly this second visit would require special attention to every detail. I therefore decided to spend a good portion of what money I had accrued on acquiring a new costume in order that I might dress myself according to the Venetian fashion, as opposed to that of my native country. A great number of strangers from various exotic corners of the known world had, over the years, chosen to reside in Venice. However, the Venetian aristocrat remained confident about the superiority of his traditions over those of any other, and, while exterior display of a different culture was tolerated, I was learning that such stubbornness was unlikely to aid one's passage through society. This second invitation from the senator afforded me the opportunity to make a larger statement about the manner in which I might henceforth conduct myself in this great republic. In my quieter moments, I had often wondered if a marriage of the finest of my own customs with their Venetian refinement might not, in due course, produce a more sophisticated man. Or, if not this, perhaps such a conjunction of traditions might at least subdue a portion of the ill-feeling to which my natural state seemed to give rise.

I woke early on the morning of my second invitation to the senator's home with my mind in a state of disarray. I soon found myself pacing the floor of my chamber, but I remained unable to locate the source of my anxiety. There were many reasons why I might feel concerned about the uncomfortable predicament that ensnared my present life, but I found this particular visitation of melancholy intensely troubling. As I looked out over the moonlit Grand Canal, which lapped pleasingly against my wall, I realized that my best course of action would be to dress and wander the cold, dark streets in an attempt to calm my nerves. It had, after all, long been my custom to explore the strange regions of this enchanted city, often mistaking the way, probing the network of back streets and the complex labyrinths of alleyways in search of both new and familiar landmarks. At night, when abandoned to serenity, her breathing light and regular, Venice presented herself as a sleeping babe upon whom one might spy with proprietorial glee.

I dressed quickly and soon found myself on the wintry Rialto bridge, from whose vantage-point I was able to watch a lean cat scurry noiselessly into a blind alley. I had grown extremely fond of the city under the moon, for it was at such moments that I truly appreciated the full grandeur of her silent majesty. Only the occasional tolling of bells trespassed upon the night, but their song, together with the sister sound of water swirling and sighing, created the most wondrous accompaniment to the silence. And then, of course, there was the moonlight, which produced spellbinding patterns as it struck the water, illuminating buildings here, and withholding its light there. Some corners of Venice appeared to have been specially chosen to be blessed with this celestial gift of light and shadow. I smiled after the cat, safe in the knowledge that the cat's response to me was not tinged with ambiguity. Fear was a reliable emotion. Constant and undemeaning. And then again, I remembered that it had been nine months now since I had happily entered Venice in that most magnificent manner: by sea. I passed through the lagoon, which enabled me to observe the towers and turrets of the city rising above the distant mist, and all around me, on the low-lying islands, I could discern the outlines of monasteries, forts and small villages. With the sea behind me, I clipped forwards at a good pace, until the city began to show herself. First the mouth of the Grand Canal, then the majestic sweep of the buildings, and then the people: Venetians. I saw them walking slowly, heads bent, going about their business as though thoroughly unaware of the privilege of living among such overwhelming beauty. These people seemed sternly unconcerned with anything beyond the narrow orbit of their own lives. I remembered.

I remembered. I had led the fighting men of my own people for many years, and had also served in battle as a General for several other nations, both Christian and heathen. But now I was confidently arriving in Venice, summoned by the doge and his senators to lead the Venetian army whenever the Turks declared their intent. But where was the party to meet me? The fanfare? The escort of lavishly attired gondoliers that were widely known to welcome dignitaries? It appeared that I would have to make do with the spectacle of the city herself turning out to greet me. I stared down at the waters flowing beneath the Rialto bridge, and I wondered if my new costume might convince some among these Venetians to look upon me with a kinder eye. It was this desire to be accepted that was knotting my stomach and depriving me of sleep, and in my distress I had once more fled to the only person I could rely upon in these circumstances: the city herself, which had remained ever faithful to her enchanted promises. Thin scarves of fog began to drift across the Grand Canal, and then in the distance, through the dank morning mist, I saw a gondola moving slowly towards me and I imagined a passenger propped up in the back, under the canopy, perhaps another victim of a troubled mind. I watched as this black gliding object, lightly powdered with snow, approached as though a heavenly vision, and then it slipped beneath the bridge and out of sight. This was my cue to turn and walk back to my lodgings. It would not be wise to find myself at the senator's dinner fatigued through a lack of sleep.

Later that same day, at a little before five o'clock, a boatman called to me from the canal that was my front highway. My Venetian attendant, without the vaguest hint of a smile or gesture of affection, brushed my new attire in the insolent manner to which I had become accustomed. I turned to him, half-hoping that he might find it possible to wish me good luck on my evening's mission, but, as ever, he chose to remain silent. I descended the half-dozen steps and climbed aboard a particularly large gondola, one that was heavy with ornaments and whose cushions bore the most fantastic embroidery. The gondolier nodded a terse greeting, which I took to indicate his disapproval of having to propel his vessel to my unfashionable lodgings in order to convey a passenger whom he no doubt deemed unworthy of transportation. I nodded back a greeting in his direction, and then settled into the well-upholstered seat. We swung out wide and into the main traffic of the canal, and I noticed that the setting of the winter sun threw a weak light on the water, a light that was held rather than reflected. Despite the heavy traffic, I felt as though I alone, in all of this great city, had an appointment to occupy me this evening. Others seemed to be idling away what remained of this day.

As we sped along, I turned my mind to the problem of why this senator had been struck with a particular attraction to myself. I had no doubt that my reputation played some large part in his fascination, but I also imagined that there was something about my knowledge of other parts of the world, of foreign adventures and travels, that appealed to his senses. Yet our first meeting had been as dull as it was short. I had simply sat before him and answered his laboured and uninspired questions as though being interviewed. I had spent much of my time looking around his room, enchanted by the huge oil paintings, impressed by the fabrics and chandeliers, and held spellbound by the long mahogany table that was being polished by a servant. I was unable to believe that this was a room in a private house, rather than a public chamber where matters of national importance might be debated. But why meet with me again? Unless, of course, he was doing so out of some misplaced sense of obligation. In the distance I heard the bells of St Mark's begin to mark the hour, and then around me other, less grand bells began to respond to the call, and then, as I looked at the shoreline, I saw a pair of monks, their invisible feet scurrying beneath their billowing robes as they hurried towards their monastery, with the fear of God coursing through their holy bodies.

The senator's house was, as I remembered it, a grand and imposing structure. To my surprise, I experienced a sense of relaxation on once again viewing its elegant façade. As I scanned the full length of its brooding magnificence, I was struck by the sight of carefully arranged flowers about its balconies which, even at this late time of the year, cast down the perfumed odours of spring. Without saying a word, the gondolier drew the vessel to a standstill and looked down at me as though wondering why I had not already understood that this place was to mark the end of my journey. I had neglected to bring some coin to show my gratitude to this fellow, but his surly manner left me feeling that my omission was no cause for regret. Pulling myself up to full height, which easily dwarfed his own stature, I strode past him and stepped upon the lowest of the steps leading up to the roughly hewn door. Such a feature of this great city I was yet to understand fully. It bewildered me that the doors to even the finest palaces in the city were often constructed of the most weather-beaten wood, a wood clearly in need of treatment and attention. As I approached the door it opened before me, as if by magic, and I stepped boldly into the interior of this great home. Once inside, the door was rudely closed upon the waiting gondolier, which caused me to smile inwardly. I followed the elderly manservant up a dimly lit flight of stairs which had never seen the sun, and along a stone-walled corridor, at the end of which I could see bright lights and hear chattering voices and much joyous laughter. The noise and light burst upon me as I entered the room, and then there was silence as heads turned, and not a few jaws dropped. I am a big man, and I had already noted that a response of some sort upon my joining a room was invariable. In fact, I had come to expect this of my unarmed entrance into any circle. However, quickly rising to his feet and defying his advanced years, the senator moved towards me with his arm outstretched. He announced my name, although I was sure that those present had already been informed of my impending arrival. Clearly, I was to be the chief amusement of this evening.

After greeting me warmly, the senator then introduced me to the members of his family. First, his lady wife, whose first freshness of beauty had long passed, yet her present visage could not totally obscure the fact that, in her earlier years, she must have been a woman of not inconsiderable charm. She smiled gently, and I returned the compliment. I was informed that the elder son, a lank-looking fellow, pursued business interests in the Arsenal in company with his father, and was heir to the family fortune. At this young man's side sat his wife, the senator's daughter-in-law, a ravishing beauty, but one who appeared to be blessed with neither wit nor humour. It appeared that her looks accounted for the greater part of her allure, and she decorated her head, hands and neck with such an abundance of jewels and trinkets that her worth might be accurately calculated in ducats. The senator's younger son could barely bring himself to raise his eyes and face me in a civil manner. He sat somewhat nonchalantly, seemingly determined to appear uninterested in the newly arrived spectacle. His dandyish clothes, which, even to my untutored eye, appeared to lack any real understanding of either fashion or taste, completed his helpless look. The final member of the group, the senator's daughter, sat silently, but with a welcoming smile about both her mouth and, more importantly, her eyes. A stranger soon learns that where the mouth may deceive, the eyes tell nothing but the truth. In common with what I understood to be the practice of a modest Venetian damsel, she showed not more than four fingers of flesh beneath the shoulders. I was placed at the far end of the table, where my closest companions were the younger son and the gentle daughter.

. . .

The meal was lavish by my meagre standards. In my own country I had, of course, eaten excessively and well, but since my arrival in Venice my diet had been confined to simple fare. However, on this evening I ate heartily and praised the senator's cook, yet when presented with wine I drank only in moderation, for I was aware that to indulge might result in a loose tongue and unpleasant consequences. And so the evening unfolded, with my person being ever vigilant. Much of the questioning was taken up by the elder son, who seemed eager to prevent any other from interrogating me in order that he might remain the focal point of the evening. Perhaps he imagined that this would somehow please his father. Whenever his dull wife tried to intervene and make a point, he was sharp in his rebuke and clearly he was uninterested in whatever it was that she might have to say on this or any other occasion. He concluded one conversational volley with the observation that, in this city of churches, palaces and canals, Venetian households did, from time to time, use black slaves. I countered with the information that I had once been held as a slave, yet, as unpleasant as this situation had been, I had survived to tell the tale. I watched this boy carefully and, deciding that the victory was already secured, I chose not to mention my royal blood, or the fact that many Romans and Greeks had also been held as slaves, and so the moment passed. Eventually the senator's daughter was permitted to make enquiry as to the customs of my country with regard to food and wine, and I assured her that they were similar to those of her own country, with perhaps fewer spices added to the meat. She nodded, as though approving of my countrymen's manner of cooking food, and then her tiresome brother once more took up his tedious line of questioning.

Some time before the final course made its welcome appearance – for, if truth be told, I was finding the whole procedure somewhat difficult – the senator brought up the thorny subject of war. He heaped praise upon my exploits in the field, referring especially to battles fought and won against the infidel Turk. He then announced that my outstanding reputation as a General and leader of men had led him to persuade the doge to dip his hands deep into the coffers of this great republic, in order that they might hire a man of renowned capabilities in the art of war. At this disclosure, it occurred to me that I was to understand from the senator that a failure on my part would be regarded as a failing on his part, too. And then, after the final course had been consumed, our dinner was suddenly at an end. The senator led me carefully but firmly by the arm, back along the dimly lit corridor, and ushered me into his manservant's company. As he did so, he shared with me his knowledge that war with the Turk was imminent. I was not to fail. I looked at this elderly man and understood that my invitation to dine at his home had provided those close to him with an opportunity to judge his prize acquisition. He was, of course, sure that he had not made a mistake in hitching his fortune to mine, but to insure himself against future difficulties he was simply seeking approval from his family. Perhaps this was the Venetian custom.

During my return journey it began to snow. Tiny white flakes spun down from the dark sky and lightly dusted the gondola with a thin salty layer. And then the pleasing tone of the journey changed as the wind began to drive directly into my face, and the flurries became bothersome. I closed the curtains to the canopy, which disappointed me, for I wished to drink in views of my Venice at every possible opportunity, but my body was as yet unaccustomed to the damp cold which characterized this winter clime. Secreted in the closed cabin of this most perfect vehicle, I felt the swerves and twists as we floated through the darkness, my senses throbbing with the perfect mystery of this journey. And then it occurred to me that the senator's daughter must live a lonely life in her father's large house. Like all the fair daughters of Venice, she was no doubt being groomed for a marriage that would be beneficial to both families and occasion the fortunes of both to swell, but, visits to church aside, I imagined that she remained alone. By the time the gondola arrived at my lodgings and I stepped back on to *terra firma*, the swirling snow was in danger of becoming treacherous. I thanked my gondolier, whose manner seemed to have improved, and bade him goodnight, and then, as an afterthought, I urged him to be careful on his return journey. He smiled in the manner of one who was grateful for the sentiment, but who wished it to be known that he knew exactly what he was doing. He did not require advice from foreigners.

After some fruitless hours spent tossing first one way and then the next, I arose before dawn realizing that, again, I needed to walk about this city in the moonlight, both to reorder my thoughts and to put into place my feelings. It had ceased snowing, but it remained bitterly cold as I set out towards the north of the city, crossing small bridges and passing stealthily through dark alleyways. The chief problem, of course, was the lady on my mind. And, like a child, I wondered if I were on hers. That we barely exchanged a word seemed to have added to the mystique of this person whom I could not dislodge from my senses. I concluded that she was, without doubt, the most beautiful treasure of Venice. Never had I before witnessed such an effortless tranquillity, a superior air of breeding both aristocratic and modest, and a strength of personality that was at once confident and gently reassuring. When this lady moved, it was as though the universe moved with her, and what light there was in the room was wholly swallowed up by her eyes. I felt as though, against my will, some part of my soul had been captured.

I stopped at the entrance to a small street which led into a square. I could see that at the end of the street there were gates, and marshalling the gates two guards. It occurred to me that this was the district about which my merchant had spoken, the place where the moneylenders resided, and never having entered this quarter, I was keen to satisfy my curiosity while everybody slept. The two Christian guards were naturally suspicious about my approaching them, but seeing that I was clearly not one of their own, and that I did not seem intent upon harming any Jew, they unbolted the gates and, after I had bestowed upon them a small token of my gratitude, they let me pass. And what a strange place was this walled ghetto. Apparently, most of the Jews did not regard this arrangement of being locked behind gates from sunset to sunrise as a hardship, for it afforded them protection against the many cold hearts that opposed their people. On Sundays and on Christian holy days, the Jews were imprisoned for the full length of the day, and they were obliged both to appoint and to pay these Christian guards themselves. In addition, they were required to pay two boats to patrol unceasingly the canals surrounding the ghetto, the outer walls of which were to be windowless. The Jews paid dearly to live and do commerce at the heart of the Venetian empire, rather than in the provinces, and penalties for offending the morals of the people of Venice were severe. Intimacy between Jewish men and Christian women was punishable by a heavy fine and up to twelve months' imprisonment, depending upon whether the woman was a public prostitute. In addition, Jews were forbidden to run schools or teach Christians in any subject, and any Jew found outside the ghetto at night was likely to be heavily fined and imprisoned. Some frightened Jews argued that the ghetto, far from affording them protection, made it easier for popular outbursts against them to achieve some focus, for the Jews were herded *en masse* and enclosed in one defenceless pen.

As I began to explore, I noticed that the streets were recklessly narrow and ill-arranged, and on either side of them immensely tall and well-appointed houses sat next to equally tall hovels. In this ghetto, the rich and the destitute lived together, the denizens bound only by their faith. Nothing stirred, and I felt as though I were wandering about a village that had been quickly abandoned in a time of plague. Not a single article of clothing hung from a window, and not a single window was ajar to allow a little breeze to penetrate. I longed to catch a glimpse of one of their beautiful black-eyed women, but the inhabitants of this region appeared to be sleeping peacefully. I neither heard the raised voice of a call to prayer, nor did I spy the night-time wandering of an exotic such as myself. Everything remained calm, and it appeared that these Jews obeyed the rhythms of day and night with a slavish adherence. I walked for some time through the maze of little streets and noticed the complete absence of shrines, madonnas, carved crosses, or images of saints. All outward signs of devotion were absent in this dark place, which led me to conclude that religious imagery of any kind probably constituted a particular sin for these people. I continued to wander, but the further I entered the ghetto, the filthier the alleyways became, and the more oppressive these tall hovels appeared, with damp staining the walls, and in certain places causing the plaster to erupt in a manner similar to boils. These towers of poverty seemed to be reaching desperately for a little light or air above a darkness and filth which seemed more befitting of an earlier age of squalor. At precisely the moment when I was beginning to feel hopelessly lost, I emerged into a small square, in one corner of which were buildings of more human proportions. At the far end of the square, and at the end of a reasonably well-paved and brightly illuminated street, I spied the gates through which I had entered this underworld. My exploration had unnerved me somewhat, for it was well known that the Jews were fortunate in their wealth. Why they should choose to live in this manner defeated my understanding. Surely there was some other land or some other people among whom they might dwell in more tolerable conditions?

Once back at my lodgings, I stood outside and stared as the sun began her morning's labour up the steep slope of the sky. Then I listened as the tuneful lament of a flute rose from a half-deserted street behind me, and I breathed a long sigh of relief. With some great difficulty I had managed to navigate my way from the gates of the ghetto and back into a world that I recognized. It was only when I stumbled upon the Grand Canal that my heart finally regained a normal beat. Indeed, it appeared somewhat shameful to me that a man who had endured many wars and faced much danger should panic on finding himself in unfamiliar streets in an admittedly civilized environment. But it was Venice herself which induced this frenzy in me, for her streets led carelessly one into the other, stubbornly refusing to reveal any clue as to where they might ultimately terminate. And then, once back in the region of my lodgings, I was suddenly seized with a desire to witness the start of the day. However, I was soon shaken from my contemplation of the sun's labours by the sight of my attendant emerging from my own door and looking upon me disapprovingly. At first I wondered if my nightly wanderings had upset him, for I could imagine nothing else that might have caused him to feel any new antipathy towards me. It was then that I noticed the letter that he was clutching. He passed it to me and, as was his custom, he chose not to utter a single word. He turned theatrically and re-entered the house, leaving me to contemplate the letter alone. Having failed to recognize the handwriting on the outside, I decided to open it and discover for myself its contents. I was shocked to find that she who had been constantly on my mind had also been moved by our meeting, but, unlike myself, she had taken the initiative and set pen to paper. As decorum demanded, she revealed little of her heart, and simply requested that I visit with her later that same day in her father's garden. According to this lady, I was to enter a gondola that would appear at a determined hour, with a white handkerchief displayed at one of the windows.

I carefully folded the letter and tried to imagine how I might occupy the anxious hours before my appointment in the garden, for the whole day stretched before me, long and troublesome. I decided to manufacture a list of tasks to which I might address myself in an attempt to stave off the worries and concerns populating my thoughts. However, I soon realized that it would be politic to address those unmanufactured tasks which might genuinely profit from my giving them due attention. To this end I composed, then dispatched, a letter to the doge himself, asking when I might be pressed into service against the infidel. I had sent an earlier communication, but had not been blessed with a reply. However, I reasoned that it could not harm my cause to ask once more. After all, I had been summoned to Venice, and was being paid handsomely to be a soldier and a leader of men. Idling away my Venetian days did not represent a good return on their investment. The problems of phrasing a letter and pressing my case, while at the same time making it clear that I wished to cause no offence, did indeed occupy a great portion of the day. However, in the early afternoon, as I stepped into the gondola that would transport me back towards the senator's house, I realized that the difficulties of grappling with phraseology had failed to soothe the anxieties which were now beginning to overwhelm me. I looked down at the water and began to shake in anticipation of the forthcoming meeting. What strange ideas must be populating this lady's mind to take a chance and write such a letter.

· · ·

I was admitted by the same elderly manservant who had received me only the previous evening, but this time he escorted me out of the back of the house and towards the garden, where the lady was waiting to converse with me. She was exquisitely dressed, and attended by a maidservant who discreetly placed herself at a short distance from us. However, she remained close enough so that she might observe, and indeed overhear if so she desired, but in order that she might appear less conspicuous she began to busy herself with embroidery. We two situated ourselves beneath a tree whose branches provided umbrella-like cover, and the lady declared that she wished to know principally of my adventures as a soldier and of the many dangers to which my life had been subjected. She listened intently, and I spun some truthful tales, but eventually I announced that I wished to learn from her about Venetian society, for I remained unclear about much of the world in which I was living. What were the common customs, the uncommon customs, the various ways in which people lived their lives? Truly, what might I expect? I fired off a volley of questions and she answered each in turn, carefully weighing her thoughts before venturing to speak. On some topics her answers were admirably brief and helpful, but on others she felt it necessary to expand more fully. In one case, she warned me against unnecessary roaming late at night for there were in Venice villains, known as *braves*, who, armed with a coat of mail, a gauntlet upon their right hand and a short dagger, were known to lurk by the waterside and attack passing strangers. Once they had stabbed their victims, and taken what booty they could extract, they would conclude the proceedings by dumping the body into the water, but apparently these days there were fewer of these villains, for the punishment for discovery was execution. Furthermore, many honest men in Venice had taken to carrying about their person a well-pocketed knife to protect their lives, and these *braves* were known to fear a fair battle. Having listened to my lady, I assured her of my ability to enter into successful combat with any, which in turn led her back to her familiar theme of my exploits on the field of battle.

Time passed swiftly, and eventually the lady's maidservant laid to one side her embroidery and climbed to her feet, which was clearly a signal that it was time for me to leave. The lady stood, as did I, and for the first time our eyes held. I had, until this moment, been careful to avoid full eye contact with my hostess, but, as we looked at each other, I knew that the stirring in my heart had deepened and I was suddenly overcome with joy. She chose to prolong the gaze and then, with what I imagined to be reluctance, she finally lowered her eyes. The lady announced that she had greatly enjoyed our discourse and, with that said, she quickly retreated and disappeared from my view. I looked all about me and I wondered what I should do, for the elderly manservant had not yet appeared to escort me back to the gondola. However, I need not have panicked, for as soon as I resumed my seat the flustered manservant shuffled into view, seemingly embarrassed that he had mistimed his cue.

That night I lay in bed and cast my mind back to the wife and child that I had left behind in my native country. I did not think of myself as having spurned them, for they were in my heart and would evermore remain there. As was the custom with a warrior, there had been no formal marriage, it being understood that at any moment I might lose my life. (It was never understood that at any moment I might also lose my heart.) My son would forgive me, for in a few years he, too, would be a man and follow in his father's footsteps. But I feared that my wife would fail to understand my present predicament, and her judgement of my character would prove to be harsh. I sat upright in bed and listened to the quiet lapping of the water below. I wondered how often they thought of me. I wondered if, as they lay at night, the moon rising late through sirocco-driven veils of mist, the warm wind caressing their skin – I wondered if, in their minds, they still held a picture of me. And if they did indeed think of me, were their thoughts always hostile, or were there occasions when I entered their souls in a benign fashion? Did it ever occur to them that I might already have made the easy passage from this world to the next and been taken up by death? But perhaps I had no right to expect anything from them. Why should they trouble their minds with me?

In the morning I awoke to the familiar sound of chiming bells, which were soon rendered discordant by the sight of my attendant entering my room with a look of some distaste etched across his face. In his hand he held a small parcel, which he delivered to my bed with thinly disguised hostility. It had already occurred to me that I might have to replace this man, and his present performance served only to confirm my feelings. I saw no reason why I should continue to tolerate such petulant displays of bad manners from this gondolier's son. That he disliked me on account of my complexion and bearing, I had no doubt, but should this failed soldier wish to serve another, then I had resolved that I would not stand in his way. I watched as he drew back the curtains, after which he strolled from the room in an unhurried manner. Turning my attention to the parcel, I was surprised to note that there was a second communication which I soon discovered to be a letter bearing the seal of the doge. Putting the parcel to one side, I quickly opened the doge's letter and learnt that I was summoned to meet him that very morning, and that I should expect a gondola before the church bells struck nine. My heart quickened on receiving this news, for I presumed that this could mean only that war was drawing closer. I then turned my attention towards the contents of the parcel. It was, as I imagined, from the lady, but upon opening it I was astonished to discover a gold bracelet that was heavily wrought but delicate in design. A short note, signed in her own hand, thanked me for sharing with her my tales. I took the bracelet and fastened it about my wrist, determining, even at that moment, that I should never again remove it.

I dressed with some haste and made my way to the Doge's Palace, taking little trouble to look about me and observe the world, as was my normal practice. Once there, it was clear that I was expected, for I was quickly delivered into an unfamiliar waiting chamber, whose walls were draped with hangings of the finest tapestry, and I was attended to in a manner which seemed to reflect my status as General of the Venetian army. The grandeur of the huge windows, and the wide stream of light that flooded the room, lent a powerfully sombre tone to the setting. The ornamentation must have cost many thousands of ducats, for at one end stood a fireplace of carved marble, lavishly decorated with figures and foliage, and above my head the ceiling was decorated with gold fixtures. Eventually I was ushered along a thickly carpeted corridor and into the presence of the doge, an elderly man, who, I soon remembered, appeared to be a trifle hard of hearing. He stood before a large rectangular mirror which boasted an elaborate bejewelled frame, and he seemed pleased to see me. I noticed that he was attended to by a half-dozen senior senators, including he who had recently occupied himself as my host for dinner. I quickly scrutinized my host's face for any sign of displeasure, but, being able to spy none, my body let out what I feared might have been an audible sigh of relief.

The proceedings of the meeting were simple. The Turks, so intelligence had informed the doge, having already reddened their scimitars with much Christian blood, were now planning to at-

tack the Venetian island of Cyprus. My commission was to re-
visit an island with which I was already familiar, this time at the
head of the Venetian army, and to subdue the infidel usurper
who was forever laying claim to this perilously situated outpost
of Christian civilization. I was to set sail before the end of the
week, and, upon my departure, I would meet those good men
who would follow me into battle. Until then, I was free to prepare myself in whatever manner was customary for men of my
region. The doge and his senators enquired as to whether there
was any issue I wished to raise. I declined, but not without some
alarm, for I suddenly realized that my head was full of thoughts
pertaining to the lady, and there were indeed questions I wished
to ask, though none were related to matters of war. I looked
somewhat useless for a moment, then regained my voice and assured these noblemen that I was happy that this time had finally
arrived. Further, I assured them that I would not disappoint, and
they seemed pleased with my confidence, for they looked upon
me with respect as I bade them farewell.

The same gondolier was waiting for me when I stepped out
from the palace and into the winter gloom. Clearly, the gondolier was under instruction to serve as my escort for the journey
back to my lodgings, but, in the manner of these people, he said
nothing and simply gestured with his head in the direction of
his vessel. I bade him be patient a while as I wished to exercise
my legs in the piazza at St Mark's and observe the winged creatures who sat in long rows, their necks drawn into their shoulders, their neck feathers bunched clumsily about their heads.
The good news that I had been waiting for with great patience
now appeared to be disconcerting, for it would inevitably mean
a period of separation from the senator's daughter. And what of
the lady herself? Would she think it forward of me to write and
suggest another clandestine rendezvous? Or would it be more
politic to allow her to initiate any further meetings? As these

thoughts tumbled in my mind, bells of all personalities and temper began to chime, and the birds took to the air with a sudden
rush of wings.

I sought out my gondolier and soon settled back in my seat,
where I listened to the backwash of the canal beating against
the hull, and the comforting drop of water as it fell from the
oar. Some moments later, I was shaken from my reverie by a
flare of light reflecting off a pile of fish that lay on the bottom
of a moored boat. I glanced about me and realized that
presently we would soon be upon the very house where the
lady resided. Upon instinct I looked up to the direction of the
balcony, then called to my gondolier and asked after him if
he could sing. He looked at me, but said nothing. In fact, he
seemed to increase his pace, but, just at the point when I was
ready to remind him that I had made an enquiry of him, he
began to steer his vessel towards the very house and to raise his
voice in a pleasing tune. And then she appeared, dressed from
head to toe in silk, the wind playing gently with her garments. I
held up my hand in greeting, but partly in order that she might
also see the gold bracelet which I proudly sported about my
wrist. The gondolier continued to sing, and people passed by
on either side of the canal, clearly fascinated by the scene being
played out before them. I was, I admit, flattered by the attention of this lady, for it seemed to my mind peculiar that one
such as I might win the affection of so beautiful a creature.
And still my gondolier continued to sing, and I gazed up at
her, then a flower was tossed down from the balcony. A
single winter rose floated in the water. And then the lady disappeared from the balcony. At that moment, and at that moment precisely, as the circular ripples radiated out from the
rose, I resolved to make the senator's daughter my bride,
whatever the consequences.

. . .

I instructed my gondolier to steer towards the bank and moor his vessel by the steps to the lady's house. He looked at me as though I had taken leave of my senses, but he said nothing. As we set a course for the steps, I managed to pluck the rose from the water and I held it up to dry. It appeared that I was already expected, for the by now familiar manservant opened the weather-beaten door and, without saying a word, escorted me through the house and into the back garden, where I understood I was to remain and await the arrival of my mistress. However, before the elderly manservant had time to depart, the lady entered in company with her maidservant. She smiled, then sat before me in all her resplendent beauty, while she that watched over her retired a short distance. I, too, sat and we began to speak at the same time, but realized our error and laughed. And then I apologized for my uninvited intrusion, and explained that on seeing the vision of her on the balcony I could not help myself. She blushed somewhat, but I continued and said that perhaps she might speak with me a little, if it were convenient, for I felt a trifle guilty that, at our last meeting, I had dominated affairs. She seemed shocked and insisted that this was not the case, but then enquired as to whether there was any subject in particular about which I wished to converse. I thought for a moment, then asked her about sorcery and magic in Venice, for I had noticed that Venetians seemed to be devout Christians and free of such associations.

In the course of the next hour, the good lady corrected my mistaken assumption and related to me many instances of superstition, some of which I knew to be true of people in other lands. For instance, to a Venetian the number thirteen, the number of Judas, is always unlucky. Further, one must carefully avoid spilling salt, and if one turns money in one's pocket at the first quarter of the moon, then it will increase during that month. (Apparently, it is also understood that hair grows and falls with the waxing and waning of this same celestial object.) I learnt that, in Venice, certain days have significance, so that on New Year's Day, to meet a humpback is a sign of good fortune, but to meet a lame person is one of misfortune. Sadly, to meet a priest means that death will occur within the year. On the Epiphany, the Venetian beasts talk to each other, but on this day only. And the dew on St John's Eve is precious and must be treasured. I spent the greater part of the hour listening to this lady's wondrous voice before the manservant reappeared and whispered to the maid, whose eyes betrayed severe agitation. The lady stood, clearly fearing discovery, and suddenly our meeting was at an end. She quickly announced that, with regret, she would have to leave. With this said, she hurried from the garden, leaving the manservant to escort me from the house.

On reaching my own lodgings, I took a seat on my balcony where, for some hours, I silently contemplated the bold nature of my unannounced visit, and worried whether my presumption would now be rewarded by rejection. Then, before I realized what was happening, the short winter's day expired and it was dusk. Below me I could see a variety of evening boats gliding by. Each had its own lantern which gleamed and played upon the water, the swifter gondolas creating dazzling tracks of light in their wake as they made their way along this grandest of canals. As night fell, my solitude was interrupted by my attendant. He presented me with a newly delivered letter which, once he had retired, I quickly opened. Unfortunately, the writing was close and difficult to read, as clearly it had been written in great haste. Because I knew it to be from the lady who had captured my heart, I could not bring myself to ask my untrustworthy attendant to aid me in the deciphering of the characters. What remained of the evening passed somewhat painfully as I looked and looked again at the letter, but it defeated me comprehensively. I retired to bed in torment, thoroughly frustrated by my inability to interpret the lady's script.

I arose at dawn and dressed quickly, for during the night I had determined a method by which I might be able to gain some understanding of the letter that lay open beside my bed. I walked quickly through the winter fog towards the north of the city, pausing only to marvel at the fact that the greater part of the world appeared to be hidden behind an opaque shroud. I soon found myself outside the gates to the ghetto, and I noticed that the Christian guards were the same fellows that I had seen on my previous visit. They seemed surprised, but not unhappy, to see me again. I offered them some coins and was allowed to pass inside, whereupon I began to search for a man who might help me. Ghostly figures were already stirring in the streets, but they moved quickly, as though frightened of holding their shape. I had determined that a scholar of some description would be best equipped for the role that I envisaged. Therefore, having finally located their place of worship in a small and unusually well-kept square, I quickly entered. Once inside, I encountered a weather-beaten, warp-faced Jew toiling over a book in the semi-darkness. He was sitting in the room in which I imagined they celebrated their unchristian service. An elegant and richly decorated place, it was furnished with a gallery which boasted the most impressive carvings. I offered up the letter to the Jew and he immediately understood what I expected of him. While he scanned the letter, he gestured to me that I should sit. Then, having examined it, he looked up at me. He did not betray any emotion, but simply began to recite to me the contents of the letter. As he began, I almost asked him to stop in order that I might press upon him the knowledge that I could read, and inform him that it was only this dense and unclear script that had defeated me. But it was too late. Once he had begun, I was intoxicated. The lady stopped short of professing a love for me, but her desire to see me again, and as soon as possible, was clearly articulated.

The scholar handed back the unfolded letter. I paid him, adding some extra for the good news he conveyed, and our transaction was complete. It was then, after a moment's thought, that I asked if I might dictate to him a letter of reply set down in his finest hand, but he had already anticipated my request. The Jew looked at me with pen poised. I was simple and direct in my affections, but the boldness of the lady's letter encouraged me far beyond what I might otherwise have dared to reveal. My passion for her I laid out openly, holding back only when it seemed necessary to do so for the sake of the modesty of he who was writing. And then, my letter complete, I asked my Jew if he would be good enough to convey it to the lady in question, but again he seemed to have already understood. The good scholar refused to take extra money for this task, and I judged by the way he looked upon me that he felt a certain sympathy for my predicament. Indeed, as I left, I am sure that I noticed a smile play around his thin lips.

Early the following morning, my attendant entered my room and rescued me from an unsuccessful night, during which I had remained painfully alert. For twenty-four hours the lady had captured the centre of my mind, creating a tortuous inertia that had rendered me incapable of any practical action. I was in no doubt that she loved me, but I knew not how to marry my life of action to any other life. Indeed, I was already beginning to fear that, should I take a chance and pursue a marriage with this young lady, immediately upon doing so my reputation as a leader of the first rank would inevitably suffer. After all, since the age of seven I had known only the power that comes through confident usage of the arm in the heat of battle. Despite my royal blood, the remote language of love had remained alien to me, for I had always refused to coat my tongue with its false words. My attendant stood before me and he repeated himself with impatience, once more informing me that the lady was waiting outside. Only now did I understand why this infuriating man had decided to interrupt my afflicted thoughts. My letter would have reached her hands, and rather than dispatch her answer she must have decided to come herself and give to me the news that my heart wished to hear. I dressed quickly, looking many times upon myself in the mirror. I was no longer young enough to pretend that I was an appealing specimen of manhood, but I remained confident that I could hold my own with any in the ring of combat. The curly-blonde-headed darlings of Venice drew to themselves cunning glances from the fair ladies of the republic in quantities that I could only dream of achieving, but my complexion was a feature that was unlikely to aid me in my attempts to attract admiration. Once more, I looked upon myself in the mirror. It was true. The wooing of this lady did indeed threaten the very foundations upon which my life was constructed, but surely it was the coward's way to remain in secure military bachelorhood and learn nothing more of the world beyond my own life. I abandoned the mirror and made my way towards the door.

She stood with her back to me, but turned when she heard me approaching. My attendant glowered in my direction, then informed me that I was to present myself within the hour at the Doge's Palace. With this said, the sour man left our presence and I simply stared at the lady. The morning light stealthily picked the blush from her cheeks, showing off her youth to its best advantage. The lady informed me that early yesterday evening she had received my letter, but once she had studied its contents, she had found sleep difficult to achieve. She had sought an audience with me so that we might converse, but even as she completed her reasoning, she apologized for the inconvenience which she was sure this intrusion was causing me. For a moment I looked at her, transfixed by her beauty, then I broke the spell and stared down at the canal beneath us, where water lapped softly against wood and stone. And then the words appeared in my mouth and tumbled out awkwardly. Without planning, I asked her if she might consider becoming my bride. To my great surprise, the child fell immediately to her knees and clasped her hands together in front of her bowed head. It was then that she told me that her greatest wish was that I should become her lord and master, and protect and honour her for the remainder of her days. With this said, I reached down and encouraged her to look up. Then I fell to one knee and sealed our union with the tenderest of kisses. Was I truly the same man who had arrived lonely and unannounced? The same man who had sailed in a state of spellbound wonder right into the heart of this city-state? The same man who had entertained a willing but subtle Venetian whore at the suggestion of my first 'master', even though I derived little pleasure from my actions? The same man who had initially struggled with the language, and who had, at times, wondered if he would ever settle among these strange and forbidding people? And now to be married, and to the heart of the society. I wondered how such a change could be wrought in a man's life, and in so short a period.

Our strategy required us to act with both secrecy and haste. That same evening, my lady would steal away from her father's house and, under cover of night, meet me in a monastery where improvised ceremonies were known to be performed habitually. We deemed it politic not to share our intentions with any others, for we imagined the objections would be many, and the obstacles placed in our path, high and perhaps insurmountable. Furthermore, the urgent details of war, as the Turk continued to threaten, were fast consuming the affairs of state and we did not wish for our decision to be in any way affected by such matters. Clearly, I had been instructed to report to the Doge's Palace for additional information regarding this Turkish peril, but I was loathe to leave my lady, and she me. We held hands tightly and resolved to meet again at dusk. However, before we bade each other a temporary *adieu*, we kissed once more, but this time with fervour.

Upon reaching the Doge's Palace, I was informed that the situation with the warlike Turk had indeed become critical. Intelligence had briefed the state that they were sailing towards Rhodes, but it was generally understood that their preferred destination was Cyprus. In addition to my position at the head of their army, the doge and his senators ordered me to assume command as Governor once I had secured Cyprus. They reminded me of the importance of this Venetian posting, implying that a great deal of faith had been placed in my abilities, for I would be replacing one of their own Venetian favourites, who, although competent, could not boast of my skills and experience. I was instructed by the doge to return to my place of abode and await the alarm. The next signal would be to advise me that I should immediately greet my army and depart for Cyprus. I thanked the doge, and his senators, and bowed low as I withdrew. As I did so, I thought to myself, I remain their General, and in a short while I will still be their General, save only for an increase in my happiness. I silently hoped for their understanding.

The late-afternoon light was feeble and it cast upon the wintry city an aspect of melancholic calm. The gondolier carried me swiftly, but silently, through the narrow back canals, where this great city appeared sluttish beneath her regal garb. I noticed a shabby row of balconies decorated with garbage and discarded furniture, beneath which flights of slimy steps led down from the now familiar battered doorways. The canal about this place smelt putrid, and I clasped a handkerchief to my nose and mouth. I had spent the latter part of the afternoon in great contemplation, much of it concerning my wife and son who remained in my native land. The word *wife* still gave rise to much private concern, but I tried to flush this anxiety from my mind. I continually reminded myself that my native wife was not a *wife* in the manner that a Venetian might understand the term, yet I wondered if this were not simply a convenience of interpretation on my part. The problem of whether I would ever return to my country, and my worries about how my new wife might be treated by my people were this to happen, distressed me greatly. As the afternoon drifted towards evening, I slowly discovered myself coming to terms with the fact that I might never again see the country of my birth. This proposed marriage did indeed mark me off from my past, and Venice, the birthplace of my wife, was a city that I might now have to consider home for what remained of my life. None of this had I hitherto seriously considered, and my winter's journey towards the monastery began to take on an aspect of finality that lowered my spirits.

The pale moon was illuminating the lagoon as the gondolier stopped in front of the small monastery. The bizarre and macabre light appeared to me a strange warning that I should quickly conclude the business of this day. I wondered if it were possible that, to this woman, a marriage to me was a mere Venetian whim that would soon be forgiven by her family. The stain of my smoky hand on her marble skin, a mark that might be washed clean in the milky basin of family love. I dared not dwell on these thoughts for too long. I looked up and realized that my bride-to-be was already present, for I could see her maidservant standing anxiously by the door to the monastery.

She need not have feared. I have always been a man of honour. I disembarked and mounted the thirty or so stone steps which led from the sea, and I entered the gloomy building. As I made my way to the side of my lady, I could see that she looked exquisite in her silken dress, with her shoulders bare, and her long hair threaded with gold in the traditional manner. However, on closer inspection I noticed that her brow was furrowed with lines of worry, and I felt guilty that my delay had induced this suffering in her. The Christian man who stood before us clearly wished to dismiss this unusual ceremony as swiftly as possible. He asked if I was indeed a Christian, although he knew this to be the case, for an unbeliever could never be entrusted with the command of the Venetian army. I spoke softly and informed him that my journey to the bosom of Christ had taken place many years before my arrival in Venice. With this hurdle cleared, little remained to cause us delay, and the ceremony proceeded apace and resulted in our soon being declared man and wife.

Some hours ago, my wife and I journeyed back to my lodgings, where I now wait for the alarm. It was a gloomy moonlit evening and, as our vessel proceeded, we were lightly powdered with snow. Only the clumsy plash of an oar as we eased beneath a bridge, or the echo of a heavy foot in a hidden alleyway, disturbed our silence. Once back at my lodgings, I dismissed my attendant for the evening and conducted my wife to my bedchamber. I had, during our silent voyage from the monastery, contemplated whether it would be proper to wait a while before taking up my rightful place with my wife, but I determined that the passion that we felt for each other should not be dammed up. She proved, as I had hoped, an eager, if somewhat naïve partner, but what she lacked in knowledge she made up for in the softness of her touch.

She now lies alone, her body illuminated by the weak light that leaks through the shutters of the tall window. She sleeps deeply, exhausted by our love-making, but also by the tension and duplicity of the past few days. I now possess an object of beauty and danger, and I know that, henceforth, all men will look upon me with a combination of respect and scorn. I also know that never again will I be fully trusted by those of my own world, both male and female, but some of this I have already anticipated. For she who has now lain with me, and before her God declared herself to be of me, this will be her first taste of a bitterness to which she may never accustom herself. That she is entirely disposable to those who profess to love her will never have occurred to her. If she remains loyal to me, there will be many new and difficult truths to which she will now be exposed. However, I believe my wife possesses a soul that is strong enough to withstand the heat of future battles.

Venice remains silent, and my mind continues to wrestle with difficult thoughts. I look again to the bed and gaze upon the sight of my wife's body. If only I were privy to her Venetian thoughts, I might begin to help her make sense of her new circumstances. And then, as night gives way to dawn, I hear the raised whisper of a messenger calling to my attendant that I should immediately depart for the Doge's Palace. Finally, the alarm. My wife stirs, and then turns to face me. Again the voice calls to my attendant with an order that he should immediately rouse me. My wife's face softens into a bleary smile and she asks if I must go. I tell her that I have to leave, but she should not worry for I will soon return. Once I have received my orders from the doge and his senators, I will once more hurry to her side. My wife smiles at me with both her mouth and her eyes.

The Venetian trial against the Jews of Portobuffole, to be heard before one hundred and fifty-two Venetian senators, began on Tuesday 27 June 1480 and continued day after day, with only two interruptions: 29 June, which was the feast of the Saints Peter and Paul, and Sunday 2 July. The defendants were represented by two lawyers from Padua, who dressed in togas and were highly skilled in oratory. They quoted all of the passages from the scripture which affirmed that, for the Jews, nothing is more impure than blood – not just from animals, from whom the Jews drain the blood after slaughter, but even from their own women. How could they possibly have been able to feed themselves on blood? They reminded those present that Jews followed the Ten Commandments, which declared that it was forbidden to kill, and the prophet Moses also specifically forbade Jews to eat blood. And then, of course, there was the cumulative evidence of the Bible. For instance, in Leviticus, chapter seventeen, verse ten, it is written: 'I will set My face against that soul that eateth blood.' The injunction is repeated some four verses later: 'Ye shall eat the blood of no manner of flesh.' The lawyers rejected as mere rumour the idea that it was traditional for rich Jews to give poor Jews Christian blood without charge, and they concluded their presentation by suggesting that the confessions obtained, which 'proved' that these Jews had sucked out the blood of a Christian child, had been elicited by excessive use of that dreadful engine of torture, the *strappada*.

The state prosecutor, on the other hand, knew the Venetian senators, and he was aware of which arguments would be most persuasive with them. He began by reciting a list of similar infanticides attributable to Jews in other cities and other towns, and provided such detail that one senator became overwhelmed and had to leave the chamber. The state prosecutor then pulled out a Hebrew book and explained that it was a Book of Prayers for everyday use. He made a doctor, who knew Hebrew, read and translate a prayer that the Jews said every morning, a prayer which contained a powerful and vengeful curse against apostate Jews who had become Christians. Servadio was asked to confirm that this prayer was directed against Jews who had dishonoured their faith in the first centuries of the Christian era, and to further confirm that the prayer had been repeated for over a thousand years. This he did. The state prosecutor concluded with the assertion that surely it was the devil himself who gave these people the idea to kill innocent Christian children, and now they must die. The lawyers from Padua did not respond quickly, but eventually mounted the weak argument that the Book of Prayers was simply a narrative text used principally for the study of the various dialects it contained.

By 4 July, the senators' levels of tolerance had reached their limit. Every day the sultry summer weather had become increasingly oppressive, and the fatigued doge had already withdrawn and left in his place an elderly councilman who, in common with the other senators, was quickly tiring of these proceedings. On the morning of 5 July, he tapped the ballot box that was before him, a sign that the discussions were over and it was time to vote. The Jews were taken back to their cells and their lawyers left the room, leaving only the senators behind. A secretary approached and began to read:

Does it seem to you, sirs, on the basis of what has been said and read, that one must proceed against Servadio and Moses, usurers from Portobuffole, against Giacobbe from Colonia, all of them wicked Jews who, by mutual consent, deliberately, and with the help, advice and favours of one another, killed a young Christian boy in the home of the above-mentioned Servadio, a boy of about six or seven, a beggar from the city of Treviso, from where he was taken by Giacobbe of Colonia, as was requested by Servadio, and afterwards was brought to Portobuffole by the same Giacobbe and by another Giacobbe? Then, at the end, they extracted the blood of the young boy mentioned above and put it in the unleavened bread that they eat during their Easter, according to their detestable habit, to scorn and dishonour our God, Jesus Christ, and his Holy Faith.

They voted first on the three who had confessed: Servadio, Giacobbe and Moses. A ballot boy gave a small piece of white fabric to each senator. Then three ballot boxes were passed around – one red, one green and one white – and each senator dropped his ballot into one of these three boxes. They counted the votes: fifty-five were undecided, three voted no, ninety-four voted yes. And so it was decided, and the secretary announced the following:

Tomorrow at the usual hour, the three will be led to a barge with oars and tied down with three iron balls. In this fashion, they will be transported along the Grand Canal, from St Mark's to the Church of the Holy Cross, preceded by a town crier who will call out their names and why they are guilty. From Holy Cross, they will return by foot to St Mark's Square. Upon their arrival, they will be made to climb up on to three high pieces of scaffolding that will be erected between two columns, and all three prisoners will be secured with a long chain; thereafter, a fire will be set under them, reducing their bodies to ashes.

The decision regarding Donato, the family servant of Servadio, now a Christian called Sebastian, was then put to a vote. Thirty-one were undecided, twelve were against and ninety in favour of condemning him. It was decided that he would be sent to prison for a year, followed by eternal exile. Solomon, the son of Giacobbe and servant of Moses, newly accused of having helped his master burn the cadaver of the child in the oven, was condemned to six months in prison and six years' exile, with eighty-two votes in favour, twenty-seven against and twenty-three undecided. Fays, Servadio's son's teacher, who was accused of collaboration in making the unleavened bread with the child's blood and then eating it too, was condemned to a year in prison and ten years' exile, with thirty-five votes undecided, ten against and eighty-seven in favour. It was decided that no charges would be proffered against Sara, the wife of Servadio, or Rebecca, the wife of Moses. As soon as the sentences were announced, the state prosecutor went directly to the prison to pass on the sentences to Servadio, Moses and Giacobbe. He then ordered that they be taken directly to church and given prayer books so they could prepare themselves to die.

In Venice, on the day of an execution, it was customary for the doge to send the same lunch that he intended to eat to those who were condemned to death. However, these Jews were fasting to atone for their sins, and their leader, Servadio, had also begged his companions not to drink, despite the fact that they were tormented by thirst. Although he did not tell them, he was also thinking that their bodies would burn more easily if they were dried up, thereby reducing their suffering and maintaining a more dignified image. At noontime, from the bell tower of St Mark's, came the echo of the last chord. It was immediately followed by another that struck mournfully, for this was the bell of the Cursed that customarily accompanied the walk of the condemned. A chamberlain appeared in front of the Doge's Palace, followed by a bodyguard who escorted the three men, who were now naked to the waist and chained together. They marched between two cordons of soldiers to the barge that was waiting for them. In the middle of the barge were three iron balls. Once the condemned men were tightly secured and chained to the iron balls, the barge departed along the Grand

Canal, approaching first one bank, then the other. A herald on the barge bellowed in a loud and monotonous voice: 'Here before you are Servadio, Moses and Giacobbe, Jews who killed a Christian child, dishonouring our Holy Faith.' Both banks of the canal were lined with people who, on hearing these words, shuddered and made the sign of the cross. Having passed through all of the Grand Canal, the party descended from the barge at the Byzantine column of the Church of the Holy Cross. The spectators who had arrived in great numbers protested when they realized that the condemned would not be immediately tortured, but would instead return on foot to St Mark's Square attached to a line of horses. They were being deprived of an afternoon of festivity.

Between the columns of St Mark and St Todaro, three pieces of scaffolding had been erected with very little distance between them, and on each one was placed an iron stake and a pile of wood. A cordon of soldiers held back the quickly forming crowd, while another two cordons of soldiers kept open a path for the imminent procession. While the crowd waited, they ate, drank, played cards and looked at all of the important people who showed themselves off on the terraces of the houses near the columns. Ambassadors, dukes, poets and many elegant ladies had made themselves available to view this spectacle. The setting sun began to animate the mosaics on the basilica, and then, once more, the slow tolling of the bell of the Cursed could be heard. At the far end of the square, figures appeared dressed in sacks of black cloth that went down to the ground and with large crucifixes embossed on their chest. Before them, they held long black staffs which were crowned with double candlesticks. These were the Brothers of Good Death, and they were followed by the three condemned Jews, whose faces were fixed to the ground. Before arriving in the square, the condemned had been exorcised in order that they might be ready to receive the

Holy Rite of Baptism. However, the three Jews rejected this last-minute offer of conversion, preferring to die as sinners. As they approached the scaffolding, the Jews began to walk more slowly. At their side was a priest who held a crucifix with both hands, and who murmured into their ears words of resignation and comfort that were usually used in situations of disaster and calamity.

Half-way across the square, Servadio, the chief conspirator, was seen to whisper to his companions. Then he lifted his eyes and began to pray aloud.

'*My God and God of my Fathers, the soul that you gave me was pure, innocent and clean, but I contaminated it and made it impure with my sins. Now the hour has arrived for my life to be taken away, the hour in which I will give up my soul to Your hand to sanctify Your name. Take my soul when I go.*'

This said, Servadio now openly encouraged his colleagues to pray, but they could only succeed in mumbling, 'Amen, Amen.' As they approached the wooden scaffolding, Servadio's fellow Jews could not continue walking, and two soldiers were forced to take the Jew cowards under their arms and drag them forwards. Once the three Jews were under the scaffolding, the bell of the Cursed stopped chiming. Servadio, however, continued to pray. The people did not understand what he was saying, and some thought that perhaps he was making honourable amends. Even when they hoisted him up and on to the scaffolding, Servadio continued to pray.

'*Hear, O Israel, the Lord is our God, the Lord is one.*'

The condemned were attached by means of a long chain to iron stakes on the scaffolding, and then the torch holders lit their torches and immediately ignited the woodpiles. The loud crackling of flames began to obscure the voice of Servadio, who now only screamed, 'One, one!' In the docks in front of the two columns, the gondolas held scores of wealthy people who wished to enjoy the scene from the water. From the scaffolding came yells that sounded increasingly like barking, and then the wind swept up the smoke and revived the flames. As the smoke cleared, one could momentarily see Moses and Giacobbe jumping back and forth, while Servadio, positioned in the middle, remained immobile as though he felt no pain. And then the flames enveloped everything, and one could see only fire. As the blaze consumed flesh and blood, the spectators, on both land and water, were deeply moved by the power of the Christian faith and its official Venetian guardians. Later, when the flames had abated, an executioner approached with a long-handled shovel. He put it between the smoking coals and when he pulled it out it was full of white ash. He threw the ash into the air and it dispersed immediately.

Eva looked all around. By the door to the boxcar a woman clutched her baby to her breast, its small mouth hammering first one nipple, then the next. After three days of travelling, clamour had finally given way to silence and people were beginning to doze off, their heads bobbing forwards like comical dolls. They were sealed in, going in one direction one hour, then back in the same direction the next. Then they would stop. Then start again. Then stop, and sometimes wait for long hours in one place. No one had offered them food or water. It seemed impossible to Eva that anyone could find sleep, for the stench from the bucket was overpowering, and its spilt contents had creamed the filthy straw. But most had already passed the stage of caring. Once again, the train jerked into motion and Eva twisted her body slightly to the left so that she could peer through the wooden slats. She saw that the morning sun had already taken the spring frost off the bare fields. She could see neither animals nor crops, just a light mist that rose even as she watched. Eva tried hard not to think of Rosa. She bent forwards and surreptitiously licked the condensation from an iron-ring that was bolted into a side panel. Then she looked at Mama and Papa, who leant helplessly against each other. Humiliation had descended upon their lives, and they sat huddled and indistinguishable from the others. Eva watched her parents, who, having tried and failed to instil some order and discipline into life in the boxcar during the first few hours, had subsequently chosen to remain silent. Other professional people had also tried to establish rules of decency, but all were shouted down. Mama and Papa were ageing before her eyes, but at least they appeared to be sleeping. Eva's anxieties about what lay ahead kept her awake, as did her fear of separation. While they were waiting to board the train, Mama had pleaded with her to fight for her life should they ever be separated, but Eva had assured her that everything would be all right. But now her Mama's fears were her own. And then Eva realized that the two old men in the far corner were still staring at her. They were bearded, and she imagined them to be religious men, but the leer which marked their faces seemed to confound her assumption. The elder of the two men wore a white scarf, and he flashed her a gap-toothed smile. Eva looked away from them both, and in her mind she edged closer still to her parents.

Eventually, of course, we found a name for the collective suffering of those who survived. These unfortunate people have to endure a multitude of symptoms which include insomnia, shame, chronic anxiety, a tendency to suicide and an inability to communicate with others. They are often incapable of successful mourning, fearing that this act of self-expression involves a letting go, and therefore a forgetting of the dead, ultimately committing the deceased, often loved ones, to oblivion. Their condition serves a commemorative function, suggesting a loyalty to the dearly departed. Naturally, their suffering is deeply connected to mem-

ory. To move on is to forget. To forget is a crime. How can they both remember and move on? This is no easy task. To be frank, people who
suffer from the extreme form of this condition are beyond all care. Eventually, they just lie down to sleep and refuse to rise up again. The truth
is, with the experience that I now have, all I have to do is look closely
into the eyes of a patient to have some idea as to the extent of the damage. But back then, before we learnt the full details of the disorder, before
we had a name for it, none of us could be sure of what it was that we
were dealing with.

I stare out to sea as the ship begins to labour in the face of the
on-coming tempest. Navigation is a skill beyond me, but I am
convinced that already we are some distance from our plotted
course, and the wrath of the storm can serve only to drive us
further from our intended destination. But these military
thoughts, as worrisome as they are, do not dominate my mind.
My wife. These days, always my wife. I recall our brief courtship
and I remember her joyful acceptance of my proposal. And I remember the secluded happiness of our marriage, and, thereafter,
the moonlit journey back to my lodgings with a new bride for
company. When, as dawn was breaking over the enchanted city-
state, the doge's messenger summoned me to the palace to receive my final instructions, I promised my wife that I would
soon return to her side, which I did. However, we were betrayed by he who married us, and her father, upon discovering
the details of our secret nuptials, raised bitter objection. This
same man who had invited me to his table, and let it be known
that it was he who had recommended to the doge that I be appointed General, now considered me to be unworthy of his
daughter's affection. My wife and I were summoned to the
palace and, before the doge and his most trusted senators, my
wife's father – this small and impudent man – accused me of
treachery, and his daughter of worse still. But this was a time of

war, and I suspected that the doge might be inclined to over-look the unusual nature of this rapid connection in order to secure my services, and so it proved. He turned to my father-in-law and declared that no impropriety had occurred and, to his mind, his General was not guilty of any wrongdoing. This was the first time that the doge had ever addressed me with the title of his General, and it caused my breast to swell a little.

My father-in-law appeared shocked by the doge's words and, indeed, he swayed somewhat. My wife stepped forwards as though she might leave my side, but something within reminded her of her duty and she remained in her place. An attendant provided an arm for the distressed senator, who was clearly in need of fresh air. As he tottered towards the door, this man paused first to curse myself and then disown his daughter, implying that there was something false in a woman who could deceive her own father in this way. He reminded those gathered that his fair daughter had forsaken many notable matches, indeed broken many young hearts, and to what end? In order that she might betray her father, her family, and the republic, and marry one such as myself? He laughed bitterly at this notion, so much so that I was tempted to remind the gathered dignitaries that I, unlike my father-in-law, was born of royal blood, and possessed a lineage of such quality that not even slavery could stain its purity. But I chose to remain silent. As he left the chamber, my father-in-law concluded his performance by reminding all present that, henceforth, this woman was not to be considered his daughter.

The virulence with which my father-in-law delivered his parting volley stung the assembled throng. However, she who was newly my wife remained steadfast in her loyalty and chose to ignore her father's foul words. I turned to the doge and asked that my wife be allowed to accompany me to Cyprus, and she who bore that name pleaded that this might be permitted. The doge, recognizing the passion between us, acceded to this request and suggested that my wife might travel to Cyprus in a day or two, in the company of an officer of my choosing. We both thanked the doge most sincerely and took our leave, in order that we might occupy what little time remained. At noon I would set sail for war, but before my departure I intended to place my wife with an officer whose ship might be expected to arrive some time after I had secured the island of Cyprus. However, before applying myself to the task of seeking out a suitable officer, there still remained an hour or two for love.

The boatswain, having completed the examination of his rigging, presents himself before me and then answers my enquiry by informing me that, to his knowledge, Cyprus still lies some way distant and beyond the horizon. He confirms that this storm will indeed make our journey both longer and more treacherous, and then this good man advises me to take shelter below deck. I thank him for his concern and assure him that I will soon join him, but, as night falls, my mind is now populated with thoughts of my homeland. Alone on these seas, and with none of my kind or complexion for company, there is nobody with whom I might share memories of a common past, and nobody with whom I might converse in the language that sits most easily on my tongue. I know leadership to be lonely and painful, especially in times of war, but this is a quality of isolation that I have never before experienced. I have no doubt that the presence of my wife would help to alleviate some of my present misery, but I can only speculate as to the degree to which she might mollify the more fundamental pain in my heart. From the depths of the ship, a junior man, a man of impeccable manners though not yet hardened in the heat of battle, appears before me. He suggests that perhaps we should turn back before we are enveloped in darkness, for some among the crew fear that the storm will be both brutal and prolonged. I look at this man and try to do so with kindness, for he does not understand. One cannot turn back. There is no turning back.

To do so would be to embrace disgrace. I cry, 'Let the storm do its work!' And then I remind him that we are soldiers. We have a task ahead of us. To turn back is impossible.

VENICE: A city that lies on approximately one hundred and twenty islands in the Adriatic Sea on the north-east coast of Italy. In the fifteenth and sixteenth centuries, the independent city-state built a colonial empire that extended throughout much of the eastern Mediterranean. During this period, Venice was renowned for the beauty of its art, the majesty of its canals, and the economic and political power of its governmental system. The city began to fall into decline in the late sixteenth century, although the city's art treasures ensured that Venice maintained its reputation as a place of great cultural significance. Today, the city relies largely upon the tourist trade for its continued survival. It suffers from polluted air, contaminated water, and is periodically subject to serious flooding.

GHETTO: It is generally thought that the word *ghetto* was first used to describe the section of Venice where, in the sixteenth century, Jews were ordered to live apart from Christians in a 'marshy and unwholesome site' to the north of St Mark's. The Italian word *ghetto* means 'iron foundry', the Venetian Jews being forced to live next to the site of a former foundry. Ghettos are generally subject to serious overpopulation, and they exercise a debilitating effect on the self-confidence of their inhabitants.

During the night, the elder of the two men hanged himself by attaching his white scarf to an iron hook on the boxcar wall. Some of the men tried to stop him, but he began to punch and kick with such force that eventually they let him be. Eva turned her face away and blocked her ears. His friend, the other man with a beard, removed him from the hook. And then again, silence. Eva looked at a woman who slept with her mouth open and wondered how she managed not to choke, for the smell was unbearable. Was she truly resting? Dreaming, perhaps? And then again, the train stopped. The boxcar was near the locomotive, so Eva was able to listen to the engine die. Silence. The world remained silent. And then, some hours later, a roar and a shudder, and once again the locomotive tugged against the weight of the train. Eva wondered if she would be strong enough to survive the rigour of what she feared was to come. She looked at her parents, who now clung to each other in a way that she had never before seen. Their faces had taken on a clenched weariness that she imagined could not be shed with sleep. And then she noticed a girl of her own age, perhaps a little older. It was her time of the month, but she could no longer hide the blood. More than any of the others, Eva felt for this girl in her moment of humiliation. Lying in straw sodden with faeces and vomit, all classes and social distinctions had disappeared. She watched as a young boy, like the rest of them crazy with thirst, licked the sweat from his mother's fevered arm. As fast as the wheels turned over, they all searched for clues that would help them to explain their present condition. And then, undernourished and tired, their minds eventually slowed to a pounding numbness, while the wheels of the train beat on.

A long-drawn-out whistle. Then a loud crash and a judder. The darkness begins to echo with barked orders. Then the doors to the boxcars roll open. Plumes of smoke spin into the night air. Somewhere in the distance, fires are burning. Most cannot stand without support. There is no time for questions. Men clamber in, odd-looking characters in striped shirts and black trousers, and they begin to kick people out and on to the platform. How is it possible to be so angry with people who have done you no wrong? And now, a sweet aroma slamming into their defeated faces. They stand and look around. Bright lights flood the dark night sky. They shuffle, unburdened by belongings which they have been encouraged to leave behind. No, I must take this with me. Have you no compassion? A single bullet answers the question. People step over the body. Children look unblinkingly at the river of blood flowing across the platform. An ever-blooming flower. Shuffle. Shuffle. Restive dogs on short leashes leap vertically into the air. Hungry. Angry. Pathetic people clinging meekly to the remnants of their lives and wondering if, through hard work, they might earn the right to live. And now the official greeters, men who are made of skin and bone. Faces hollowed, skulls grotesquely visible, temples sunken in, ears standing out. Men who are acclimatized. They cast sidelong glances, they wish to speak, they know too much, their tongues have been removed, they have dared to survive this long. They address nobody in particular. You are eighteen and you have a trade. Give the child to its grandmother. Give away the baby. And now, at the end of the long platform, a uniformed man who possesses the gift of supreme confidence in himself. He waves first one way, and then the next, first this way, and then that, with no regard for affiliation. Destiny is a movement of his hand. Perhaps a quick question to make sure. Looks can deceive. How old? Healthy or ill? The old, pregnant, young, short, infirm. This way, please. Walk quickly. Roll up. Roll up. Already, a loudspeaker is blasting instructions to remove all clothing. Remove artificial limbs and eyeglasses. Tie your shoes together. Surrender any undeclared valuables and claim a receipt. Children go with the women. Where are we? The thin and the handicapped, this way, please. All gold rings, fountain pens, and chains. Roll up. Where is God? Where is your God? An old woman talks quietly to herself, as though out walking in pleasant hospital grounds. The blunt end of a rifle crashes against her forehead. Melting before this brutality like snow in the sun. Roll up. Roll up. A uniformed adolescent kicks an old man. Then he laughs. The old man stops and stares. I am your father. He reloads his weapon. I am your father. Each time he fires the young man laughs louder. I am your father. And then the young man removes his pistol from its holster and shoots the old man in the head as though he were a sick dog. I am a bookkeeper. I am a carpenter. I am a dentist. To the left. To work. Only later will they appear in the Register of the Dead. I am pregnant. Her name will appear nowhere. Not even counted. She joins the right-hand column (five abreast) that wheels towards cleansing. A belt of rubbery flesh for a waist. To the right, please. Hang your clothes neatly. Remember where. Put them on the hooks. Here is the towel. Here is the soap. Here is the towel. Here is the soap. Undress, please. You are going to heaven. Sanitary belts are ripped off. Blood everywhere. Shame. Shame. Now! These men without the breeding to look away. Shower. For the lucky ones, no gas. Thank you, God. Uniforms. Barbed-wire everywhere. With electricity. Everywhere barbed-wire. Sky above. Where is God? Where is your God? Mama and Papa are to go one way. Mama squeezes my hand and whispers. Everything will be fine. Papa looks at me and speaks the same words with his eyes. And then it occurs to me. He has known all along. Since the time in the café, the couple opposite us, furtive lovers, and the waitress bringing wine and coffee for father and daughter. And then Leyna. Papa knew then, the day of his friend's funeral, that one day he would have to say these four words to his youngest daughter. Everything will be fine. But now the time has arrived and Papa has no words left. He turns from me and wheels to the right. Mama's eyes are full of tears. A woman pushes me in the back and I stumble forwards and in a new direction. And then all about me I hear voices, at first quiet and nervous, and then stronger. We stare to our right at those who continue to wheel towards cleansing. May His great Name grow exalted and sanctified *Amen* in the world that He created as He willed. May He give reign to His kingship in your lifetimes and in your days, and in the lifetimes of the entire Family of Israel, swiftly and soon. *Amen. May His great name be blessed for ever and ever.* May his great Name be blessed for ever and ever. Voices are raised. Everybody continues to stare to the right. The chimneys bellow smoke. A sweet aroma. We breathe deeply on the air that will enable us to live. We fill our lungs and stare. Plumes of smoke spin into the night air. A red glare. The smoke whispers the truth, but, at this moment, none wish to listen.

My hair is removed by a woman who wields large blunt scissors. The woman seems to relish the thought of inflicting pain. She speaks: While you were still going to the theatre, we were already here. Now she smiles at me. The hair on my head, the hair under my arms, the soft hair between my legs. Go ahead and pray. But you know where your mother is, don't you? I look around. Our heads are strange and knobbly. We all look the same. Grotesque figures, naked and without hair. Right up in that chimney, that's where she is. And then we disinfect our feet in violet water. And then we shower. And then a powder of some sort is sprinkled on us, and we scramble for clothes. I try to forget my name. I decide to put Eva away in some place for safe-keeping until all of this is over. But already Eva refuses to be hidden. There is no new name in my throat. Eva refuses to disappear.

For three whole days we endured the furious onslaught of the sea, before our battered vessel finally arrived at Cyprus. It was dusk, and a large contingent of my army were gathered on shore to meet me, with relief written large upon their faces.

Clearly the storm had propelled them in a more logical direction, which had enabled them to make good time and a safe landfall. After greeting my men, and receiving the welcome news that the Turkish fleet had fallen victim to the might of the sea, I asked to be immediately conducted to the bosom of my lady. My lieutenant, Michael Cassio, a Florentine intellectual and arithmetician, assured me that she who I now called wife was safe in the company of my Ancient, to whom she had been entrusted. It appeared that there would be a few days in which to luxuriate while we waited for news from Venice and, this being the case, I immediately determined that I would divide these precious days between my wife and my officers. It was important that I rested, for I freely acknowledged to myself that I was no longer the young Titan who bestrode the battlefield in days past. After a night of sweet slumber, I would begin to embrace this free time to learn yet more about these people who were clearly to be my new countrymen. This island of Cyprus, to which fate had deposited me safe in both body and mind, would serve as the school in which I might further study the manners of Venice, before eventually returning to the city to embark upon my new life. However, my first action as both General and Governor was to order that revels should commence within the hour to celebrate both the drowning of the heretical Turk and the happy and fortuitous marriage of their commanding officer to fair Desdemona. It was at this point that Michael Cassio took me to one side and conveyed to me the intelligence that my father-in-law had died shortly after my departure. Whether from grief, or anger, or some other cause, he chose not to disclose, but I thanked him for the information. According to good Cassio, my wife had betrayed no outward sign of mourning, so again I confirmed my order that within the hour revels should commence, and I charged my men that they should busy themselves and prepare for a night of celebration that would live long in the memory.

OTHELLO: A play by William Shakespeare. Probably written between 1602 and 1604, and first performed in 1604. The principal source for the play is Giraldi Cinthio's *Hecatommithi,* a collection of Italian stories first published in Venice in 1566, and used by a number of Elizabethan and Jacobean dramatists as source material for their plots. Out of one key sentence in Cinthio's story, Shakespeare wrote the early scenes of the play.

It happened that a Virtuous Lady of wondrous beauty called Disdemona, impelled not by female appetite but by the Moor's Good qualities, fell in love with him, and he, vanquished by the Lady's beauty and noble mind, likewise was enamoured of her.

Each morning, while waiting for sunlight, she sighed (The worst part of every day. I open my eyes and I feel pain.) and faced the truth about her situation. (How long, winter? How long?) *I spotted her among those lost souls, just as she was knotting the rope around her neck. Mama! I cried, Mama! No! And she looked at me and spoke softly, all the while continuing her preparations. She said, but I am not your Mama. I knew that she recognized me, but she did not want this filthy rag for a daughter. I began to laugh, as though it were a joke. I wanted to shame her into recognition. And then she stopped, and she took the rope from her neck. So you have come back to me, my child? She touched my arm. Yes, Mama, I've come back. And then she smiled sadly. And now Papa flooded the dream world. He was dressed elegantly, and walking down a broad avenue near the City Hall.* She prayed that she might be left undisturbed, for everybody knew that one should never wake anybody having a nightmare. Reality was much worse. Nightmares were acceptable. *He approached the man and asked pleasantly, 'Excuse me, could you tell me where the American Embassy is?' The man looked him up and down, as though unable to comprehend this impertinence. (He was a man some years younger than Papa.) Then he stepped back and struck Papa a blow with his walking stick, a blow that sent Papa sprawling to the ground. I looked on, but said nothing. I watched as the younger man walked off into the afternoon sunshine, and then Papa looked up at me, his face red and marked, and he assured me that it did not hurt.* Six people on a plank of wood, on top of them another layer, below them another layer, one turns, all turn, packed like livestock, frozen nights, reach the bucket or let go on the wood. Hold on. Hold on. Sleepless nights. Newcomers quarrelling, cursing in a new language. Hateful people. Stubborn moonlight flooding through panes feathered with frosty patterns. And then it is morning. Rise and shine. A sleeping partner has given off enough warmth to enable her to sleep for a moment, and dream. Human life is cheap. (I sometimes think that I would even kiss one if it meant that I could live.) Young bodies rusted like old taps. (Squeeze it, turn it on, drip, drip, rust coating my fingers if it meant I could live.) Valueless. (Perhaps there is to be no continuity to my story?) Unless she changed her attitude towards herself and others, she was going to die among squadrons of furious flies. (In the morning, a wealth of corpses. I look and wonder, if I survive, and if I should meet their husbands or children or parents, and if they should ask me about their loved ones, what should I say? Should I confess to the terror in their eyes? Should I say that at some point during these squalid years we all wished to stumble forwards on our swollen feet and simply fall into the ditch. Easy. But to try to survive was terrible. Should I tell them this? That the body begins to eat itself. Fat. Flesh. Muscles. In this order. Unless one fights hard, there is soon only enough strength left to flick the switch and turn out the lights.) But this death is a trivial affair. It has become a habit, like the habit of the lice to quarry their way to the armpits. Only typhus is feared, for the head bursts, the body trembles, the intestines and stomach are stricken in agony, leaving one to wallow in pools of excrement of one's own making. The rest is routine. Every day, there are examinations. Men and women in name only, an unaesthetic drop of menstrual blood signalling death, a tongue coated in a white deposit signalling death. Dragged across the courtyard by the ankles, the head banging out its final resistance. But they must remember to wash with the coffee, they must remember to try to keep clean. Picking at each other's lice like monkeys. Now reduced to a small tangle of bones covered with skin that is stretched tight and stained with bruises and bites. Bald heads and powerful eyes. These were women who once made love, decaying now like discarded and foul-smelling fruit. Buried in their own filth. (Buried in one's own filth.) Hungry enough to gnaw on a shoe, forever relieving themselves, stinking skeletons. Repulsive. It is in the natural order of things for the elderly to die before the young, for the adult to die before the child. And still they come. Newcomers. With no understanding of the language that is being barked. And on some days the smoke pours so powerfully from the chimneys that daylight cannot break through. (I once passed close by a chimney. Ash-freckled snow skirted its base. A seasonal cape of good cheer defaced.) They look at the guards. These newcomers don't know the words to this song. Random history by chance gave you your precious golden face, but measured time will carry you off to a bloodless place. But perhaps they will learn the words. Some of them. (Look at us! I plead with the newcomers. Do you not understand?) And the newcomers look at these monkey-people with shaved heads and they feel compassion. But the monkey-people have nothing to give except glances and whispered warnings. The monkey-people no longer hear the silence. They no longer ask the question, where will they put us? She once helped a pregnant woman to flush a child from her womb. (I told her. We were once you. Healthy, with beautiful figures. With long hair. (Mama and Papa still exist in my mind.) And breasts.) Her full breasts, soon to disappear. An imaginary pebble near the nipple, distorting the length. Then the sack will shrink. Shorter. And then she will become a man. No breasts. Plumes of smoke. (Margot was to be lived for. Only Margot now.) The newcomers must remember their names. Without a name, nobody will know who they are. Nobody would know who she was. Morning. Good morning. On the floor, mice have frozen to death next to scraps they were too weak to bite apart. She must use the latrines. Quickly. But in the barracks there are no latrines. (I try to forget that I am aware that to befoul the body is to befoul the spirit.) Quickly. In this place, only buckets that have to be used at night. Buckets that are soon filled. And, come morning, spilt and emptied, for it is easier to carry a bucket that is only three-fourths full. Come morning. Quickly. Public humiliation. No privacy. A tiny building ankle-deep in human waste, a smell that chokes like a cloud, squatting like birds on a wire, showering each other, exploding, quick, hurry, this is no temple of reflection, no paper, nothing to clean with, beaten with a club, diarrhoea sticking to clothes, dropping down legs, nothing to wash with, a cold in the bladder means you can wash frequently with urine, dreaming of the bucket which, when full, spills against bare legs, repulsively warm, it offers some heat. Quickly. Outside. (I feel guilty, for Papa always said that I must never sit on a strange toilet seat.) In the sky, shifting clouds. (Before I work I need food.) A piece of bread is a lifeline. So hungry that at times they behaved like wild animals and would unthinkingly have murdered for food. (I disliked the dirty, uncultivated people from the east.) A hungry body is an affront to human dignity, but why waste time? Why water a dying tree? (Why waste time on these people?) Tin plates of soup. A few grains of barley floating in warm water. A lump of mouldering bread. Coffee? Water to which bitter black colour has been added. She uses the warm liquid to wash her hair. Nothing is wasted, nothing is saved. The only safe storage place is the stomach. A diet designed to kill within weeks, unless one could steal. (Everybody is a part of somebody else's game. That much I understand.) Lick your spoon. Lick your spoon. No clock. No time. Now only work. March to work. The ground wounds easily beneath the foot's heavy passage. Slow, vague thoughts filter through their confused minds. Today, they continue to burn bodies. (I burn bodies.) Burning bodies. First, she lights the fire. Pour gasoline, make a torch, and then ignite the pyre. Wait for the explosion as the fire catches, and then wait for the smoke. Clothed bodies burn slowly. Decayed bodies burn slowly. In her mind she cries, fresh and naked, please. Women and children burn faster than men. Fresh naked children burn the fastest. Do not look at those who watch. (I always know where the nearest guards are. I always know what they are doing. I never volunteer for anything.) Tonight they will jackal to each other as they dull their minds with king alcohol, and then they will vomit like pigs. (I do not look at them. Fifty lashes. Or a quick shot and a short journey to heaven.) One woman attaches a written message to a stone and throws it hopelessly towards the fence. Frostbite has already removed her toes. She cannot dance. They make her dig her own grave, her shovel scraping against the stubborn earth. The dull thump of clay as it is tossed to one side. And her companions look on and dare to weep. She climbs in and lies down with her arms folded about her chest, her shovel by her side. They place the gun barrel almost at her temple. Then shoot. Her head is bent backwards and her bared teeth are visible. One eye stares vacantly into space. Dear kind mother earth, we tear deep wounds into your holy body. When it rains, the earth turns to thick mud. (Standing in mud up to my ankles.) A terrible thirst caused by stench and smoke. But now to the ravine. But before they leave, a quick shot and another one in heaven. Death has swept another soul from off her feet. Sashaying musically across the floor, twirling and pointing, arms thrown wide, head tossed back, death is so happy, so fleet-footed, so free. A tempting invitation. And at the ravine the ground is moist, the graves eight weeks old, and she pulls out parts – heads slushing easily away from bodies – and she puts them into buckets, and then she carries them back to the fire to burn. And then she goes back to the ravine. Old sites, up to the knees in foulness, pulling flesh from bone, joy, look like you are working, or digging, and any who find time to pray will die of an active mind. Look into the dead faces. Eyes sunken and dimmed, eyes which once flickered with happiness. Mouths that once gave wise counsel and encouragement, now hang agape. (I long for fresh bodies.) Look, over there. (Please do not let me discover anybody that I know.) Night falls with the weight of a hammer. We go back. Carrying tools and cauldrons, a heavy load. But pain can be conquered in a way that hunger cannot. Shuffling along on her spindly legs, her dry shrunken lungs gasping for air. Damaged bodies. A forest of barbed-wire illuminated by powerful lights. So bright they render the whole scene a photograph. And again the moon. (I look at the moon. Still pregnant. Every month pregnant.) Standing in line with people with big heads, and within their big heads only the eyes are living. Always the eyes. A piece of black bread, four inches thick. Whispering. Bread? More bread? Twenty-five lashes with a whip in exchange for the chance of somebody else's bread. This is good business. Good business. Will anybody trade bread for cigarettes? Or coffee? Or anything? Whispering. Bread? More bread? (I don't trust anybody.) Don't trust your best friend. (I look out for myself.) Don't get sick. It is evening. And they are counted into the hut. People's mouths move, their faces ablaze with indignation. They shout orders. (No words reach me. Inwardly I remain calm. I simply stare. Suspended. A young woman-foetus. Slowly turning.) Rats feed on human bodies. Dead or alive. The distinction is irrelevant. All night, she brushes mice away from her eyes and lips. There is a small stove with three feet. But no fuel. *I cannot keep my feet. I cannot eat or drink. It is morning. I drag myself out of the hut, but fall motionless to the ground. My colleagues begin to march off to their work sites. I summon what strength I have and stand, but that is all. I cannot move. I simply watch them disappear from view.* Between us, enough Hebrew to recite the basic blessings and prayers. (My parents believed just enough so that nobody could accuse them of being either disrespectful or ignorant.) *Death swims before my eyes. Alone in the yard now. My head slumps to one side. A prod in the back brings me back to consciousness. The man is standing over me, a smile frozen on his lips. I am aware of his health. He holds the gun lightly and allows his fingers to play with it. And then he points the gun at my head.* An early dream. Too early to dream. Six people on a plank of wood, on top of them another layer, below them another layer, one turns, all turn, packed like livestock, frozen nights, reach the bucket or let go on the wood. Hold on. Hold on. And somebody whispers, did your family light Shabbat candles on a Friday night? (And I laugh.) And somebody spits then asks, did you wash any bodies today? (And I laugh.) Everybody laughs. She laughs quietly. Stupid questions. And somebody laughs then asks, did you witness any men reciting the Kaddish today? Too much. (I cannot laugh.) Six people on a plank of wood. Tonight. (I remember. Sometimes Mama lit the Shabbat candles. A beautiful, delicate glow. No smoke.) No smoke.

What I now know of the condition I've learnt largely because of Eva Stern. Not because I possess any intimate knowledge of her case history. I hardly knew her. I interviewed her just the once. But it was she who started me thinking about the problem in general. These days they call me an expert, or more properly a specialist, but initially I could find only the odd article. I have to admit that I was guessing as I was going along. Not entirely satisfactory, but I couldn't afford to be too precious. These people's conditions were generally chronic. They needed time to forget, on the one hand, and on the other hand time to learn to trust people again. Sadly, neither of these processes can be rushed. Eventually, we all have to submit to the whim of time. However, I couldn't help wondering what the situation must have been like over there. I knew there had to be thousands of these survivors, and as a result there would be countless fellows doing research in this area. After the situation with Eva, I thought about doing a paper myself. About their clearly defined emotional anaesthesia, or psychic numbing. Eva, in fact all of them, they were so detached. But, at least to begin with, I didn't have enough information.

My wife smiles, and I reach over and clutch this faithful jewel to my bosom. The light from the lamp illuminates the sheen of her skin and I almost swoon with delight. She is both smooth and unblemished, and beneath her breast I can feel the gentle pounding of her heart. Her legs are gracefully entwined in the confusion of the sheet, but with one hand I reach down and strip away the offending garment. Tonight there is no reason to worry that our bedroom hours might be interrupted by messengers from the doge, or concern ourselves with the furtive nature of our coming together. We are man and wife in a union known broadly to all, and acknowledged by the doge himself. There is time for love, then our revels, then more love. And then, when my duties here on Cyprus achieve a happy conclusion, we shall return home to Venice and commence our new life of peace in the remarkable city-state. She whispers my name. And again, my name.

Margot died on a cold grey morning in a country that was not her own. After she left her parents, and her sister Eva, she spent eighteen months in hiding at the top of a house in a tiny room which held only a single bed, a chair and a tall wardrobe. She was not allowed to leave the room, she was not allowed to use the bathroom, she was not allowed to have any contact with her former life. Her Mama and Papa had explained to her that, depending on how things developed, the hiding parents might let her live openly among them. Alternatively, for her own safety, they might choose to lock her up. They chose to lock her up. On the day of their separation, Eva sat on Margot's bed and stared idly through the window as her sister packed her suitcase. As the day faded, Margot told Eva about some of the things she had discussed with her new friends. The most important news was that Peter had heard of Uncle Stephan, and apparently their uncle was a real hero. And then the man arrived, pocketed the money and took the seventeen-year-old Margot away, and from the moment she stepped out of her parents' four-storey house she was no longer a child. A nice couple, they climbed the stairs, and brought her food, and permitted her to whisper her Jewish prayers, but otherwise she was to be quiet at all times. (They told a frightened Margot about the searches. Many had been discovered. And there were terrible rumours about their fate.) Above her bed they hung a crucifix, which she ignored. They encouraged Margot to practise how to hold her nose so that she might sneeze quietly. Quiet, like a cat. Eventually Margot discovered an imaginary friend named Siggi, who never spoke. And from behind closed doors, Margot listened to her country change, while inside she, too, was changing. To experience loneliness at any age is painful, but so young, and without the warm memories to offset the bewildering isolation and the worried speculation. It marks a person. She could feel this. A year passed and she grew accustomed to watching the early daylight at the edge of the curtains, and then witnessing the sun lighting up the floral pattern of the wallpaper. She thought all the while of Mama and Papa, and she tried to forgive them for turning her over to these people. In particular, Margot thought of her little sister Eva, and how once, when they were younger and playing together, she had kicked her. Margot thought endlessly of her cruelty and she hoped that her dear sister might have forgiven her. Apparently, there was no way of communicating with Eva. Her hiding father told her that things were very bad, and then one night, when his wife was out, he came to visit her. He looked at her, and touched her, but Margot dare not scream, for to scream would be to betray her hiding place. (*Right now you're a very pretty girl, but as you get older your racial character will show.*) And then he kissed her, and he tried to open her lips with his big mouth, and Margot felt the weight of his heavy hands upon her. How hard this man concentrated as he pushed, the beads of sweat popping on to his brow, individual, evenly spaced. Margot began to count. Siggi said nothing. And then he peeled himself clear of her body and left. Inside she bled, and her mind tumbled down a flight of stairs and struck its head. During the night, the rain fell like applause and Margot remembered that Papa used to say that a storm was nothing more than God moving around his furniture. In the morning she awoke to discover her nightgown gathered up about her waist, and her face bathed in the thin spokes of light that filtered around the edge of the curtains. As she lay curled in shame, she realized that her swollen tongue was now too large for her dry mouth. She made a decision. Margot swung her legs off the side of the bed and felt the damp chill of the linoleum. She would cut her hair short, her thick fluent hair that Peter liked to touch. Cut it off. When, a week later, the man visited her again, she slid to the floor so she would not fall, and then she screamed. Both she and her hiding parents were escorted down the three flights of stairs and emptied out into the street. The light dazzled her and she raised an arm to protect her eyes. The hiding parents went one way and Margot another, towards a train, her hands lacing and unlacing as she walked. One year later, in a country to the east that was not her own, she died on a cold grey morning, naked among naked strangers. She paid dearly for the sin of being born. (*Did you think of me that morning as I stumbled naked and shivering towards my death? Did you think of me?)*

The process of gassing takes place in the following manner. The helpless victims are brought into a reception hall where they are instructed to undress. Most keep their underwear about them, but they are quickly encouraged to remove these last vestiges of modesty. In order to maintain the illusion that they are going to shower, a group of men dressed in white coats issue each person with a small bar of soap and a towel. The victims are then ushered into the gas chamber in such ludicrous numbers that the illusion is immediately shattered. In the gas chamber there is no room for the victims to turn around, let alone raise their arms up above their heads. In order to introduce yet more people into this limited space, shots are often fired to encourage those near the door to push towards the back. Those in the far corners are sometimes crushed to death before the procedure even begins. Once everybody is inside, the heavy doors are slammed shut, and sealed and bolted from the outside. There is no escape. After a short interval, which allows the room temperature to rise to a desired level, men wearing gas masks and bearing canisters of the required preparation clamber up on to the roof of the building. They open trap doors, then shake the contents of the cans (which are marked *Zyklon B – for use against vermin*) – a product of a Hamburg-based company – into the traps and then quickly retire. This product is a cyanide mixture which is known to turn, at a predetermined temperature, into a noxious and highly effective poisonous gas. After only three minutes, every single inhabitant in the chamber is dead, and nobody has been known to survive the ordeal. The chamber is then opened and aired by men who, for obvious reasons, must still wear gas masks. After five minutes it is deemed safe, and new men appear – prisoners – who cart the bodies on flat trucks to the furnace rooms where the burning takes place. The hearths of the furnaces are charged with coke. Once the cremation chamber has been brought to a good red heat (approximately 800° C), the corpses are introduced. They burn rapidly. As soon as the remains of the corpses have fallen through the grid to the ash-collection channel below, they can be pulled forwards by means of a scraper, towards the ash-removal door. Here, they should be left for another twenty minutes to disintegrate fully before being scraped out and into a container. In the meantime, further corpses can be introduced into the chambers. All bones will have disintegrated, but some small particles may remain. The ash is white and is easily scattered.

Once Gerry returned to England, he wrote her many imaginary letters. *Dear Eva, I think I ought to explain . . .* But he never sent any of them, preferring instead to believe that the strange girl would soon forget him. However, his conscience troubled him. If, when he asked her, she had said yes, then he was convinced that he would have made whatever arrangements were necessary. He would have told her everything, and then taken a chance and brought her back to England. They might have had to wait a couple of years before they could actually get married, but he'd have done it. That's what everyone wanted after the war. A new beginning. A chance to put things behind them. To begin again. But when he got back and saw Noreen and the kiddie, he began to write the letters in his mind. I mean, Noreen wasn't a glamour piece or anything, but he had made a commitment. *Dear Eva, I think I ought to explain . . .* It was silly, really. For one thing, how could he have afforded it? It was bloody hard work to get a job again. Nobody gave a bugger that you'd served king and country. So bleeding what, mate? You were over there with your foreign crumpet, while we were stuck here getting bombed on. Triumphant England didn't live up to his expectations. Things were bad for everyone. And so eventually he stopped writing imaginary letters. And, soon after, he saw Iris, who was dancing unconsciously to the static crackle of a wireless as she rearranged cups on her tray. She was a waitress in the tea shop that Gerry stopped in on his way home from the factory. It was the sign above the door, which boasted 'A good selection of cakes and pastries', that first caught his attention. Gerry liked the familiar tinkle of the doorbell, then the pleasing rush of warmly scented air as he edged his way in and found his usual seat in the corner by the tall glass window. From this position, he could gaze out at the tide of people who washed by in both directions, but inevitably he was shaken from his day-dreaming by the elderly woman with her notepad and her hair that was tied back in a frighteningly severe bun. She took his order and, soon after, his tea would arrive at the table with a clatter. And then one day he saw the girl dancing as she rearranged cups on her tray, a new girl with eyebrows plucked into dark arches. Gerry looked at his watch and realized that they would be closing up in ten minutes, so he deliberately waited until she came to his table to take away his cup. 'You're new here, aren't you?' She smiled, and Gerry could now see just how young she was. Sixteen at most. But she refused to reply. And so it went on, day after day, week after week, with Gerry being unable to torment a conversation out of her reluctant person. His sole knowledge of this girl's background was her name, Iris, which he discovered only by overhearing the elderly woman shouting at her when the girl appeared to be slacking. Eventually, Gerry accepted that his infatuation with the girl was leading him nowhere, but it had served the function of removing Eva from the front of his mind. He no longer peered anxiously down the hallway in case a foreign-looking letter lay by the door, nor did he worry about whether he should say something to Noreen about the Jewish girl. Gerry's conscience no longer troubled him. Although he had given up hope of winning her over, Gerry still sat in the tea shop, in the corner by the tall glass window, and stared at his Iris. He particularly enjoyed watching her when she raised her arms to tie back her hair. It occurred to him that young girls needed protecting. But Iris would be fine. She knew how to look after herself.

I have made a friend. Bella. Bella with the dark complexion. Her eyes fenced by crow's feet that mark her out as one who has toiled in a southern sun. (My skin as white as paper.) They have given Bella an easy job, packing down the top of the pits. I share my bowl of soup with her. Carry me, Bella, and I will carry you. Bella tells me there are rumours that we will not win. She speaks as though everything is a confession. I tell Bella, no. No. You must see your parents again. You are only seventeen. We lie together in the hut. I look at my Bella. Her brown eyes clouded by cataracts. I am twenty. Bella, I want to live to love. To believe in something. To believe in somebody. Because of Bella, I hope with reckless vigour. Men do not know the landscape of women. Your hair is growing back. I am a virgin. Tell me, have you had a boyfriend? A kiss? Yes? In the folding places of your body? I need a piece of bread. We need a piece of bread. But somebody must remain alive to tell all of this, Bella. It is senseless to die now. I need to see Margot again. And then, one morning, I look across at my Bella with her sleep-shaped hair, and I know that soon I will be on my own again. Life continues to drain from her. Too weak, now, to steal warmth from my body. I press close to her, as though my life might pass into her body like a fever. But she continues to leak. Seepage. The most undignified of all diseases. Flooding the cracks in the wood, dripping into the faces of the women below. Speckling them. It is winter now. Our second winter. And bitterly cold. The roll-call. I am going to be late for roll-call. Dear Bella. Bella with fine straws stuck through the holes that pierce her ears, keeping them in readiness for the earrings that she still hopes for. Dear Bella, it is easy to be selected. Swollen legs? A forgotten head kerchief? A soiled uniform? Step forwards. Goodbye. A scratch on a leg? Puffed with malnutrition? Step forwards. Goodbye. A flick of a riding crop to the right. Goodbye. The other women, they cry now, please, Eva. Eva, please. Bella is gone. My Bella is gone. She is no more. Eva, she is no more. Colour your hair with this charcoal. Twenty and I am going grey! Look strong. Get up. Fresh air. Fresh air. The other women. Their feet wrapped in straw that is held in place with cloth and string. Dirty spoons attached to their waists by cords. I ask them, are you still women? Look at my swollen feet. The other women drag me away from my Bella. I am screaming. Look! In my Bella's crabbed hands there are still signs of life. I cannot leave her like this. A cage of bone. As I stand in the courtyard, I know that I will have to find Mama again. The wind continues to collaborate. It makes us shiver in front of these poorly educated people. I will have to find Mama again. Meanwhile, dear Bella. Bella with the dark complexion. Dry my face with your breath. Your refusal of this world has not gone unnoticed. Death will want me too. Death is hungry. Always hungry.

And so you shadow her every move, attend to her every whim, like the black Uncle Tom that you are. Fighting the white man's war for him/Wide-receiver in the Venetian army/The republic's grinning Satchmo hoisting his sword like a trumpet/You tuck your black skin away beneath their epauletted uniform, appropriate their words (*Rude am I in speech*), their manners, worry your nappy woollen head with anxiety about learning their ways, yet you conveniently forget your own family, and thrust your wife and son to the back of your noble mind. O strong man, O strong arm, O valiant soldier, O weak man. You are lost, a sad black man, first in a long line of so-called achievers who are too weak to yoke their past with their present; too naïve to insist on both; too foolish to realize that to supplant one with the other can only lead to catastrophe. Go ahead, peer on her alabaster skin. Go ahead, revel in the delights of her wanton bed, but to whom will you turn when she, too, is lost and a real storm breaks about your handkerchiefed head? My friend, the Yoruba have a saying: the river that does not know its own source will dry up. You will do well to remember this.

We rise with the sun. I turn from Giacobbe to Moses, then back to Giacobbe. My brothers, do not let them see you weeping like this. Today, we must leave this cell and begin our final journey, but let us do so with dignity. There will be no tears and no pleading. We will maintain our fast and continue to refuse to drink water. We are going home. I look again at my companions, but they continue to weep copiously. I redouble my efforts. The journey to the north by water, and then back here to St Mark's on foot, is designed to humiliate us. But they are not our masters. We must obey only God. Let them take away our sons and baptize them. Let them pour scorn on our women. If we have done right by God, they will capture only the outside of our people, but not their souls. Do not weep. Please, do not weep. (*In Portobuffole, I was respected. My family never cheated anybody. We lived modestly and we celebrated our holidays in peace. We respected your traditions, we made charitable contributions towards your institutions. Yet now you people pluck my beard, you stone my children, you defraud me, you mock my clothes and my religion. I tell you, I have never heard of this boy, Sebastian New. I have never seen such a boy. I know not what you are talking about. My wife is suffering, my family is drowning in tears. Why? Who is this Sebastian New? What are you talking about?*) My brothers, let them burn our bodies. If this gives them pleasure, then let them burn us. But our souls do not belong to them. Have you lost faith? (*To whom will Sara and my children turn? You have destroyed our small community.*) Do not search for God in this moment of grief. You will move too quickly to find his true depth. Trust him. Today, as we leave this cell and feel the ground beneath our unsteady feet, we must walk with confidence towards our fate. These Venetians may be uncoupling us from this life on earth, but we are journeying towards a greater place. (*Who is this Sebastian New?*) To these men's ears, my words are stale. Giacobbe and Moses continue to weep. The sunlight begins to pour into our cell, the light raking down the wall, then pooling on the stone floor. I am thirsty, but I will not drink water. We must refuse to drink water.

My friend, an African river bears no resemblance to a Venetian canal. Only the strongest spirit can hold both together. Only the most powerful heart can endure the pulse of two such disparate life-forces. After a protracted struggle, most men will eventually relinquish one in favour of the other. But you run like Jim Crow and leap into their creamy arms. Did you truly ever think of your wife's soft kiss? Or your son's eyes? Brother, you are weak. A figment of a Venetian imagination. While you still have time, jump from her bed and fly away home. Peel your rusty body from hers and go home. No good can come from your foreign adventure. A wooden ladle lightly dipped will soon scoop you up and dump you down and into the gutter. Brother, jump from her bed and fly away home.

Eva slipped and fell into the snow. She scrambled quickly to her feet, but could feel the warm trickle of blood where her left leg had hit against something hard – probably a rock. She knew that later it would hurt, but later did not matter. She ran on. Behind her, the soldiers' voices grew louder and more animated, but it was the barking of the dogs that frightened her, for she felt sure that at any moment they would be allowed off the leash. It was foolish of her to imagine that in her condition she might outrun grown, healthy men. Dogs would find her easy sport. If only she might be scooped up by some large celestial hand and gently deposited across water and into some other world. The soldiers would gather in a breathless huddle and call off the search. They would knock their tightly packed cigarettes out of their boxes, light up and agree that she was more trouble than she was worth. That she would not last the night. That the wolves would get her. But Eva ran on, furiously weaving her way through the trees, diving beneath branches and stumbling over exposed roots, until she saw the small house in the clearing.

She threw her body against the wooden door, which immediately gave way under her timid weight. She pushed it shut behind her. Eva looked down at her leg and saw the blood. Only now did she feel the pain. It shook her so hard she whimpered. And then again she heard the dogs. For an instant, she had imagined that she might have thrown the soldiers off her trail, but now there was only one last hope. She hobbled across the dark deserted room, through another door, and into the storeroom at the back. Once there, she called to her Mama, who was too weak to answer with anything other than a whispered, 'Eva.' At least Mama was safe. Outside, Eva could hear the soldiers who seemed now to have surrounded the house. Why was she so stupid? Why lead them to this place? She could have kept running past the house, deeper into the forest, until the dogs caught her and tore her limb from limb. At least Mama might have survived. But this way? It was madness.

Eva began to climb up the narrow wooden ladder, pushing hard with her good right leg and dragging her lame one behind her. Dogs can smell blood. The storage platform, which would normally bear the weight of hay, was empty apart from the shivering bundle that was her Mama. Eva pushed herself off the top rung of the ladder and, using her elbows, she slithered across the floor and folded herself tightly around Mama, as though providing her with a protective blanket. She heard the outer door

*fly open with such gale-like force that Eva knew it must have been
kicked clear of its moorings. Men and dogs roared furiously, and Mama
trembled and muttered her one word, 'Eva.' Eva offered her Mama a
thumb to suck on and waited, and wondered if, lying here in the vast
expanse of this platform, the soldiers might mistake them for a mound
of abandoned garbage. And then the inner door thundered from its
hinges. And Eva heard the baying. (Of course, the dogs could not climb
the ladder.) And then the creaking of the ladder as the soldiers mounted
its rickety structure, and the triumphant shouting, and the laughter, and
then she felt the warm thuds as the bullets found scraps of flesh in
which to nest.*

I have tried to stop dreaming, but it is difficult to control my
mind. I sleep as I walk. There is much to look at as we snake
through the narrow lanes. It is a new world. Trees and hedges,
and small fields. The wind surges again and the snow begins to
flurry then swirl. Under the weight of snow, the trees are beginning to stoop over like old men. I fall, then quickly clamber to
my feet. The wind tears the breath from my body. I want to live.
The snow that already lies on the road makes it difficult to
walk. I walk as though each step will be my last. Eva. I remind
myself. My name is Eva. I am twenty-one years old. I have
shrunk into womanhood. Mama walks beside me. We are people without expression, our backs bent, our heads low, a weary
caravan of misery. They are taking us to another place. Goodbye, camp. To another place. Camp, I will never see you again.
Another place. Camp, I will always see you. After two years, another place, but we know not where. I look at Mama and ask
for forgiveness. Her eyes dim, and she looks at me and says, 'But
you have done nothing for which you need to be forgiven.' I
brush snow from her lips. Death on this road is a different affair.
Lips turn blue, then the heart stops. Life is abruptly terminated.
A snow-frosted mound. I cannot find Mama. I have spilt this

life, but I will be more careful if you give me another one. *I came naked from my mother, and naked will I be taken back. The Lord has given, the Lord has taken away; blessed be the name of the Lord.* I sleep as I walk. Each step is torture. My wet feet, my wooden shoes, my blisters popping like tiny balloons. I eat the snow from the shoulders of the person ahead of me. I have no body. It is my soul that is now being punished. The sky, the horizon, the fields are all garbed in white. My companions tumble into the ditch. We pass people who refuse to see us. Is this a dream? I find it difficult to control my mind. How will they cleanse the earth after this?

SUICIDE: An act of voluntary and intentional self-destruction. St Thomas Aquinas (1225-74) claimed that suicide was a mortal sin because it usurped God's power over human life and death. However, neither the Old nor the New Testament directly forbids suicide.

In this new place, there is no work. We seldom see guards. There are no roll-calls, nothing but typhus and death. (When we move we flutter like helpless, jittery chickens.) With no routine, it is easy to give up and die. So easy. Four months now and no work. It is spring, but winter remains tethered to us, reluctant to leave. We simply sit in the barracks and wait. Death waits with us, visible, staring us in the face. We simply wait. The toothy grin of death. Again, I have lost Mama. Somewhere on the road. I thought of lying down and giving up, but I willed a way to continue. During the day, I go outside and sit with my back up against a wall. I have discovered a place where I can find what little sun there is. Winter sun. I sit where I can see most of the camp. Men and women lining up to taste a thin trickle of water from a pierced pipe. Troops of cattle. To their side, sick animals lying in pools of their own filth. Glazed eyes. A crazy bowel, perpetually active, shouting its protest. Life leaving without a real struggle, collapsing and tumbling in upon itself. No killing. No last words. No cruelty. Just death. Compared with the last place, there is little noise. I do, however, notice the birds. I envy them, for they can fly wherever they wish. But they keep their distance.

At first I had no idea where she found the knife, but it seemed to me that it could not have been too difficult for her to obtain one. After all, we didn't consider her a suicide risk. But then, when I thought about it, I realized that Marjorie, the nurse, had probably sent the knife to her room with Mr Alston. Eva was supposed to use it to cut the cake that her friend, Mr Gerald Alston, had brought for her. (No. I'm telling you, doctor, I saw it with my own eyes. To start with, they were dying at the rate of a couple of hundred a day. We had to get bulldozers in to move them. They were just too far gone to be brought back to life, just crawling out into the sunlight to die. Feeble it was. Bloody feeble. I saw a woman choke to death on a spoonful of water. I saw it with my own eyes. I can't ever forget that, ever. It'll be with me till the day I die, it will.) *There was no reason to think that she would do something irrational. I know now that they suffer feelings such as imagining that they should have died with their families. But back then, I hadn't done any research. Quite simply, I didn't know the danger. She didn't talk much. In fact, I don't think she said anything to anybody. Including myself. But there would have been time for all of that. She wasn't considered to be a serious problem. There were no seizures or fits. But, sadly, we were wrong. There was a problem. There was also a lot of blood. She cut the right artery, as though she knew what she was doing. A lot of blood.*

. . .

It is night. I prefer it when it's quieter. I have endured the day. I did not talk. I have seen the doctor. I have a private room. I have seen Gerry. There is something about this hospital that reminds me of the barracks at the end. (During the day, I go outside and sit with my back up against a wall. I have discovered a place where I can find what little sun there is. Winter sun. I sit where I can see most of the camp.) Since Gerry's sudden departure, I have stayed in bed. Propped up on my new pillow. I keep thinking that something is about to happen. But nothing has happened. Nothing is going to happen. And so life goes on. And so hope is finally extinguished. (Men and women lining up to taste a thin trickle of water from a pierced pipe.) This is the first time that I have ever been in a hospital. It makes me think about Papa. I can see the silhouettes of trees outside the window. English trees. Gerry's trees. Gerry brought me a chocolate cake. A peculiar gift. But there is nobody with whom to share it. Neither Margot, nor Bella. Only the girl who followed me across the water. I hear the murmur of voices in the corridor, and then I notice a crack of light beneath the door. There is a wide-hipped gully in this mattress. I am slightly uncomfortable. I am also unhappy. Now the light in the corridor is turned off. Objects are muddled in the dark. But I can still see her. The girl who followed me across the water. Perhaps she wants the cake. Gerry's chocolate cake. It is night. I hear the sound of coughing from another room. The other girl, with the swathe of red around her mouth. She is still here. Waiting.

I sit on the train and stare out of the window. Light rain carried on sea air. We are leaving the coast. In the distance, white wisps of smoke rise from chimneys. I try to avoid those who stare at me, for their eyes pollute my confidence. There are two others in this compartment: a man who is preoccupied with his newspaper, and a young woman, perhaps in her mid-twenties, who, when I first sat down, seemed keen to talk to me. She appears, however, to have now decided that it is best to say nothing. I am pleased. My foreign voice will only jump out and assault her. Somewhere lurking at home, by the fireplace, I imagine there is a man who provides her with some reason to live. It is raining heavily now. The drops smash against the window. I have a suitcase. We pass through green fields divided into squares that resemble pocket handkerchiefs. Tidy. Everywhere fenced off from everywhere else. Cows have rushed to shelter in one small corner. And then I see an untended graveyard. Weeds grow wildly. So this is England. And then, some time later, the train pulls into a station. A huge black cavern, full of smoke. And people. The man folds his newspaper neatly and stands. He opens the door and passes out into the corridor without so much as a word to either of us. The woman also stands and reaches up to retrieve her suitcase from the rack above her head. She speaks in a cathedral whisper. 'This is London.' One of her teeth is marked with lipstick. I, too, have a small suitcase. I stand and smile at the woman, desperate that she should say nothing further to me. I reach for my suitcase and avoid eye contact. But once more she speaks. 'Goodbye now.' I have no choice but to look at the woman. Her smile is the smile of a woman who has been sorely disappointed by a lack of conversation.

I stand in the middle of a great rush of human activity. It is difficult to know which way to turn. All around me there is a purposeful haste. Faces are set, minds focused. People swing luggage carelessly, as though clearing a path for themselves. I stand with my suitcase. Gerry's letter said come to England. He said he still wanted to marry me. He could not find Margot, but he said we could make a new life together. And so I boarded a train that furrowed its slow way across Europe towards the English Channel. And now I am in London with Gerry's address and no idea of how to get there. (He could not find Margot, but I will find her. He invited me to come at my leisure, and so come at my leisure I have.) I pick up my suitcase and begin to push my way towards the exit sign. It is evening and the sky is a dirty grey colour. The wind hits me forcefully and I bend into it. To my right, there are a line of people waiting for a taxi. I join the line and glance at the piece of paper in my hand. Gerry's address. I know that everything will be all right once I see Gerry.

The taxi driver does not say anything to me. We seem to have been driving for a long time, perhaps too long, but it is difficult for me to judge. These streets flow carelessly, one into the other. I want London to be a different place. A happier, brighter place. I am hungry. The driver stops outside a house that is joined to the houses on both sides of it. Some children play in the street. Young, dirty children dressed in tatters. I reach into my bag and pass the driver a note. 'Thanks, love.' There is no change, but I cannot argue for I do not know if he has cheated me. He looks at me with an invitation to leave his taxi. To leave his city. To leave his country. I will leave. I step down from the taxi and close the door. The children stop playing. They look at me and my suitcase. Number thirty-one. I see the door. A woman walks by, her scarf flaming in the wind. It is a small house. Gerry did not promise me a large house. He did not promise me anything on a grand scale. He did not, in fact, promise. But I have fallen and landed in a place where, despite the lack of promises, I have come to expect. I walk the three paces to the door and knock lightly. Gerry? There is no fence, no garden, nothing. This house opens right on to the street. I do not like this. It is not safe. And then the door opens. A woman with short blonde hair. A child clings to the hem of her skirt and looks up at me. She holds a wooden baking spoon in her hand. Behind her, I see two apples on a small table. I have caught her at an unfortunate moment. I have to speak. This is the wrong house. 'Gerry?' I ask. She takes her time. She looks down to my feet and then up again. 'He's out.' She pauses. 'What do you want?'

I believe the suitcase caused her to behave coldly towards me. It is one thing seeing a strange woman on your doorstep. It is another thing seeing a strange woman with a suitcase. Such a person has come to stay. I imagine these hospital people think I have come to stay. At their hospital. I fainted. I have no memory. And now they tell me I am unable to function. (This afternoon, you'll see the doctor. Then they'll get you a private room.) They cut up my lunch for me. (Cottage pie and vegetables. Green beans. Sauce. Bread and butter.) Into the smallest, silliest pieces. They lay my knife and fork to sleep next to each other. I prefer not to eat. Food that is carved for a child. I am twenty-one. I look out of the window at the trees. I look out of the window at the grass. I love nature. England, through this window, is green and happy. Should I explain to them that I came only because Gerry asked me to come? (But last night, in the pub, I finally abandoned words.) I still have the letter. I can show it to them. He asked me to come to England and marry him, and so I came. But he gave me hope where none existed. (This afternoon, you'll see the doctor. Then they'll get you a private room.) I wanted nothing more than to be the source of happiness for somebody. Is that too much to ask? A sudden burst of rain sends my mind spinning. I still dream.

Margot and I sat together in the park and watched the small children playing on the grass with their parents. It was late afternoon and the light was beginning to fade. Beyond the children, and behind a tall screen of trees, was the lake, whose surface was being gently combed by the wind. Gliding across it slowly, and with wilful deliberation, were two rowing boats that seemed determined to be swallowed by the encroaching gloom. I looked again at my sister, who seemed to have rushed into womanhood and left me behind. The way she spoke, the manner in which she walked, even the manner in which she sat next to me, made me feel awkward. (These days, she sat with her legs crossed, one on top of the other.) We had always shared everything – toys, books and secrets – but now she was different. She told me things that I didn't know, which made me realize that there were other things that she knew which I didn't know. She had secrets. Then one of the small children, a girl with a yellow bow as big as a bat tied to the top of her hair, fell over and began to cry. Her mother came rushing towards her, and gathered her up and into her arms, and the child immediately stopped crying. Margot smiled. How many babies do you want, Eva? She asked me this question without turning to look at me. I followed her eyes to the drama on the grass, and then looked beyond this scene and through the screen of trees to the lake. There was only one rowing boat left, and it was now limping its way towards the small wooden jetty. Two children, I said. One boy and one girl. Margot nudged me and began to laugh. You're so conventional. I want to have three children. Three boys. Or three girls. Or four, maybe. And once more, without realizing it, Margot had managed to make me feel stupid. I knew she didn't do this on purpose, but it took all my strength to stop myself crying. I wanted to tell her that I had thought about having children. That I knew that a child does not choose his name, or his parents. That when he enters the world, he finds either a place of love or a place of hate. I knew that children are either a result of longing or a mistake. That they need to be given space to live. Margot, I have thought about these things. But I said nothing. We sat together and watched as the mothers led their children away. And then, in the distance, as the final boat nudged up against the jetty, and the park became enveloped in darkness, I saw the man take the older children and walk them to a large ditch, where one by one they were thrown into the fire. I listened to their wailing above the crackling of the flames. Having dispatched the last child, he walked back to where the infants were huddled with their mothers. One by one, he picked them up by the legs and smashed them against a brick wall. The pulped corpse of the infant was then pushed back into the mother's arms to prevent unnecessary littering. I saw Margot standing with three dead babies in her arms, the blood flowing freely from their crushed heads. They were boys. Dead boys. Margot! I cried. Margot! But she did not hear me. She stood with her three dead children and refused to answer me.

The orderly is standing over me. You want me to call the doctor for you? Lady, you all right? He is leaning against his broom and looking down at me with concern. You gotta calm down, girl. This kind of carry on won't do you no good. It is still afternoon. The tea is cold. They were telling the truth. I did see the doctor. I am in a private room. I have no idea of how long I have been asleep. If I talk out loud in my sleep, what language do I speak? The wooden chair is empty. I move my head slightly so that I can see the orderly's face. The pillow is wet, my hair lank with sweat. Girl, you need a next pillow. The man hesitates for a moment. It is only when he puts aside his broom that I remember that I do not talk. (Last night, in the pub, I finally abandoned words.) His is a statement, not a question. I soon come back with a next pillow.

Of course, Gerry was at home. Hiding behind the door. Back at the camp, he had impressed me as a quiet and reasonable man, one who even shared his provisions with ladies. One morning, he came to me by my wall, where I sat hoping for sun. He came to me and brought me his army rations: a package containing biscuits, dried fruit, chewing gum and cigarettes. He never asked me, did you survive because you slept with a man? (Others asked this question, but not Gerry.) But of course, Gerry was at home. He emerged from behind the door and said something to his wife, but I couldn't hear. I looked at him and noticed that his trousers were thick, with turn-ups at the ankles. Then Gerry stepped from his house and led me quietly through the streets of London, not offering to carry my suitcase, not saying anything beyond, 'We'll have a drink, Eva love.' He cracked a smile. 'There's a nice pub just across from the tube station.' And so we walked on through the streets of London, neither one of us saying anything. I moved with the frantic beauty of a late butterfly, but he did not seem to notice. And then we passed a man who looked at me, then flicked a cigarette end that quickly arched and then fell to the ground, having described a tight burning parabola. I feared this kind of sudden dramatic action, and a chill ran through my body. But Gerry didn't notice. As we walked on, I looked all about me and decided that I liked these streets which, the cigarette-man aside, seemed to tolerate my presence. I liked Gerry's London.

'Park yourself in that corner. It's snug over there. I'll get us a drink.' As he spoke, Gerry fished in his pocket for money. I obeyed his instruction and sat in the corner on a stool that was covered in balding crushed velvet. I watched him walk across to the bar, where a large man spoke to him. The barman was prematurely grey, his hair parted in the middle, and he wore a jacket and tie. He had the sort of face that belonged to a cigar. Clearly, appearance counted for much with this man, and I imagined that it was he who polished the brass pumps and pipes in this pub. Then Gerry looked over to where I was sitting and he smiled at me. The barman stole a glance. They were talking about me. I looked down at the table and waited for Gerry to return. In the ashtray, ashes. 'I got you a gin and tonic.' I looked at his beer. The glass was impossibly huge. 'Well, drink up then.

It will steady your nerves.' Cubes of ice swilled noisily in the bowl of my glass. The other people were smoking, sitting in pairs, whispering to each other. It was unacceptably intimate. 'Drink up.' I lifted the glass to my lips, but the smell was overpowering. And then the taste. It burnt me. 'I can get you something else.' He spoke with fake enthusiasm. And then there was a deep silence, broken only by the sound of Gerry drumming a peeling coaster against the edge of the table. 'The wife. Well, I told her you were a bit crackers. I'm sorry, but I had to tell her something.' Please, Gerry, do not do this to me. Do not be somebody else now that you are back home. A woman started to play the piano in the corner. 'I think I need another pint. You all right?' The wooden panelling was brown, the carpet was brown, the wooden tables were brown. I could feel the tingle of gin and tonic as it coursed through my veins. 'Look, I won't be a minute.' I watched him go. I don't want to be hurt again. I won't be able to survive being abandoned again. Not again. Through the window, I saw people snaking along the evening street. I hid behind the curtain, and I realized that Gerry had probably said all that he was going to say to me. I watched him now, laughing with his friend at the bar. No, Gerry. No. Surely you are better than this?

The doctor sits opposite me. In this room, some of the furniture is covered with white dust sheets. There is a thick rug on the floor and a pair of noisy radiators against the wall. 'It's bitter outside for this time of the year.' He notices me looking around his makeshift office. A desk with a solitary chair in front and one behind, a single bed, and a metal filing cabinet. The other pieces of furniture are shrouded. Behind the doctor's desk, there is a small uncurtained window, and on his desk there is a single flower in a thin vase. I look into this tall man's face. His eyebrows run into each other, and then his mouth moves strangely, as though he is trying to overcome a yawn. 'We're putting you in your own room.' I look beyond him to the window. It is early afternoon. Then I hear the sound of feet pounding their way towards us and a sharp knock and a door opening. I turn around. 'Hello, dear. How are you?' This woman's manner is too familiar. As she moves, she releases the scent of a cheap perfume. 'A cup of tea, doctor. Before she settles into her new room.' She glances from me to the doctor, then back to me. 'Or perhaps you'd like your tea upstairs after you've finished with the doctor?' The doctor motions for her to set down the tray, which she does. Then she smiles. 'A mixture of plain biscuits, with one or two chocolate ones.' The woman hovers. 'I've put clean towels on the chair for your bath. I'll see you up there, and let me know if you need a top-up.' Only now does the woman turn to leave.

'You know where my office is if you need to speak to me. We just need to examine you for a few days.' The tea has gone cold. In the useless afternoon light, I have sat in silence and cast my mind back across the past few years. My cheeks are tight with dried tears. If only I had a photograph, so that people could see who I was. Whenever I fell over, they would be able to look into my bag and see Eva. This hospital worries me. They have dressed me in slippers and a dressing gown. They have taken my suitcase. They have fed me lunch that was carved for a child. This tall doctor, with long fingers to match his long legs. Now he leans back and stretches. Then he stands and walks a few paces. I expect a less animated gait from a man of his height. But there is a curious optimism to his movement. Again he sits, this time on the edge of his desk, his knees forming twin-pointed hillocks on which he now rests his flat palms. He leans over me. 'You see, one must have patience. It takes time. Last night, the people in the pub, they were frightened when you started shouting. Do you remember?' I do not know what in the world he is talking about. 'When they brought you here, we

195

just gave you something to make you sleep, that's all. You've
been doing very nicely.' Now I feel the doctor's bony hands on
mine. 'Why did you write the letter, Eva? Mr Alston. I mean,
Gerry. He has a wife and child. As you can imagine, this has
caused him some difficulties.' He takes his hands from mine.
'Did you write the letter so that you might prove something to
somebody, is that it?' He does not seem to understand that I do
not talk. Last night, in the pub, I finally abandoned words. 'Ah
well, we'll get Marjorie to brew you some more tea. Then you
have a nice hot bath and take a nap. I think you'll like your new
room. We can speak again later.' I scrutinize this doctor's face,
but then I realize that he cannot see, on my shoulder, the butterfly that I have become.

She followed me across the water. In fact, she follows me everywhere. I have had to learn to tolerate her. I arrive somewhere,
then she arrives moments later. I leave for somewhere, then
moments later she, too, leaves. At first I used to panic and cry,
but she would not listen. The other girl has a jagged slash of lipstick around her mouth, red like blood. I have tried pleading
with her. I have said, 'Please, I have done nothing to you. Why
do you torment me like this? Can you not just leave me alone?'
But she will not listen to me, and I still hear her padding along
behind me. Whenever I turn, I see that pitiful face. I thought
that maybe on the ship across the water I could fool her. I could
pretend to be her friend, then, when she tried to nudge up
close to me, I might give her a push and topple her over and
into the sea. This was to be a new land, a new beginning. I
didn't want her to follow me here. That would not be fair. But
when we arrived, there she was, dressed in those same rags,
standing behind me, waiting for me to decide my next step.
Nobody else notices her, even when she tries to reach out and
hug me, nobody sees. Stay away from me! I scream. But nobody
sees her, nor do they hear her whispered promise that she will

live with me as long as I live. I know that it was she who ate the butterfly on my shoulder. Stay away from me! I scream. But nobody sees her.

The orderly brings me a pillow and a visitor. Gerry. It has taken Gerry all day to show his face. He sits on the wooden chair to the side of the bed. Beyond him, the curtains are drawn back. My head is propped up on the new pillow and my arms lie outside the white sheet. He is a smaller man without his uniform. He has brought me a chocolate cake, and a knife with which to cut it. He can barely look at me as he tells me that he feels some shame. His voice drops a note. He was confused. He wanted me so much. Men do awful, unforgivable things in war. I listen. He does not mention the letter that I signed with his name. Perhaps he is not such a bad man. But it no longer matters. I want to ask him: Gerry, is this England of yours any place in which to plant tender shrubs? Of course, I do not ask him. I simply watch him. Has he forgotten the well that a generous word can sink? Say something, Gerry. Eventually he stands. 'I have to go.' I say nothing. 'Eva, I asked about your sister. Nobody knows anything. I don't know what else to do.' He looks as though he is going to cry. For a few moments our eyes meet, then he lowers his head and turns away. Does the sight of me frighten him? I now weigh more than sixty pounds. Not much more. But more. I watch him leave. The poor man. The poor, sad man. And now the doctor comes in. He takes the chair that has recently been vacated by Gerry. He begins quietly. 'Would you like to see him again?' I shake my head. 'Now, Eva, are you sure?' I do not want to see this Gerry again. I am alone. I look at the doctor, but he fails to understand. I am alone. He waits a few moments, then hauls himself to his feet. 'Tomorrow, then.'

It is night. I hear the sound of coughing from another room. The other girl, with the swathe of red around her mouth. She is still here. Waiting. I look at her and wonder why this sad, unhappy girl persists. The coughing stops. I know that somewhere, buried deep inside me, is a place where I will be able to lay down in peace. And this other girl will not be able to follow me. But until then? Can I ever be truly happy? Dear Bella, without you this is not happiness. Mama. Papa. I do not know in what strange land you are buried. Or what stubbled growth or building defaces the earth above your precious bones. But I am tired. And I want to come home. For us, the hinge of generation will not move. That morning, walking to the train station, with our suitcases. A human river of shattered lives. Passing houses that had become our prisons and our tombs, the train door opening with a grating sound, one pail into which we must all relieve ourselves, stopping for hours for no apparent reason, the morning mist rising from the fields, the smoke. Mama. Papa. Dear Margot. The smoke. Once again, I hear the sound of coughing. The other girl is looking at me with sadness in her eyes, so I reach over and take first one hand and then the other. Don't worry, I say. Everything will be fine. Please. Don't worry.

HE had been watching her for a long time. She sat alone across the room, her face an impassive mask, while the other women swirled and dipped in large gestures of exaggerated joy. The hard afternoon light had long since faded, and the room was increasingly dominated by shadows. Because she was sitting, it was difficult to tell whether she was tall or short, but this woman was beautiful. He could not take his eyes from her. When the other women were passed over, they lowered their eyes and remained seated as the music played. One or two among them would occasionally betray a look of frustration, but this woman, who nobody asked to dance, simply sat as though she was indifferent to people's attitudes towards her. Once more, the music stopped and partners were hastily exchanged, and he watched as, again, this woman was ignored. She uncrossed then crossed her legs.

(Together with my parents and my brother and sister. (In our village, nobody had ever seen a light bulb or a telephone. Of course we were unprepared.) We lived as farmers and weavers. Out in the desert, you flashed your lights to attract our attention. And then you herded us on to buses. Now I can smile about it. We had never been on such a thing as a bus. And yes, it was frightening. At dawn, we discovered that we were travelling through a desert that was littered with the skeletons of camels and goats. People looked around. Not everybody was here. It was impossible to take everybody. Relatives were being abandoned. And then on to the embassy compound, where we were stored like thinning cattle. Grazing on concrete. And from the embassy to the airport. We just let it happen. I was lucky, for my parents, and my brother and sister, were relatively healthy. But many people were weak with malaria. It is true, many people were dying.)

Some of the men travelled in from nearby kibbutzim, but the majority lived in the city. They were elderly, mainly bachelors or widowers, but among them were those whose loveless marriages had long ago turned stale. A few among the young women were prostitutes, but the greater number of them were students, or unemployed actresses, all of whom were paid a small sum by the management to dance for a few hours each week. The management's chief source of income were the men, who were required to pay an annual membership fee for their weekly flights of fantasy. Other activities were continually promised, such as outings to places of historical interest, informal dinners, and lectures by prominent speakers on issues relating to the culture and arts of the country. However, in the two years that he had been a member, he was not aware of any other club activities, beyond these weekly dances each Wednesday afternoon.

Ten years ago, after his retirement, he had decided to sell his city-centre apartment, for he imagined that the profit would ease his remaining years. His new apartment, a twenty-minute bus ride from the centrally located club, was comfortable although somewhat noisy. In the beginning, it was the construction teams who disturbed his peace, for they seemed eager to work around the clock. These days it was just people's children, always shouting and playing at all times of the day and night. A little over two years ago, he had nearly died. It was after his recuperation that he decided to join the club, for, with neither work nor family to occupy him, he had finally admitted to himself that he was lonely.

Eventually, he found the courage to cross the floor and ask her to dance. Without saying a word, she stood and eased her slender body into his arms, allowing him to hold her in a manner that was both respectable and intimate. People were watching. He steered her backwards and into the cluster of dancing couples, in the hope that they might attract less attention if they could edge their way towards the middle of the floor. However, her dancing seduced his attention with its grace and surety of step, and he soon forgot his cowardly plan. He hardly noticed when the music stopped, but, as she turned to walk away, he found himself clumsily reaching out and touching her arm. The music started and he stepped towards her, and once again they began to dance.

After her arrival, she had undergone two years of intensive language study, and then she had trained as a nurse. However, at present she was not working. She would say nothing more. He suggested that he might be able to help her, for he was a retired doctor, but she continued to stare straight ahead as though he had not spoken. Her eyes were the deepest black, which made the white about them appear ivory. Her hair was also black, and short and tightly curled. It appeared to have been sheared, rather than cut, close to the natural shape of her head. He began to feel self-conscious, aware for the first time that his feet may not be moving in time with the music. And then there was the closeness of her body, and the warm strange smell of her person. Suddenly he wanted to stop this dancing, and to sit down and talk to the woman. This was a ridiculous charade. He was making a fool of himself with a woman at least fifty years his junior, whose behaviour seemed designed to remind him of the frailties of old age. None of the other women had ever made him feel this way. In the two years that he had been coming to the club, it was precisely the awful reality of these frailties that the young women seemed temporarily to erase from his mind.

(On the plane there were no seats. Just mattresses on the floor where we could squat, but most remained standing. We were frightened. Together with my parents and my sister and my brother, I prayed. And then a man died while we were in the sky. My sister and I wondered, in this new land, would our babies be born white? We, the people of the House of Israel, we were going home. No more wandering. No longer landless. No more tilling of soil that did not belong to us. What is your name? Malka. Malka, do not be shy. You are going home. And when we arrived, and stepped down off the plane, we all kissed the ground. We thanked God for returning us to Zion.)

At the end of the dance, it was a polite convention for the man to retreat and allow another to stake his claim. However, he knew that nobody would challenge his right to dominate this woman's time. He asked her if she would share a drink with him at the bar. Generally, the woman was expected to feign sur-

prise and then agree. Drinks cost money, and so this arrangement kept the management happy. But when he asked this
woman, there was no fake surprise. She simply shrugged her
shoulders and led the way from the dance floor to the small bar,
where she quickly found a seat on a tall stool and he, somewhat
less quickly, joined her. For a moment he stared at her, and then
eventually she smiled. It occurred to him that she might be
laughing at his expense, and he swallowed deeply.

They each drank a glass of white wine, but there was little attempt at conversation. He asked her to dance again, and so she
emptied her glass and slid from the stool. As they turned among
the other dancers, he whispered that he would prefer it if they
could stop at the end of this dance and perhaps talk properly.
Beyond the knowledge that she was presently an unemployed
nurse, all he had managed to glean was that she was nearly
thirty, and that she lived with her parents and younger sister at
the edge of the city in one of the developments into which her
people had been placed. She refused to be any more specific
with regard to her domestic arrangements. She also volunteered
that this was her third, and perhaps final, time at the club. The
manager had informed her that, if nobody danced with her this
time, then she would not be allowed back. As she told him this,
she again shrugged her shoulders, indicating that it mattered little to her, one way or the other.

When the music stopped, he followed her back to the bar. A
new song began to play, one of his favourites, but he was glad
that he would no longer have to dance. He wondered if she realized just how old he was. Most of the young women guessed
him to be about sixty-five, which meant they really thought
him to be seventy-five. He was proud of his condition, but
whenever he thought of this he chuckled, for what else would
one expect of a doctor? Until the heart attack, he had been

blessed with perfect health. However, he knew better than most that it was impossible to insure against the ravages of old age. And then he remembered his manners.

'Another drink?'

Suddenly he was afraid that he might lose her.

'Or perhaps I could buy you dinner this evening?'

She nodded, and then climbed from the stool. For a moment he imagined that she wanted to dance to his favourite tune, but the somewhat impatient manner in which she was staring at him left him in no doubt that she was now ready to leave.

As they left the club, he noticed that there were only a few minutes of daylight remaining. The sky was darkening, but thin light still filtered through the clouds. He panicked and wondered where he could take her. Although she did not look like a prostitute, one could never underestimate people's imaginations.

'Do you have any particular place in mind?'

It was a foolish question, for it was clear that this woman had little understanding of society. He imagined that her visits to the club provided her with an escape from the claustrophobia of her family, and the stubborn manner in which they probably clung to their traditions.

'Why don't we go to a hotel?'

He turned to face her. He assumed that she must be making a reference of some kind to a hotel as a place to eat, but before he could disguise the embarrassing transparency of his own bewilderment she spoke again.

'Or perhaps your place is suitable. I am sorry, but I have no money.'

He turned from her. It was impossible to deny that it had not occurred to him that at some point he might meet a young woman on the dance floor who might offer him uncomplicated pleasure. Over the years there had, of course, been entanglements, including one protracted relationship with a musician, a cellist from Austria, whose daughter he had treated for bronchitis. Now, as he looked back almost thirty years, he had come to recognize this as probably the love of his life. Not including, of course, his wife. Since Renate, the cellist, there had been occasional and generally unsatisfactory encounters which had at least avoided the unpleasantness that he imagined an exchange of money would introduce into the whole business. However, these casual encounters were no longer validated by the thrill of pursuit and conquest, nor were they legitimized by passion. It seemed that the ladies, often grateful patients or freshly grieving widows, were, like himself, acting out some physical pantomime in which memory played an increasingly large role, and in which pity, from one to the other, seemed to be the dominant emotion. How could he tell this strange woman that he did not want a prostitute? He wanted a companion, someone to talk to, a friend even. But he had no desire to offend the woman.

He looked at the hotels that lined the seafront – tall, concrete structures without any character, to which businessmen or package tourists confined themselves. He could not take her back to his apartment, for even if he was lucky enough not to meet anybody on the bus journey, he failed to see how he might get her into his apartment without someone noticing. To his neighbours, he was a respectable retired bachelor doctor, and the ladies who visited him either did so in company, or appeared to be decent enough not to warrant any comment.

'Did you have any particular hotel in mind?'

The woman shook her head. He searched her face for any sign of fear, but he could detect none. And then he pointed to the nearest hotel, one that lay less than fifty yards from where they were standing.

'Perhaps this one here?'

She said nothing and again the man re-examined his own motives, for he doubted that he would be able to fulfil whatever expectations this woman might have. He spoke quietly.

'Are you certain about this?'

The woman shot him a puzzled look, so he pressed on somewhat awkwardly.

'Well, we can eat first. They have a restaurant, I'm sure.'

They were given a room on the seventeenth floor, with a large bathroom and a broad view of the sea. He slid back the glass doors and walked out on to the balcony.

'It's very pleasant out here.'

She explored the room. On either side of the large double bed were matching tables and night lamps. A small desk and a chair, a standard lamp, and a lumpy two-seat settee completed the furniture in the room. The pictures on the wall were of views that she imagined related to a different country, for the greenness of the grass and the large mountain ranges suggested a more temperate climate. She sat on the settee. This was her first time in a hotel. When her family first arrived, they had been housed in what they were told was a hotel, but within a few weeks she came to understand that, in reality, the place was something called a hostel. And a hostel was most certainly not a hotel. The conditions were intolerable, but she had promised herself then, during her first weeks in her new country, that one day she would stay in a real hotel. She was not going to be cheated.

She was anxious to be seen to be behaving with dignity, so she rose from the settee and inspected the spotlessly clean bathroom, which boasted its own hairdryer and weighing scales. Having done so, she returned to the room and sat demurely on the edge of the bed. Then she changed her mind and crossed to the balcony. He pointed.

'The sea is very calm.'

She stood behind him, close enough that she could hear him wheezing slightly.

'Looking at the sea always makes me want to travel.' He paused. 'Even at my age.'

He turned to face her, and she smiled at him, which caused him to lower his eyes.

They stepped clear of the lift and discovered the hotel lobby to be crowded with people. Those coming in from the street were closing umbrellas and shaking off their coats, while those ready to depart were reluctant to venture out. What had begun as a light drizzle had now turned into a downpour. He looked at the woman and spoke jauntily.

'Just as well we are staying here and eating in the grill.'

She said nothing as he led the way across the packed lobby to the oak-panelled reception area of the hotel restaurant. Troubled thoughts were erupting with frequency now, but even as they formed, he pushed them nervously to the back of his mind. He was simply having dinner with a young woman. That was all. They were ushered to a table by the window, and, once seated, he ordered white wine and steak, while his guest decided upon a large salad.

'Two years ago I suffered a heart attack,' he said. 'That's when I started to go to the club. It was important that I should start getting out a little.'

He watched as she pushed the lettuce about her plate, as though uninterested in eating.

'It's funny, but even I panicked when it happened. But, of course, I knew that it was a coronary.'

He laughed slightly, anticipating his own humour.

'If only I'd been able to treat myself, I could have saved on the hospital bills.'

She would not rise to meet his conversation. Did she understand what he was saying? Perhaps it was simply a problem of language and culture. He decided to forgo dessert.

(The mayor of the town in which we were first placed complained. He had requested that he be sent only those who could sing and dance, so that he might form a folklore group for tourists. Everywhere, we were told the same thing. First we will teach you the language, then when you leave the absorption centre you will be able to study at the university. Don't worry, your parents will find work. The first day that my mother saw a television set, she pushed a broom through the screen. There was a fire on the programme that was being broadcast and she tried to put it out. In our country, we did not eat in public. In our country, we had never seen a classroom. These things were difficult. In our country, we were not used to relying on outsiders. And then, as we learnt the language and your ways, our parents felt as though they were losing us. It was hard for them. They were no longer responsible for their children. Have you seen the ugly housing at the edges of the city where we live? My brother is in the army now. But my parents, they are sick. After the absorption centre, they are frightened of white walls and white coats. They simply watch television. My mother is tattooed on her face, her hands and her neck. She finds it difficult to leave the apartment, for people stop and stare. And my father is incapable of adjusting to this land of clocks. I try to honour him as I would do in the old country, but it is impossible if he will not change. So we do not speak, and when I get a job I will leave. Three women in one small apartment. At certain times of the month, he says, we women pollute the place with our presence and so he will sleep outside. My sister cries. Like my mother, she does not go out into the world. Malka, stay with us. Stay with us, please. Please, Malka. I ask you, is this home? And yes, I went to your university – I am a nurse – but I cannot find a job. Four of us, we live in one cramped apartment. This Holy Land did not deceive us. The people did. The man at the hostel, he said to us, 'Welcome, my black brothers and sisters. You are helping us to understand what we are doing

*here.' Is this true? Are we helping you? I know now what a stamp is. I
can use a telephone. I, too, can turn night into day by simply pressing a
switch. I wear shoes. I have seen a highway. But please. My people
never killed themselves. Hunger, yes. Disease, yes. But never this problem. During Passover, we kill a lamb and sprinkle its fresh red blood
around the synagogue. But not here. You do not allow this. You say you
rescued me. Gently plucked me from one century, helped me to cross two
more, and then placed me in this time. Here. Now. But why? What are
you trying to prove?)*

The meal was largely unsuccessful. The waiter offered him the
opportunity of either paying directly, or putting it on the bill for
the room. He chose to pay in cash, for he remained unsure if he
would, in fact, be spending the night in this hotel. They left the
dining room and sat together in the small hotel bar, a glass of
whisky before each of them, the piano player hammering away
in the corner to little effect. She sipped at her drink, and then
she wedged an ice-cube between gum and cheek and waited for
her mouth to go numb. Once it had done so, she spoke.

'You can be honest with me. You do not want us here, do
you?'

'Not everybody feels that way.'

He looked around the bar, but apart from the white-jacketed
man serving drinks, and the two American tourists watching
CNN, the place was empty. Nobody could hear their conversation, especially above the clatter of the piano.

'I am asking you. You, a doctor. Why do they train me as a
nurse?'

'Well, why not train you as a nurse?'

She laughed.

'You do not understand.'

Now the alarming question was beginning to take shape in
the forefront of his mind. What did she want? Was there to be
some attempt at humiliation?

. . .

While she was in the bathroom, he stepped from his clothes and slid into bed. Ashamed of his body, and unhappy with the scar that ran the full length of his upper torso, he chose also to switch off the night lamps. The moonlight streamed into the room. With the curtains drawn back, it was possible to watch the sea, calm after rain, and to become transfixed by the sight of the surf as it tugged continually against the shoreline.

'Why did you turn out the lights?'

There was a note of bewilderment in her voice. She continued.

'I can't see you.'

'Why do you want to see me?'

He laughed and tried to make a joke of it, but there was silence. And then she spoke.

'Do you not wish to see me?'

She was naked. Tall, smooth and graceful, she was carved like a statue. Before he could catch himself, he heard the words fall from his lips.

'I would like to be your friend.'

She stepped into shadow. Then she slid into the bed, taking care not to touch him.

'But you *are* my friend. I have been here six years now, and no man has seen me naked. I am not that type of woman.'

He turned to face her. She spoke again, this time in a hushed voice.

'You did not look as though you would hurt me.' She paused. 'And I have never stayed in a hotel.'

'But won't your family worry?'

Now she turned from him and lay back on the pillow. She fixed her eyes on the ceiling.

'My family worry about everything. Maybe, like my brother, I will join the army.'

She paused, then looked back at him. She lifted her head from the pillow.

'You may kiss me if you wish, but I prefer only that. I am sorry.'

In the morning, she was gone. His first thought was to make sure that his wallet was still in his jacket pocket, but he resisted this ungenerous impulse. He rolled over to the part of the bed where she had slept. There was still an indentation where she had lain, but no warmth. He had spent most of the night staring at this woman, trying to understand why she had chosen him. Was there some quality he possessed that she had observed? Perhaps other women could see it too? (Did she feel sorry for him?) During the night, the sheet had slipped down to her waist, which allowed him the opportunity to examine her skin. If he had been younger, then maybe. But she belonged to another land. She might be happier there. Dragging these people from their primitive world into this one, and in such a fashion, was not a policy with which he had agreed. They belonged to another place. He thought of her now, taking the first of the buses that would carry her back to her cramped apartment. And then, upon her arrival, he imagined she would have to endure her parents. And her sister. Their questions. Their unhappiness. But there had been a private adventure. (For both of them.) The club, the hotel, the dinner, the bar, the room, the bed. She had lived. She was living.

He paid the bill and stepped out into the bright morning light. It was a fine day. He walked slowly along the promenade that ran between the hotels and the beach, and passed the poorly arranged concrete benches, in that most faced each other rather than the sea. He had thought of taking a stroll down Dizengoff Street and sitting with a coffee, but he knew that soon he would not be alone. Inevitably, someone would interrupt his privacy with their unsophisticated questions. What are you doing in town? So early? I saw you last night. With a black woman. No, it was you. I am sure of it. He saw a bench which nobody had yet claimed and which, unlike the others, enjoyed a clear view of the sea. He sat heavily and tried not to think of his wife and child. But it was useless. Every day, assaulted by loneliness. Every day, eaten up with guilt. His only companion was memory, and how he struggled with the burdensome weight of this single relationship. He now understood that to remember too much is, indeed, a form of madness. And he understood that people are not made to live alone, neither when things are good, nor when they are bad. These inelegant attempts to heal the lesion in his soul. The woman on the first of the buses that would carry her back to the edge of the city. He did not want anyone to feel sorry for him. He, too, had lived. He remembered the garden with its wooden bench. And the two sisters who played beneath the wide branches of a large tree. They chased each other and screamed gleefully. Then they stopped and the older girl spoke first. 'Uncle Stephan. Are you leaving us?' He smiled. They were pretty girls, with dark eyes and long black hair. They would become beautiful women. And now the younger sister spoke. 'Tell us, Uncle Stephan. Tell us.' Again he smiled, and then he looked down at the space between his feet. The grass was yellowing in the sunlight. It had been an unusually hot summer. He was definitely leaving his wife and child and returning to Palestine. A decision had been made, but these two girls were not making it any easier. And then he looked up. Instinctively, he raised one arm to touch Margot's cheek, and then he stretched out his other arm to beckon Eva. But they did not see him. They simply saw strange Uncle Stephan staring at the yellowing grass between his feet. The sisters looked at each other, and then Margot began to laugh. And then again, they began to chase one another, their voices becoming louder and more excitable as their pace increased. And now he called to them, but they did not hear him, for his weary tongue was unable to bear the weight of these children's names. Strange Uncle Stephan, staring at the yellowing grass between his feet. It was Margot who decided that it was too hot to play, and that she and Eva should go inside. Uncle Stephan watched as they skipped away and left him alone on the bench, his arms outstretched, reaching across the years.

A NOTE ON THE TYPE

This book was set in a version of the well-known Monotype face Bembo. This letter was cut for the celebrated Venetian printer Aldus Manutius by Francesco Griffo, and was first used in Pietro Cardinal Bembo's *De Aetna* of 1495.

The companion italic is an adaptation of the chancery script type designed by the calligrapher and printer Lodovico degli Arrighi.

Composed by Dix, Syracuse, New York
Printed and bound by Quebecor Printing,
Fairfield, Pennsylvania